Warwickshire County Council

LEA 5/21			

This item is to be returned or renewed before the latest date above. It may be borrowed for a further period if not in demand. **To renew your books:**

- **Phone the 24/7 Renewal Line 01926 499273 or**
- **Visit www.warwickshire.gov.uk/libraries**

Discover • Imagine• Learn • *with libraries*

Warwickshire County Council

HOLLOW IN THE LAND

JAMES CLARKE

This paperback edition first published in 2021

First published in Great Britain in 2020 by
Serpent's Tail
an imprint of Profile Books Ltd
29 Cloth Fair
London
EC1A 7JQ
www.serpentstail.com

1 3 5 7 9 10 8 6 4 2

Printed and bound in Great Britain by
CPI Group (UK) Ltd, Croydon CR0 4YY

A CIP catalogue record for this book is available from the British Library.

ISBN 978 1 78816 3521
eISBN 978 1 78283 613 1

MIX
Paper from
responsible sources
FSC   FSC® C020471
www.fsc.org

For my mum and dad

VALLEY. N. (PL. VALLEYS)

1 a low area between hills or mountains
2 an extensive, more or less flat, and relatively low region drained by a great river system
3 any depression or hollow resembling a valley
4 a low point or interval in any process, representation, or situation
5 any place, period, or situation that is filled with fear, gloom, foreboding, or the like

noun HOLLOW IN THE LAND

synonyms
basin, canyon, combe, corrie, dale, dell, dene, depression, dingle, dip, gap, glen, gully, hole, pass, gorge, HOLLOW, *ravine, rift, slade, strath*

Below the Wind Farm

—

ON THE MOOR OVERLOOKING THE VALLEY was a wind farm. You could get there easily via the root system of track built for the maintenance guys, and each turbine made a wild sound if you got close to it. According to Ada Robinson the swoop and turn of those forty-metre blades fucked with your spatial awareness. You'd be standing at the foot of one, looking up, and the razors would come at you at such a pace and angle that it could do all sorts to your head, especially if the clouds were being sent in the opposite direction. She'd said all this to Harry Maiden a few days ago, but now, wandering between the turbines for the first time in search of Ada's putrid-smelling Border Terrier, Harry had no idea whether or not she was right.

It was so misty that he couldn't see more than five feet ahead. He kept stumbling upon the turbines, the structures looming so suddenly from the murk that you could be forgiven for thinking they'd sprouted from the ground and were ready to rocket free, maintaining their course into the sky. Harry had spent the last fifteen minutes maundering through this place, and picking his way around each turbine's broad metal base was beginning to make him feel as if he was sneaking between the legs of an enormous wintery monster.

Ada had never really displayed much affection for the terrier anyway. The creature had belonged to her husband, Martin, who had left her to go travelling somewhere in Asia, so it was a trophy of sorts, albeit a sentient one. Harry pictured the look on Ada's face when he brought the dog home. Her hand might slide up his shoulders, her fingertips graze the nape of his neck. She was the sister of a lumpy colleague of his who he had yet to figure out. At the quarry they called Ada's brother Jolan Rob; Jolan drove the dumper trucks and gave Harry a lift to and from the site every day. A couple of years ago Jolan had taken a tumble from his truck's hopper without a helmet. Landing badly, he'd suffered a depression fracture of the skull, somehow managing to come through the ordeal with relatively little fallout for the quarry's management. Surviving and saying what the bosses told him to say to the health-and-safety investigators meant Jolan now had a job for life. It meant easier shifts, extra holidays and pretending you hadn't noticed when he said something odd, when the corner of his mouth drooped or one eye did whatever the hell it wanted.

Before they left that morning, Ada had specifically told Jolan not to let the dog off its lead until they arrived at the moor where they could keep an eye on it, but midway up the bluff Jolan had untethered the creature's collar with a shrug. The dog duly disappeared and now Harry was striving after it, coughing up a smoker's gobbet here and there. His bearings were lost and his patience had thinned. Jolan was following somewhere. He better had be.

Sick of the mist, Harry scrambled through the spiny bunches of gorse populating this subsection of hill, and stopped to whistle. Ada's dog had a stupid name that he couldn't bring himself to say out loud, so it was a matter of this, of calling unintelligibly to it in a higher register. He'd always found it odd that people talked to their pets in such silly voices, yet here he was partaking in the same theatre. Harry supposed it was what he'd signed up for when he agreed to this endeavour behind Jolan's horrid little terrace. He'd only agreed to come along because he thought Ada would be joining them, but she'd been struck with a headache almost as soon as she stepped into her walking boots. Harry, she'd said, falling lavishly against him. Could you help me to my chair, please? *Thank you.*

Harry hadn't known Ada that long, let alone that she suffered from headaches. He'd started at the quarry that autumn after returning to the valley where he and his wife Jenny had grown up. Like Jolan, it was Harry's job to shift the compacted knots of sandstone around after they'd been removed from a hill that had been so over-mined it now resembled a giant piece of cake with a bite taken from it. Harry had been placed on Jolan's team, and for some reason Jolan had taken a shine to him. This was strange because Harry was far from outgoing and resisted meeting new people, especially those who tried as hard as Jolan did to be liked. The pair had been muddling through this terse dynamic when it came up that they lived near to one another, and seeing as Harry hadn't a car, would he like a lift?

It made sense to take advantage of a free ride, even though Harry knew Jolan shouldn't be driving after a head injury, so he'd agreed to the offer, heroically putting up with Jolan's insane speeding and the daily attempts to coax him indoors for a drink. For weeks Harry had refused Jolan's invitations. He'd said no so many times that there had to come a yes at some point, if only for the lifts' sake. With that in mind he eventually found himself scraping the residue from his work boots on the steel mat on Jolan's front step, and entered the house hoping for a glass of something strong to take the edge off another day. Ada had been waiting by the kettle. She explained to Harry that since her husband disappeared, she'd been unable to afford the rent. She was staying with her brother until she got her head together, while her children were being looked after by their grandmother for the time being. Ada had a baggy purity that Harry liked, an obtainable quality. The cuppa at the Robinsons' had become a pot now, a regular thing.

Harry found the dog in a clearing way below a farmer's field. The terrier had wandered down the escarpment in pursuit of a sheep that must have slipped through a fence hemming the elevated meadow, then fallen off the crag to where it now lay, at the bottom of about eight foot of stone and boulder reaching up a messy face of rock and fern.

If you could see past the hazing flies and stillness, you could be forgiven for thinking the creature was asleep. But when Harry knelt close he could see that its eyelids were shut, locked forever, and the eyeballs had been reduced to a gloop that eked from beneath the lids in thick, ketchup-red tears. The sheep had died alone. Perhaps it had bleated awhile before submitting to the pull of what cannot be avoided.

Ada's dog had lost interest in the sheep. It nuzzled at a scent along the boulders, then, sensing Harry, it gave a cursory turn of the head before scampering up the rock. It was a sharp and wiry ratter, an agile thing.

Robbo! Harry called. Fucking dog's here.

He drew the line at picking the animal up himself. He'd seen how dogs behaved – there was just no way. He sat on a rock to wait. The fog had cleared enough to reveal a hill marbled with russet and green, and above it turbines that spun sedately, looking so out of place up there that they could have been built by aliens. A bird flew above the wind farm in the sifting cloud; it resembled a punctuation mark against a page. Even *that* had slowed, hovering as if suspended from an invisible length of wire. Harry watched the bird. He saw it dive. He missed its return thanks to Jolan, who chose that moment to burst into the clearing.

David!

Jolan hitched his saggy jeans up around his waist and paused, apparently perplexed by the sight of Ada's busy dog, the expired sheep and Harry smoking. Between his damp breasts and broad belly line, Jolan had a smiley face of sweat illustrating his T-shirt. Harry studied the pink crack of scar riven up Jolan's head. Tearing through his crew cut, it looked melted on, a puckered centipede that reached behind one ear, forming an unsightly keloid. On sunnier days you could make out the raised brushstrokes of tissue along the perimeter of the scar: the trail where many stitches had woven Jolan's scalp.

Here he is, said Jolan to the dog. Where you off to, pal? Where you going?

The terrier cocked its head, its front paw raised. Its beard and whiskers shone, its coat ranging in colour from brown–black to light brown then back again.

How is he? said Jolan. How's my boy?

The dead sheep stank. It had been a juvenile, its tail not long removed. Harry's father had often spoken of docking the lambs on the farm he'd grown up on, not far from here. The pensioner as a boy, strapping delicate shins into snapping braces and tying the cords around the tails so men could sever them with the metal snips. Some stories you never forgot. Blood saturating cotton and forearm while local events were discussed, football scores, whatever daft thing a family member had last come out with. You'd not feel as sorry for 'em if you'd seen a sheep with its back end eaten to the bone by fly strike cause its fucking tail's been left to infect, Harry's father had once said.

Davey, come on now … come wi' your Jo-Jo, Jolan cooed as he eased the dog's leash from his pocket. He jangled the leash, but this prompted the terrier to clamber further up the rocky mound. A breeze stirred David's coat: a bristle caused by wind when seemingly there was none. Harry headed around the boulders so that between Jolan on one side, him on the other and the sheep carcass in the middle, the dog's options were limited. Or so you'd think. Harry had to laugh as the animal slipped into a hole at the top of the rocks and vanished from view.

It took Harry and Jolan a long time to clear enough space in the boulders to see where the dog had gone, but once they'd crawled through the gap they realised that the animal had led them into what was undoubtedly a very large cave. Harry used the torch application on his phone, and noticed that Jenny hadn't bothered to message today. His wife had been faffing around on the kitchen worktop with a watermelon when he'd left for work that morning. For after lunch, she'd said, maybe tea. Knowing full well that Harry didn't like watermelon, thinking he didn't know that the moment he left the house, she upended a secret litre of vodka into a hole bored in the top of the fruit. After finding the boozy remnants of the previous melon, Harry had considered saying something to Jenny like he used to do when he found the empty bottles hidden all over the old house, but this time he'd decided to let her continue eating her way to inebriated peace. Turning a blind eye to how she dealt with her sadness had started out as an act of weary compassion, but had since become a means of salvaging a quieter life. Because there was no other way of putting it: these days Harry's wife was easier to be with when she was drunk.

The mediocre phone torch didn't reveal the whole chamber. What it did show, if you got about a yard away from the walls, was clefted and hoary limestone, time-rippled, set; a very different quality of rock from the sandstone that Jolan and Harry worked with every day at the quarry.

Harry shone the torch on the spot where the boulders must originally have come down. There were what looked like carvings in an alcove there: three skulls. For some reason he wasn't afraid. He put a finger in one of the eye sockets and wondered who the last person to do this very thing had been.

Can you see him? asked Jolan.

No, replied Harry. You'd think it'd be warmer in here. He hugged himself. Fucking animal.

They advanced until they arrived at the edge of a second chamber, managing to pick their way through a chorus of dripping water, delving into what Harry supposed was the essence of the earth itself. He traced his fingers up the cave's walls yet could find no more carvings. By now they were as deep into the cave as they dared go, and Ada's dog was nowhere to be seen. There was no light in this place – there wasn't supposed to be. There was just a phone torch piercing the blackness, its glare swiftly lost.

*

Harry arrived home to find Jenny asleep on the couch with a thoughtful expression on her face and 'Cheree' by Suicide playing on the stereo. She'd eaten – for there was an open jar of greengage jam by the cooker and a paring knife jammed into the melting butter pat – then likely made a start on unpacking the washing machine, forgotten what she was doing and opted for music. A solitary wedge of melon lay on the rug while additional rinds were discarded in the bin as if various smiles had been cut from the faces of green jack-o'-lanterns. The TV flashed merrily. People with fine teeth conversed mutely on the flat-screen.

Upstairs, Harry fetched the big torch. The spare room where it was kept was criss-crossed with washing lines on which many shirts were strung on hangers. Varying from colour to colour, sweet-smelling, soft, the shirts looked surreal suspended there without the men to fill them. Not one of them belonged to Harry, who washed and ironed his own clothes because Jenny never felt like it after laundering for other people all day. She and Harry had bought the laundry business when they returned to the valley after the ordeal with Jenny's ectopic pregnancy finally drew to a close. Having the foetus removed had rendered Jenny infertile, depressed, so they'd opted for a new start in an old place, somewhere they could get on with their lives without being bothered, knowing it would be just the two of them now.

Harry knew Jenny blamed him for how things had turned out. The single cycle of IVF valley women her age were granted courtesy of the NHS had failed, they couldn't afford to go private and, as for adopting, who wanted to deal with another man's mistake? Harry recalled the door slamming when he told his wife this.

The finality of the sound.

Although for his part Harry blamed Jenny too. Because he was certain that if she could have, his wife would have opted to proceed with the ectopic pregnancy, preferring to risk her own life rather than going on after what had happened to their would-be child, leaving him alone. Jenny would have preferred that tragedy to the complicity of elective surgery. After all, there is romance to tragedy and Jenny had always been susceptible to romance.

Harry put his nose to a shirt. He loved doing this. The wholesome aroma of the fabric softener reminded him of riding his bicycle as a kid, behind the gritstone terraces, the neighbours' pegged bedsheets flapping from the washing lines strung across the track. He used to cycle into the drifting cloth, burying his face in something clean, the fresh rectangles.

Downstairs, he saw that Jenny had the robin book out again. She was obsessed with the damn birds, convinced their lost baby was trying to communicate with her in the form of one. This delusion had originated during a walk through the roving dunes of Formby last year. Overcome by yet another wash of grief, Jenny had turned towards the churning boundary of the ocean where she happened to witness an extraordinary flitting ball landing on a jumble of bricks buried in the sand. The delicate bird stared at Jenny and broke into song. You never saw robins by the sea, she said. The bird was a messenger. It was their son.

Rosy blotches of watermelon juice had made the pages sticky. Today's robin had a rotund chest of vivid watercolour, true crimson, its twig legs melded to a scabby tree stump. Harry wasn't sure if robins had empathy in their black eyes, or if the artist had just managed to imbue this particular depiction of one with some soul. *Jesus*, he was getting as bad as Jenny – she had a whole scrapbook of this shit upstairs. He stood and watched her sleep for a long time. He lit a cigarette with a match. He left the room.

Ada took the news of the dog's disappearance from the couch, covered by a woollen blanket, a damp flannel draped across her forehead. Unreliable light broke through the gap in the drawn curtains and caught the eddying dust spores that settled on the coffee table, upon everything. The room smelt strongly medicinal, a combination of the calamine lotion Jolan used for his eczema, and the Olbas Oil Ada said helped curb her sinusitis. Grown tall outside the window was a lush bower of blackberry. Looking out, Harry noticed some lip-stained urchins picking at the vines, stuffing the nobbled clots of fruit into their mouths. Three long-haired elders watched from across the road, necking cans of lager bought from the Booze Buster around the corner.

Harry listened to Jolan's benign, supplicating apology with his arms folded. He was trying hard to ignore Ada's resemblance to Jenny, the way she lay, half-stirred, her gentle face reaching the lip of the couch's seat. She was a shapely woman in her early forties. He was a neglected husband whose drunk wife joked about his pattern hair loss. Harry touched the nascent pebble of cruelly revealed scalp, the fronds of crown hair he had gelled upright in an attempt to disguise his bald patch. *An egg in a nest*, Jenny often called it, delighting in mentioning it in front of other people. Stop being so sensitive, she used to say.

Least we know where he is, declared Ada, sitting up. I just don't like thinking of him on his own down there.

She glanced at Harry, who had to stop himself from taking her hand. There was just something *to* this woman. The fact that he was sure he could have her was eight tenths of it, the fact of his boredom and Ada's apparent understanding of him made up the remainder. Of course Harry couldn't imagine himself without Jenny, and the thoughts of his wife finding out about his trips to the Robinson house were terrifying, but he couldn't escape the niggling desire to have his own way. After all, if something as tiny as an atom could be split, there seemed like no good reason why you couldn't do the same thing with something as big as your own need to possess what you shouldn't. Harry could divide his affections in two. A fire engine hurtled up the Bury Road.

Using the wind farm as their compass Harry and Jolan navigated their way towards the cave. Jolan wheezed all the way up the brow, carrying a greasy box of fried chicken and a holdall packed with nine-inch candles. The sound of him massacring the bones and licking his fingers, his greedy, scything breaths, Harry tried to ignore. Jenny still hadn't been in touch. She was probably lounging in bed, floating through the cottony inter-zone between sleep and consciousness. Harry pictured their room. Even their private quarters were draped with the bil-lowing laundry of local strangers.

They left the path to pick their way through the furze. Harry swatted away a horsefly while a group of goldfinches fussed in a sour-smelling hawthorn nearby, the tree contorted as if suffering the most agonising arthritis. He would ease onto the bed that evening and ask Jenny how she was. She would call him darling, and he'd feel awful, he knew he would, each hand resting in his lap, unable to hold his wife because she didn't like to be touched when she was hungover and had got drunk all day and didn't want him to know about it.

As soon as they arrived in the clearing Jolan tossed the cardboard box of chicken bones into the undergrowth, then he crawled through the boulder gap. Harry found his atten-tion commanded by the grassy altar. The way the sheep was splayed was hypnotic. A shimmering square of sunlight drifted over its corpse.

With the aid of the torch and following the dim parade of Jolan's candles, the two men explored the cave. Its ceiling was low at first, fraught with curtains of bumpy stone, but it quickly rose to over twelve feet in height, ribbing the hill's interior like the insides of a fossilised whale skeleton.

Clumps of rock shaped like busted popcorn kernels inter-cepted the tunnel leading to the next cavern, the overhangs forcing Harry and Jolan to duck, the narrow walls glistening, chilly to the touch. The sound of water was back. Their boots upon the rock. There was a cooling draught; where did it come from? They were of the hill now, no longer on it, and the further Harry went into the cavity the more urgently he wanted to go as deep into this place as it would allow him.

In the next chamber they set down the last of the candles, lit them and cast the torch. Harry would plait piss if he had ever seen anything this spectacular. They were in a limestone grotto, an ancient place. The light they brought proved it, searing vectored shadows up tall undulating walls that could have been made of cream slime, on stalactites, stalagmites, dense columns linking ground to ceiling.

Moisture glittered everywhere. Thousands of years of seepage had left amazing deposits up every surface, forming claws of hardened calcite, free-standing knuckle sculptures, bubbled flowstone lumps. The cave's walls fed into the darkness, ridged, almost blossoming, the shapes trapped in sequence, rough yet smooth, sometimes seeming as if they'd been coated in wet batter, the liquid dribbled over the rock and suspended there for many centuries.

Harry could run tours in a place like this; he'd be on TV. His giddy torchlight guided him along sheets of mineral that reminded him of tripe hanging from the cave's roof, upon hundreds of tiny stalactites emerging from the ceiling as slender worms. It picked out calcite deposits so wide and delicate that his light beamed pinkly through them. Robbo, what've we gone and found? he said, but by then Jolan was in the next chamber facing an underground lake. When Harry followed the torch's beam, he too saw, at the water's edge, a glowing pair of discs: animal's eyes. The timid sound of whining filled the cave.

Ada insisted on celebrating with a drink. Jolan had left her and Harry alone because he'd the petrol-station boy bribed into letting him use the red diesel reserved for agricultural and construction vehicles; he had to fill the car's tank up before the boy's shift finished. David lay in his basket performing the occasional wild spasm. Since the terrier's dank rescue and its journey home in the holdall, it had done nothing but shiver. Covered in blankets, the dog could have been mistaken for a furry baby.

Harry and Ada took about two drinks to lurch together. Ada kissed differently to Jenny: she was fiercer, more mechanical. Midway through the embrace, Harry opened his eyes and saw that Ada had hers open too. She was watching him. He pulled away and wiped his lips on the back of his hand.

The sound of the front door slamming and Jolan's ludicrous moan interrupted the syncopated dry-hump Harry had going on a short while later. He and Ada parted then staggered their arrivals downstairs, Harry visiting the bathroom on the way, splashing scoops of water over his face before entering the living room where he found Jolan knelt in prayer and Ada with her cheeks flushed, her furrowed brow misted with sweat.

The dog lay dead in its basket, its tongue flopped from its mouth like a pink shammy leather. Harry tried not to look at Jolan, whose eye had done that weird thing again.

Well, he said.

He must have caught a chill, said Ada.

Jolan rocked back and forth. My fault, he kept saying, *Oh, Jesus.*

No, Jo-Jo, said Ada. Harry, tell him …

Harry stuffed his hands in his pockets. It *was* Jolan's fault. He approached his colleague. Weren't to be helped, he said gruffly. You weren't to know.

Jolan bear-hugged Harry's legs.

Never mind, said Ada. He died surrounded by the people who loved him.

Yes, said Jolan. Yes.

We'll sort him a proper grave, mate, Harry added, extricating himself from Jolan's clutches and looking at Ada, who he now felt strangely intimidated by. She was the only woman since Jenny who he had ever acted on an impulse around, and he worried now about his capacity for venturing into tempting places, of substance dark.

Later that day he pushed into the cave for a third time, the most exercise he'd had in weeks. He set down Jolan's tool bag in the second chamber. Jolan had been in tears when Harry left, prising out a patio flag with his bare hands in order to transform the panel of soil beneath it into a grave. Harry said he'd be back with a surprise. Ada had watched him coolly as he left.

It would take a while to knock out the stalagmite: needing the conical edifice in one piece meant taking his time. Harry had selected a marker fit for a dog's grave: a formation from the cave's rear that people wouldn't be able to see when he opened the place up to the public. *Maiden Voyages*, he'd call it: a tenner a pop for a tour of the awesome caves below the wind farm.

Harry knocked a dent free of the stalagmite with the hammer and chisel, then he knocked away another, working around the circumference, deeper, carefully, until the whole thing came loose in his arms. He heaved the stalagmite by its trunk into his backpack, then headed back towards the cave's entrance. He'd just arrived at the crawlspace when he heard a ruffling, feathery sound, and what he could *swear* was birdsong.

He whirled around to face the call, but saw only those carved skulls: three pitted and amused faces leering at him from the rock. In that moment the stalagmite Harry had planned to present Ada with weighed many tons, and at the same time it weighed nothing at all. He got to his feet. There was the most wondrous definition to this cave. Its scope and depth brought him back to Jenny and the days when they were making a foray into a life together. The Bridestones were a throne of rock overlooking Todmorden and the Calder Valley, and he and Jenny used to hike there, each of them tiny against the cliffscape. Jenny always packed a lunch: triangulated sandwiches and 10-pence packets of crisps, a plastic bag with a stash of ice in it to keep their drinks cool. She always knew what to do. Once, when Harry stumbled upon a lapwing nest in the grass, Jenny led him away before the dive-bombing parents returned to protect their young. Later, they wrapped themselves in their coats and a tartan picnic blanket, and lay on the roof of Harry's car listening to CDs.

Harry dumped the stalagmite on the ground and hurried, drawn, he didn't quite know why, to the cavern with the lake where they'd found Ada's dog earlier that day. That clever draught created wavelets here. Harry could see a letterbox-shaped crevice above the murmuring water. He edged around the lake until he could shine his torch into the fissure, discovering a greater treasure within the tear: a magnificent stalactite of dazzling alabaster white. Perhaps Jenny could display it on the hearth.

Harry dragged himself into the crevice and began to climb. There were enough handholds to think of this gap as another obstacle course at a jungle-gym, the kind he would have taken his son to when the boy was older, had he had the chance.

The stalactite emerged from the rock like a canine tooth from a gum. Harry began chipping at it. He had just the room to work, pinioned at a right angle in the crevice, back against one wall, feet upon the other. His devoted breath swirled from him in the radiance of the torch trapped between both tense legs.

He worked for a long time, striking chisel with hammer, clinking until the stalactite was ready to come away, realising as it teetered and dropped how heavy it was going to be, and not just how tired his legs were, but how rash he'd been.

The stalactite landed immensely in Harry's lap, the impact knocking his feet loose and sending him down the vertical passage, three, four feet, where he caught his back on a ledge and came to a halt, stuck at the waist, his legs dangling, he wasn't sure where. The hammer, chisel and torch splashed into the lake. Harry had at least kept hold of the stalactite. He breathed in the cold, his blindness total. The blood clammed his shirt as he cradled his wife's gift. Thousands of years it had taken for this strange monument to grow, and he had broken it away with remarkable ease. Harry rested his head against the pitiless stone. Outside the day would be escaping, its sun setting, the golden sleepers of light navigating the first winding flush of the sweet peas staked in his garden miles away. The creepers had exploded recently into glorious flower. Jenny had planted the seedlings earlier that spring.

This Strange Light

THE MESSAGE CAME THROUGH AT DUSK, a phone call when silence had grown customary between the sisters. The mobile vibrated in the car's door well but Annie didn't know who was calling – she was panting in the back seat beneath Jethro, watching him peel off the condom like it was a strip of Sellotape. Snow tumbled outside. Sticking already, it began to coat the wall surrounding the reservoir. It disappeared into the water and dissolved on the road. Annie often thought what a sight she and Jethro must make when they were entangled in their duty vests like this, a rustling mass of hi-vis and polyester. She would have laughed aloud at the thought if it hadn't been for the Airwave terminal bleeping on the dash. It wouldn't have been a happy sort of laughter anyway.

She played Alex's voicemail back when she could, managing three listens in the McDonald's car park a little later. Rosie Shannon was dead, and did Annie want to come and pay her respects? Jethro returned with a hot paper sack of food and two noisy pots of Coke, and he passed the whole lot to Annie through the passenger window. Dinner came free of charge, such were the privileges of law enforcement, although Annie wouldn't manage her fries. As the steam from her burger drifted around her, she realised she was going to cry. The Airwave terminal bleeped with another bulletin. *Burglary in progress.* This time Annie answered its summons with the siren, accelerating beneath the turnpike, second exit. She loved the urgency of the response car. She felt Jethro's hand upon her leg. The tears finally came as they picked up speed. The clarity of the road seemed fitting: bad things still happened on nights as beautiful as this. Rosie only had me, Alex had said in her message. I suppose now I only have you.

Annie lay with Mark later that morning. This shared time when he was waking and she was about to sleep felt important. As a low-ranking uniformed officer with little chance of promotion (she knew that now) Annie's life was spent in the throes of shift work. Her cycle was divided into two earlies, two lates and two nights followed by four days off, which meant she had a fractured social life at the best of times and barely knew what day of the week it was. This seemed to suit Mark. Since leaving the design agency and going freelance, he could work from home in peace, see his friends whenever he wanted and have Annie around sporadically. Annie eased a finger under the determined elastic of the faded knickers Mark enjoyed teasing her about so much, and removed them. Next, she used a big toe to free herself of each sock, then unfastened her blouse and bra while staring at the lunar terrain of the ceiling. Speckled, flaked. Several strands of Mark's chest hair had gone the same colour.

Annie changed into the baggy purple T-shirt she kept stowed under the pillow.

Wake up, she said.

Mark didn't stir.

Mark.

Still nothing.

Annie rose from the bed. Fatigue-sensitive to the morning chill, she stepping-stoned to the window using the clothes Mark had left all over the floor. Her view was of a pragmatically laid-out arcade of businesses and flats. In one of these flats, the place above the barber's, lived an unsympathetic-looking neighbour in his mid-forties. Annie would often see the man at this time of day, and wondered if they would nod at one another, as they did now, if they ever made eye contact out in the real world. She breathed on the window and wrote her name in the steam for him. The other side of the glass was dressed by snow as dense as mashed potato, and the geraniums Mark had planted in the sill box were all dead. As a Routemaster splattered through the slush below, Annie pressed the lump that had recently emerged on her left breast. The bus shook the entire flat. The silence that closed in after it had gone felt gigantic.

The seat belt was a pain in the neck all the way up the M6 – then again, perhaps Annie was being sensitive. It took four hours to get to the valley: a sodden vein of towns running through the West Pennines where you still got comments about how you lived from people you no longer knew. There were many extinct factories here, a textile mill converted into apartments, more bakeries than you'd expect, and more takeaways. Just off the roundabout in Rawtenstall town centre was a market where, by night, bored youngsters languished in the shadows like packs of jackals.

Annie steered the car up a buckled drover track leading to Arnold Grange, a former farmhouse horseshoed by a fine belt of land. This isolated and whitewashed building had been Rosie Shannon's home for the last three decades of her life. Since she took over the place former chicken coops had been fitted with glass and transformed into miniature greenhouses, glittered bunting was strung from guttering to eave, and teal and silver streamers dangled from the trees. Anything that could house a plant did so: buckets, kitchen sinks, steel bathtubs. Even a basket still attached to its bicycle was packed with verbena, the bike's spokes laced with long grass and browned-up forget-me-not.

Annie halted the car and made her way along a barked trail

that met the front door. She could see the rugged staircases of the hills, the bifurcating townships of the valley. Although people said places like this never changed, Annie didn't think that was true. In her experience everything evolved by increments, whether you were paying attention or not.

The door swung open to reveal Alex, who no longer looked anything like her older sister. A lot of blonde hair smothered her shoulders now, a haze of rosacea bubbling up either cheek. Alex called herself an artist, and she dressed with an artist's pliancy, wearing a green blouse buttoned, matron-like, to the top, a huge fluffy cardigan and navy blue culottes stopping shy of either ankle. Although you could no longer tell there were two years between them, if how Annie felt most of the time could be captured on another face, Alex's was it. Alex was the better-looking sister and from an early age Annie had known it. As a consequence she had developed a less outgoing personality, and still found herself jealous of her sister's spacy, heavy-lidded eyes, because they made Alex seem like she was hiding something, which had intrigued people, especially boys, when they were young. That was a long time ago. Annie set down her rucksack and entered the house. She was about to speak when Alex pulled her into an embrace.

It's good to see you.

It's good to see you too.

The glass table bore two urns. One held the cremains of Rosie's husband, Joss, a solicitor who'd suffered a heart attack on the brink of early retirement, sliding off the bench in the garden like scrambled eggs from a plate. The other contained what was left of Rosie, who'd been rushed into A and E after eating what turned out to be death cap mushrooms. Rosie's heart was damaged, her liver and kidneys. After living through sixty summers, she had spent her last evening on earth in a shroud of violet light because the intensive care ward was in a south-facing wing at the top of the hospital, and her bed was stationed by the window.

Joss's ashes had been waiting to be reunited with Rosie's for fifteen years, and now that the inquest had delivered a verdict of death by misadventure, the cremation had been allowed to take place, and the wait was over. Alex was pretending she was okay with everything.

Surprised you managed the time off, she said.

We were between shift cycles.

Makes things easier to arrange, I suppose.

Annie nodded. Her sister didn't seem able to look at the urns.

What did you tell them? asked Alex.

I just said she was my aunt. They were pretty understanding.

Annie wasn't sure if Alex's snort was intended to register disparagement, amusement or plain doubt. She began to fiddle with the copper bracelet that was supposed to protect her from arthritis, and watched Alex delve a hand into an upper cupboard, shadow cloaking her sister's features. Well, she said, they really were.

The spacious kitchen was unusual in that there were no windows, so the deep stretch of garden on the other side of the wall could only be imagined. An empty bird feeder would be there, as would Rosie's manky trellis, crucified against the fence behind Joss's bench. The death caps had grown at the foot of the kinked crab apple tree near the compost heap. What had possessed Rosie to gather them and add them to her soup?

Annie gripped her mug and held it out for the ice-dusted bottle of vodka Alex drew from the freezer drawer. Bearing the old Weetabix logo, the mug must have been sent off for decades ago. It hadn't been cleaned properly in about as long, the tobacco-tan of brews gone by circling its inner base like the rings of a severed tree trunk. Rosie Shannon had loved trees, and once single-handedly saved an ancient oak the council were planning to cut down by chaining herself to its mesh of upper branches while swathed head to toe in coloured ribbons, singing songs of protest. Annie smiled as the vodka arced into her mug. It was syrupy with the cold and would be the better for it.

There was a slight challenge to Alex's voice as she raised her mug. *Na zdrowie.*

The language of their parents. Was she being ironic? It was Annie who visited their father and his new family every summer in Krakow. Alex, who'd taken their mother's death from cancer particularly badly, hadn't spoken to their father since moving in with Rosie, at least that's when Annie dated the fallout. She felt like sighing. *Cheers.* She lifted her mug and set it down again.

Alex snorted for a second time, then drank. She'd moved into Arnold Grange after Rosie was widowed and the reasons why were nobody else's business. The two women were initially bonded by outrage, meeting at a protest outside the Florist's, the quietest valley pub, where a local hunt convened, a survivor of the national ban thanks to a loophole in the law that made it legal to use dogs to flush wild animals out, as long as it was for a bird of prey to hunt. This loophole meant that while a falconer was paid to have his raptor sit in nearby trees, valley men of narrow prospect could wear crimson jackets and drive their hounds through verdant country in search of foxes.

So how long do I have you? said Alex, draining her vodka, wincing.

A couple of days, replied Annie, taking a sip and doing the same.

I thought you might want to stay a bit longer.

After that it comes out of my holidays.

What, a couple of days?

Yeah.

Annie.

Don't bloody start.

Alex's hand was freezing. Annie pulled hers from under it, the legs of her chair roaring up the tiles as she pushed away from the table.

The next morning Arnold Grange was frigidly cold. Annie had only stayed here once before, and it had been like this then.

Leaves blown under the beds and in the summer, flies. All kinds of flies. Although it was an old house and therefore difficult to heat, the chill tended to creep indoors because Rosie Shannon made a practice of keeping the window of the second guest room open to accommodate the traffic of good and bad spirits. It appeared Alex had been maintaining the tradition since Rosie's passing.

Annie drew the blanket to her chin and hiked her legs up to her backside. She'd told herself she hadn't slept because she should have been on the night shift back in London. In another life she and Mark had known this time as the 'raver's dawn'; deep basslines aching above smokestacks and warehouse roofs, the sky different every time you looked at it. Mark had just finished his graphic design MA at John Ruskin when they met. He'd been beaten up one night whilst waiting for a taxi, and Annie, off-duty, had found him. His face, bloodied in an attractive way, was a picture when he found out what she did for a living, but he wasn't put off. Until she met Mark Annie hadn't realised she'd been waiting for the breathless trepidation of being noticed, letting someone in. Plausible deniability went right out of the window a month later when Mark pressed that chalky pill into her palm. Annie had known what she was doing. She hadn't cared.

What's up? she said to the door.

Alex shuffled into the room. How did you know?

Annie stifled a smile. I can smell your hair from under that rubber johnny.

Alex made a ditzy face. Beneath her shower cap her hair had been slathered with tomato ketchup because the pipes in Rosie's house were made of copper, and turned blonde hair green.

Shit, I forgot.

I don't know how.

It's gross, isn't it?

It really is.

Still, it keeps my hair the right colour, and it's cheaper than installing an air filter, said Alex, stepping closer. I came to see if you wanted breakfast.

Annie began to muss her own hair in the window's reflection. Cut into a bob and black now. Black for many years. She slithered out of bed and attempted to touch her toes. She could *feel* her lump.

I don't eat breakfast.

Oh.

Don't be like that ...

I'm not.

It's fine, said Annie, flopping onto the mattress. She had a message on her phone from Jethro. He was so much younger than her, it was crazy, but six months ago he'd snagged himself on her Hiatts. Pausing to untangle himself, the beat of collusion between them had been unmistakable.

How did you sleep? her sister asked.

Work boring x

Home too Xx

Annie?

What?

I said did you sleep okay?

Fine, yeah.

You look exhausted.

Thanks. So do you.

While Alex ate, Annie looked around upstairs. She could never resist sniffing about in other people's houses. She told herself that she was only keeping her eye in while she was off-duty, sort of in the same way that an old car needs driving to be kept roadworthy, but she also knew that always having an excuse ready if she was caught told its own story.

Her bare feet felt delicious on the dry, painted floorboards, on the jazzy rug stretched lengthways down Rosie's hall. She'd just showered and her legs were blue-red and freshly shaven. Candles and raffia were in abundance in the corridor, gemstones and birthstones glimmered in a shelving unit outside the bathroom, and a beaded curtain guarding the spare room clacked softly.

Alex slept in Rosie's room – Annie wondered for how long. There was the glass Rosie used to keep her false teeth in. Surely it was the same one Annie had seen when she first stayed here, stumbling in search of the toilet and catching Rosie, the person her sister had chosen above all others, napping with some false teeth in the tumbler by her head. A pickled grin with a virtual stranger snoozing next to it.

The second guest room had mealy wallpaper with a pattern of peach flowers that looked like wet tissue, abstract flamingos. Dream catchers, dolphin posters and mandalas were strung and tacked and a chair made from intricately looping cane stood beneath a bookshelf filled with self-help books and biographies of people who were no longer famous. Annie stepped around the bed to shut the spirit window, her towel slipping into a heap at her ankles. As she crouched to gather it about herself, she accidentally knocked the bedside table and put it at an odd angle to the rest of the wall. There she noticed a grainy black stain: a damp cumulus smearing the wall's surface.

Engine oil? repeated Alex.

I think so, yeah.

That's weird.

I mean, why would that be there?

Alex replied that she had no idea, but there was a furtive quality to her voice that Annie knew she would later question. Earlier, half-naked, she had strafed the wall with her pen-torch, illuminating the crude mottled stain that would never dry. Someone had made a good fist of scrubbing it away.

Did Rosie drive? she asked.

Cycled. She took the bus when her arthritis got on top of her.

Wasn't handy, nothing like that?

God your accent, Annie.

How do you mean?

Alex's voice cracked. Oh, I dunno.

Alex had been like this since Annie left home at seventeen,

ignorant of the fact that it was her fault, unable to accept that external modes of softening such as a gentler accent, painted nails and statement hair, were really examples of how a person could harden.

Some things about me were bound to change, Annie said, braking the car at some traffic lights, the supermarket beaming ahead. They were shopping for Rosie's long-delayed wake, which would be held at Arnold Grange. Afterwards guests were welcome to stay, then the following morning whoever wanted to could accompany Alex on a hike to the moor where Rosie's ashes would be scattered over Lancashire, dwindling, gone.

There was the earthy smell of muck-spreading in the air, and Annie found this oddly comforting. She touched her lump for the umpteenth time that day, hoping to come to a kind of familiarity with the fleshy bolus's weight, the pressure's pain, and said, When did you find this stain then?

Have you a coin for the trolley?

Annie fished her purse out. Soon after Rosie passed? A couple of days? A week?

Oh, how should I know?

Well did you at least report it, Alex?

Course I fuckin' did.

You can tell me if you didn't, you know. It's okay.

Jesus, am I being interviewed here?

No. Annie handed over a pound coin. I'm just wondering.

Alex said, The police haven't exactly been responsive. From day one it's been uphill with them.

That was a *no* then, and was that a dig? Annie checked her phone. Mark had texted a picture of the TV, his feet up in front of it, a bottle of beer. He was watching *Under Siege* by the looks of it. Again.

Cuts. We have to justify looking into as much as a broken nose these days. And reopening a case after an inquest's verdict …

Annie made a blade of her finger and drew it across her throat.

Alex tutted. Never mind. It's over now.

Is it?

Course it is.

Because when you think about it, I can't see Rosie being stupid enough to pick death caps, never mind eat them. Didn't she know about stuff like that? Herbology and shit.

Not really, no.

Well, what about that spare-room window? It's always open. Someone could easily have got in.

Oh my God, said Alex. Will you just leave it?

Better an empty property than a bad tenant, Devon Yarbo's place was proof enough of that. Everybody called Devon 'Mugabe' because of his resemblance to the infamous Zimbabwean dictator. He was an old friend of Alex's who'd joined her at various protests and gotten friendly with Rosie in the process. A chef at the Toby Carvery where Alex once waitressed, Mugabe was doing the food that afternoon and needed a lift to Arnold Grange.

His shabby dwelling was surrounded by Heras fence: a static caravan set on the outskirts of an abandoned quarry-cum-shooting range. Mugabe had moved to the valley from Nottingham in search of a woman he'd met online, and although the relationship hadn't lasted he'd decided to remain where he was. The city was the death of art, he said, and in a place like the valley where you didn't suffer the distraction of high wages, where violence was as much of a normality as boredom, you had to focus the mind, appreciate the landscape, internalise. In short, what had driven Annie from the valley was what had persuaded Mugabe to stay.

He'd made the rented caravan his own. A hand-built veranda was balanced on a dodgy parapet, while stored beneath were faded Calor gas canisters resembling rusted bombs. Clay sculptures were set about like chess pawns. Varying in size, Mugabe's golems were a febrile orange; they had puckish lips and cretinous brows, and were fashioned in a shanty kiln of brick and concrete. A sun lounger demonstrably saw little action whereas a plastic chair was surrounded by grub-shaped dog-ends and empty, warped beer cans. Mugabe's gleaming silver Granada had no hubcaps and the bonnet was open. Music that Annie regarded as clever and unlistenable played from a little radio, everything powered by a generator that chugged fumes and a carbon funk.

Alex tapped the caravan's door with her house key, then pushed inside with Annie following. The curtains were drawn inside and a laptop covered in stars sat on the table, an open chat window on the screen beaming the caravan's main source of light. The whole place stank of feet. Mugabe was standing in profile, pissing in the sink.

Hey, hey, he cried. Hang fire!

Jesus. Annie pushed out into the yard, the door clappering against the caravan wall. The last time she'd seen Mugabe she and Alex had been seventeen. He'd sold them two tabs of LSD, to make their day more interesting, he claimed, because skiving college a couple of times a week so they could skip a random train, travelling all over the country in search of they didn't know what, had taught the latch-key sisters that one satellite town was as dull as any other, so why not spice things up a bit? Because acid was way more intimidating than the cheap beers they'd been used to, Annie refused her tab. Alex took both then spent the entire journey to Stoke locked in the toilet. Annie managed to get her sister off the train but by the time she was able to coax her down to any semblance of normality, they were badly lost. November, darkening fast. Annie would never forget the scabbed wen under the stranger's eye, the rote way he itched it as he told her, No, he couldn't direct them back to the station, made as if to walk away then came at her from behind, dragging her into a ginnel while Alex hallucinated obliviously twenty yards away. That was the day Annie decided to join the force, pinned by a stranger on a pile of flattened cardboard boxes, rain as white noise and a kind of incantation escaping her lips, no one around to help when there damn well should have been.

Toilet's broke, Mugabe said, tipping his pork-pie hat at

Annie and squeezing a fat burst of sanitiser gel into his palm. Greying now, he had that same ready-to-smile face, the same coda tattooed in capitals across his knuckles. NOW + THEN, the hands said.

Annie watched her sister approach Mugabe and thread her arm through his. She was astonished to see Mugabe kiss Alex fully on the mouth.

Devon, I brought my big sister.

Mugabe's mouth made a wet sound. The broken rocks of the disused quarry behind him and Alex made them look as if they were in another country.

How you doing, girl? he said.

Annie nodded. He had engine oil coating his arms.

She's giving us a lift, said Alex.

I remember you, said Annie.

Likewise, Mugabe replied. You're the policewoman.

They took the lengthier route, the scenic route. In just a few hours' time the Shannons' ashes would be scattered. The snow had gone; it was a bone-dry day, a crumbly sort of sky, not the kind you'd choose what was left of you to become nothing beneath, thought Annie. Although that certainly wasn't up to the Shannons any more.

Mugabe sat in the back while Alex spoke to him in that didactic way of hers. The pair were planning an installation that was to be projected against Arnold Grange's exterior. Scenes and stills, mainly: pylons regimented like guardians across vast meadows, lost stags with branch antlers patrolling deserted dual carriageways, tins of glue acting as vambraces for tree boughs and leaking PVA sap. Alex had already begun work on the stop motion footage, the flickering Super 8 stock of shifting stone and soil, broken thorns, gulls with ragged paper serviettes for wings, mad kids in cardboard masks, a coleslaw of Crayola defacing their blank features.

Mugabe lapped it up. We show a bench with a dead guy's name on it, he said.

Maroon eyes. Scrawny as fuck. Annie had to check herself, keep her eyes on the road.

Are you allowed? she said. You know, is it all right to just beam all this shit onto someone's house?

Rosie's house, said Alex. And we're not planning on showing it to people.

Well what's the point in that?

Some work you just do, said Mugabe. Most of my stuff, if it was for the public I wouldn't enjoy it.

Annie tried to ignore his beaming, flat teeth.

We all need something to help us handle how hard life is, Mugabe added.

It's still Rosie's property. What about the family? Her kids.

Rosie doesn't have kids, said Alex. She was an environmentalist.

Didn't have.

Right. Alex flicked on the radio, a respiration of static filling the car, the odd word striving from the fuzz as if someone was trying to contact them from another dimension.

So who does the house belong to if there's no next of kin?

Me, said Alex.

Seriously?

Hard to believe, Annie?

You're the beneficiary of Rosie's will?

Alex shrugged. It was a surprise to me too.

The car crested the hill before Annie could respond, the windscreen revealing elevated land, private land. An antic tube of smoke smudged the point where the hilltops met the skyline. Mugabe pointed at the ritual. Shep Summers's land, he said. They're burning the heather to regenerate it for grouse coverts.

Ready for the glorious twelfth, said Alex bitterly.

Annie directed the car into a lay-by so they could watch the smoke coiling on the fleecy plateau, winding about itself and unravelling again like acrylic ink dropped into a tank of water. None of Summers's men were manning the fire. Une-venly-spaced ragstone butts for the shooters to hide behind had been erected, grass-topped, evoking Dark Age defensive outposts.

Summers reopened the grouse shoot's application before Rosie was even cold, said Alex.

Smoke lapped beatifically across the hills, dimming the light.

Bastards, said Mugabe.

How did he react to Rosie's injunction? asked Annie.

Stop it, said Alex.

How do you think? Mugabe said.

Annie turned in her seat. A grouse shoot will bring a lot of money to the area. A lot of jobs.

A lot of bullshit, said Mugabe.

Pinching the bridge of her nose, Alex muttered something Annie couldn't make out.

That doesn't mean they would have *done* something to Rosie.

Oh, Lex, you reckon? Mugabe said. Look at all this, soon as she's gone. They don't give a shit about the place. The rain's gonna flood off the hills. Where'll it go? We ain't got no forests any more. Then there's the emissions, you know, from the peat, as well as ...

He gestured at the smoke, his chapped hand so close to Annie's face that she could smell the caramel of old tobacco on his fingers. Cocoa butter. He had slick brown chef's burns up his wrists. And they'll cull the wildlife, Mugabe said. The birds of prey and the whatsit, stoats.

Stoats? said Annie.

It's not funny, girl.

Oh, is it not funny?

The land wasn't made to be messed with.

Do me a favour, mate.

What it is, is what it is.

Arnold Grange was decorated with pictures of Rosie, Joss Shannon absent from all but one. Rosie playing with her cat. Rosie after retiring from the university, youthful trips to Kenya, Nepal, Nicaragua. The last years of her life spent with Alex had been extremely well documented. Rain fell almost apologetically over the valley.

People went wild for Mugabe's vegan buffet. Annie had to admit it tasted okay, lingering at the side of the room, her mouth packed full of lentils. Funerals killed her. In another life Rosie was still alive. In another, Annie was dead. So was Alex. So was everybody else. Each guest was being themselves, *in a way*. Annie could hear them chatting about their loft spaces, yoga sessions, their children's lives. There was a lot of talk about 'how well' Alex was dealing with everything.

After people had eaten they sat in a circle to share memories of Rosie. When it was her turn, Annie talked about seeing Rosie chained in that tree. A cuddly woman who had described everything as 'brilliant' and 'fantastic', and now she was gone. Everyone wanted to know what Rosie had sung, but Annie couldn't remember.

Later she sat beneath the urn, overshadowed by a photo of Rosie as a girl, a booksniff, no doubt, well-meaning, proud and credulous, somewhat difficult to placate. Alex was drunk, so open-featured you could read the happiness on her face as if it was plastered across a billboard. She'd done very well from all of this. The once struggling artiste.

Catching Annie's eye, Alex made her way over and stood by her side, seeming uncertain, no chair to hand.

I loved her to bits, you know.

I'm sure you did.

Fancy another drink?

Thanks, but I'm trying to lay off all that.

The sisters were quiet for a long time.

So when you thinking for tomorrow? said Annie, standing up.

Well, I want to catch the sunrise, if there is one.

It'll be nice seeing them off together, won't it?

Together?

Rosie and Joss.

Alex might have nodded. She might have shook her head.

They've waited a long time, said Annie, pausing. This wasn't what she wanted to say. She had a good idea how *that* conversation would go.

It will be good seeing them reunited, she added. After all these years.

Fuck, Annie.

What?

When did you get like this?

Like what?

So browned off all the time.

How do you mean? I'm not browned off.

Alex chewed her bottom lip. You must be, or you wouldn't be constantly trying to get a rise out of me.

Annie could practically smell the leguminous scent of the wet fields beyond the block of wired glass in the front door. I've upset you, she said. I don't know how, but I've upset you.

You're so cynical the way you go about it.

All I was saying was it would be nice for them to be together again.

Alex laughed. Do you think they care what happens to them? They're dead.

And you say *I'm* cynical.

Funerals are for the ones left behind. They're for us. I haven't decided if I'm scattering them together yet, all right?

The executor's right.

If you like.

Very nice.

You know, Annie, you're going to make yourself ill if you go on like this.

I beg your pardon?

I said you're going to make yourself *ill*.

Annie batted the wine glass from Alex's hand.

The urns were unexpectedly light, the sky madly spangled with stars. The door to Arnold Grange clicked behind Annie, who made her way up the fell at this early hour, an hour for weeping brows, the going steeped in bog and a terrific sucking of the boots. The ground reminded her of chocolate pudding.

From the tor's pinnacle the view spanned many miles. It was a pleasing height that happened to overlook Shep Summers's scorched land. Annie unzipped the backpack. The contours of the fells made her feel dizzy if she stared too loosely at them, as did the banded bronze hues of the Shannons' urns. Some way off on Scout Moor was Shep Summers's barn, twin marquees protruding from it, emitting the tireless rhythm of a rave. Acid-house music palpitated across the valley roof. As Annie tried to smile at Alex, she passed her an urn. Neither sister spoke. They unscrewed the urns' lids and set the contents free. For a brief moment the tipped ash resembled intertwining ribbons. Alex released a glottal sob as the strands disappeared together. She hugged herself, her shoulders rising, falling. Annie reached out to try and comfort her, but a deep cough racked her lungs and she had to bend double and cover her mouth with both hands. All around the two of them a strange mauve glow had begun to striate the heavens. Morning was coming. It was here already. In fact, it had been here the entire time.

A Broken Drey Won't Save Them

———

THE SKY HAD BEEN GLOWING COALS when Molly went to fetch the fuel that morning, and that meant rain. He could see the murky distance of it through his work glasses: a haemorrhage of cloud visible through the splots of old resin. He checked his strop, which was safely slung around the tree's pole, and, one and two, adjusted the climbing spikes jammed into the crannied bark. Thirty feet in the air with a chainsaw dangling on a rope clipped into a harness, and below you: your groundsman, Nick, gazing up from the forest floor, yawning gormlessly.

Molly brought the saw up to himself, his name emblazoned in scruffy capitals down the handle with a black marker pen. He flicked the choke and squeezed the throttle, then he brought the roaring blade down into the branch. He always savoured these first applications, the cutting chain forcing itself into the wood. The main incision was easy and then the arm of brash was sent tumbling to the ground, narrowly missing Nick by a couple of feet.

Once the brash had been cleared an extended series of stumps laddered up to the tree's crown. Above that, its heat thwarted, the sun had become a blob of melted tallow that glowed over the valley scrub. Nick skipped back from the final plummeting branch and stuck his tongue out to catch a flake of sawdust: swirling mist the colour of custard that fell upon everything: the pine cones, the pine needles, the truck. He caught a flake and spat it out. Now that the brash was piled before him, he'd drag it to the dirty yellow chipper parked at the top of the bank. Here he would break the brash apart so Molly could feed it into the chipper piece by piece. This task, unenjoyable at the best of times, would be done by hand because Nick had failed to earn his chainsaw licence last month. Although Molly hadn't said so yet, Nick knew better than to ask him to shell out for a second attempt on the qualification. He would have to get used to not being good enough.

Molly shimmied up to do the tree's crown. Once that was gone, he'd climb to the ground and make a gorge cut in the uncarved totem pole the tree would be reduced to. Then he'd push the pole over and divide it into logs of descending size. Molly gazed at Nick, that pumped-up bumpkin. He had a fantasy where a tree's pole caught Nick's sternum, another where a bough wedged into the kid's blocky head. At that angle, with that weight, Nick's tattoo-sleeved arms would twitch as his body went into shock, the last vestiges of life's current flickering free of his fingers as if Nick's corpse was casting a final spell. Molly didn't know how he'd break the news to Nick's father, but he would be unsparing about it.

Nick was transfixed by the huge plume of sawdust that erupted from Molly's saw way above. The smell of ruptured pinewood was everywhere, reminding him of the builders' merchants where he'd been taken as a kid, running his hands along the planed lumber, savouring the fresh char scent of cut planks. It was mostly him and his dad back then. Nick's mother Jade was always away, at least in Nick's memory she was, off on another *stint*, which was what Nick's father called the times where she periodically disappeared in search of things, being *You know, just different*, elsewhere.

Although Jade had never made it any further than Bolton,

she always came home after the promise of whatever had coaxed her away this time had exhausted itself, and Nick genuinely appreciated that. I'm just up and down with it all, she used to say, I don't know what it is. And Nick understood, he even respected his mother's unswerving faith that life had the potential to get better if you kept trying. He never let on though, that each time Jade left him, he would draw doodles of her in the margins of his school exercise books. He never told her about the time he found her hairbrush down the sofa, how he kept looking at the thatches of dead hair woven through the tines, missing his mum and feeling foolish, aged twelve. Nick used to tell himself that Jade would take him with her the next time she went away. He even came to believe that her stints were scouting exercises, that Jade was planning a new life for the two of them. He didn't like thinking about that any more. He supposed he didn't need to. After all, he was a man now, he had a perfect BMI, he even had his own car. Jade had been impressed by *that*. If there's one thing people addicted to the next destination understand, it's possessing the means to conveniently get you there.

Watching Molly mutilate yet another tree, Nick wondered how his mother would feel, *hypothetically*, if she knew he'd lost his virginity the other week to Molly's daughter Louise? After all, the experience had been something to savour as much as fear, and one thing Jade had taught Nick was that pursuing what scares you was worth the effort if not always the reward, because you learned to push yourself, which was at least something.

A harrowing crack resonated throughout the wood.

The tree's crown was tipping, falling ...

Thump.

When the day had stilled, Molly picked his descent down the tree's remains, slicing the high upper echelons of the pole into sections and shoving the new logs to the forest floor. Everything was taking place through the grille attached to his hardhat, which was there to protect him from the gore of sap and woodchip but had the added benefit of setting him at a glorious remove to the rest of the world. The mufflers played their part too, covering his ears and stymying all noise. Molly was convinced that this distance was the main reason his old boss Teddy Lowry had started the tree-surgery business after returning from the first Gulf War. The helmet takes us back, Lowry used to say, meaning, *it kind of did*, and while Molly had never fought for anyone but himself and never would, he understood what Lowry meant: you can lose yourself handsomely amid racket and mess.

Nick scratched his bare arms. They were torn by the branch spines and irritated by the sap. Hungover, he'd forgotten to wear a long-sleeved shirt today, and after vainly searching for his work boots had settled for wellingtons instead. Climbing out of the truck that morning, Molly had said Nick would have to make do, then promptly given him jobs that accentuated his mistakes.

Clear fucking brambles. Clear fucking van then stomp branches while I set fucking chipper up.

As a rogue branch scored another painful line up Nick's wrist, as a nail drove itself through his wellington boot, piercing the space between his big and second toes, he'd thought of Louise, and how her skin tone nearly matched the colour of his bedsheets. The miserly clank of her earrings. The contrite way she'd smoothed her psychology coursework out after Nick had trodden on it. Had Molly worked out what had happened between them? Did he already know? Had he *always* known?

Molly first took over the business after Teddy's run in with the chipper. The number one rule in this gig was that you respected the equipment. Teddy had forgotten that and now Molly could still see the accident in his more static moments, those lonely times when the slowed world seemed to have defiantly reduced itself to only the broadest definition of what it was supposed to be. Witnessing an unexpected sunset, smelling the exhaust fumes of a traffic jam, listening to Louise chatting on her phone – when the terrible beauty was at its bluntest, Molly remembered the blood. There was so much of it. An unbelievable amount had cascaded, pumping vibrantly into the space where Teddy's arm had been. *I've got you, mate. I've got you.* The tourniquet Molly made from his own shirt hadn't been good enough. He'd got crazy and used Teddy's dog tags, which promptly formed compression marks on the ravaged stump. When he was better, Teddy donated the tags to Molly and to this day Molly still wore them. It felt right to. They were a kind of rosary.

The final log tumbling, he descended the last couple of feet of pole, knowing already that he was barely going to cut the crown apart with the big saw. The carabiners, his loops and the gaffs on his spikes sounded almost like spurs as he turned to Nick and pointed at the truck, smirking when Nick obeyed the silent instruction like he was supposed to. Gestures were all Molly needed to make himself understood. This was what it was to be the boss.

Talk about heavy. Nick lugged the enormous section of felled tree as best he could up the bank. Louise had been waiting at the bus stop the other week with a local boy named Cribbins who lived around the corner from her. Cribbins was a loner with white-blond hair and a strange tic that caused him to blink a certain way, first shutting both eyes at the same time, then the left eye, followed by the right, always in that order. He and Louise were travelling together because a valley man reportedly dressed in Rockport shoes and an Adidas tracksuit had been exposing himself to local schoolgirls, which wasn't surprising, thought Nick, given how some of them dressed. That April day Louise's skirt had been rolled high at the waist to make it shorter at the hem, and she'd worn pop socks rather than tights, which were the first things that caught Nick's eye, Louise catching him ogling her legs.

You work wi' my dad, she'd said.

Nick stopped. He had a plastic bag with some lottery scratch cards, a bottle of Malibu and a frozen pizza in it.

He keepin' you busy? asked Louise.

Hard at it, replied Nick.

Hardly at it, said Cribbins under his breath.

Nick pretended not to hear. Where yous off to? he said, concentrating on a puddle at his feet that had the complexion of a rainbow.

Louise didn't answer. She bit her bottom lip.

What's so funny? asked Nick, worried he was blushing.

Really laughing now, Louise replied, We seen you coming out the shops before an' Cribbins here said he reckons you look soft.

Cribbins nearly tripped into the road. I never did!

You what?

I never said that!

He went, Them muscles aren't real, said Louise, nodding at Cribbins. He reckons you're on the 'roids.

Nick shoved Cribbins. These feel fake to you, you little prick?

He presented his bulbous arm to the younger boy, the traffic surging by as Cribbins was forced to reach out and feel Nick's muscles.

Satisfied, Nick insisted on his firmness to Louise next. Feel these and fucking tell us they're not real, he said, again worrying about his face, which felt ready to ignite when Louise flicked her cigarette into the puddle, gripped one of his deltoids and squeezed.

A kingfisher-blue flame sprang across the puddle's surface. Cribbins kicked the fire out and Louise's fingernails left crescent marks in Nick's skin. Nick was soon driving his boss's daughter home via his place.

The next bit of the memory was the good part, but up the bank a peculiar sound had broken through the dull chug of Molly's saw, which was set to standby. Nick couldn't see what it was. The noise had come from his right, but now that the chainsaw had started again every other sound was being drowned out.

He waited until he was rewarded by a shift in the pine branches. He swallowed as he approached the movement, scrunched his sappy hands together. There was definitely something lying within the brash.

Molly spotted his groundsman prodding at something with his wellington boot. He killed the saw and called out to Nick, then strode over, the visor of his helmet sliding up with a crunch, revealing his flimsy work glasses and a sallow, unshaven face, eyebrows conjoined at the bridge of a roman nose.

For some reason thinking Molly was about to strike him, Nick flinched. Delighted, Molly said nothing because, for him, quiet victories were the kinds to be prized above all others. He watched Nick trying to act like he hadn't just embarrassed himself. The kid even stuck his chest out as he said, There. He pointed at the branches. There's something in there.

Molly lifted the topmost limb. Nick was right. At their feet were three translucent pink sausages with membranes covering their eyes and scrawny tails dragging limply from their rears. It was three baby squirrels lying in the mess of a broken drey. They must have fallen some sixty-odd feet.

Tree rats, Molly said, regarding Nick's dumb, ruddy face, that pierced eyebrow. The kid was goggling, the surest sign yet of the kind of naivety Molly despised most. He would have filled in a small-beer guy like this a few years ago, when the country wasn't so damn PC, when you spent your days loitering in the shadows of the boarded-up precinct of shops in the centre of Rawtenstall, and weekends inveigling your way into the Embassy Club, searching for girls or waiting until you got a pussy like Nick on his own. Molly actually saw himself as a fair and decent person. The way it was in the valley, you made weakness see itself. And if weakness could take many forms, so could the way you dealt with it.

Molly, Nick was saying.

Molly looked up. What?

I said what do we do?

Molly licked at a cold-sore he could feel coming. He nodded at the chipper and shrugged.

Nick faced the bank. It had become a wet incline of trampled sward, part-padded by a beige layer of sawdust. The chipper looked almost self-aware, its carbon-smeared, mud-flecked yellow panels picked out against the natural backdrop of the last problematic trees overlooking this beautiful row of stone cottages. The cottages had been here for years but had recently been conjoined into a glorified tunnel by their new owner and his tasty wife Shelley. Nick couldn't remember the guy's name but he'd seen him at the rugby club enough times. He was one of those thick-necked types who thrived in factions and were incapable of admitting they were wrong about anything. The man had never spoken to Nick or any of his friends, not because the only reason they frequented the clubhouse was the cheap drinks – although Nick suspected that was part of it – but because callow youth just wasn't worth the time of day. It had come as no surprise to hear that Molly was friendly with a guy like that, even though the idea of Molly having friends was incredible to Nick. Between them, Molly and the man had plotted the downfall of these graceful pines. The agreement was for Molly to quietly remove them from public land, cut them apart and prise them out, stumps and all, then dispose of the woodchip so an application for planning permission for an aviary-like extension to the back of the cottages could go ahead. My kind of job, Molly had said as he pocketed the elasticated wad of money. I'll get it done. But it was clear to Nick that all things were now secondary to these squirrels.

He was facing Molly and breathing heavily, he realised. Maybe we could hide them, he said, till the mum gets back.

Rain beat a tempo on everything, making the forest hiss.

Fetch the shovel, Molly said. Hurry up.

While Nick jittered over to the truck, Molly crouched to examine the kits. They had blind, bulging eyes. Wretched little monsters, he thought. Look at them, writhing and crying when he'd always thought them mute. He hawked a fluke of mucus up and spat on one. The phlegm slapped the kit's body and slid down the cobalt tinge of its organs, which were just visible beneath its latex skin. A lot of fuss, Molly said. A lot of fuss.

Nick returned. The idiot had left his gloves and helmet by the chipper. Molly gazed at the kits one last time. Baby birds, mammals, a few larger things too, he'd euthanised it all. If it wasn't him today, it would be a cat or fox later on, something else and not as quick. He accepted the shovel and speared it in the ground. This would be the penultimate act before the pub, then home, where waiting for him would be Sal. He wasn't sure how he'd even met his wife. He'd KO'd on a night out sixteen years ago and come to at her place: a bedsit in Stack-steads with an ethereal fish tank on a shelf, a wall of DVD's and an ironing board in the kitchen behind the couch. In Sal's bed Molly had faced a mirrored wardrobe that reflected his own groaning expression back at him. This strange, crass woman had acne scars and a partially infected dolphin tattoo. Not to worry, Sal said, we didn't do it, but she said it in a way that made a fool of Molly. Molly made up for his failure then dressed with unease, caught the bus home and didn't even tell the boys at the Woolpack what had happened. Sal tracked him down at the pub twelve months later. The baby had golden balls in its ears and blue shadow daubed around each eye. She's yours, pal, Sal told him. Her name's Louise.

Nick watched Molly clear the area around the squirrels. It would be easier to gather them on the shovel this way. Maybe he could take them home, raise them up. They mewled in the undergrowth, as if in agreement. How many animals had been slung into the cuboid gears of Molly's chipper in the past, gripped by tail, claw or wing, bodies chewed by the blades and scattered in the mulch? He could feel a lump in his throat at the thought of it.

Then the shovel was being passed his way and Molly's visor had been lowered and his helmet's mufflers were down.

Nick gawped. Look at him, thought Molly, puppy tough.

The gel in the kid's hair was being rained in creamy tracks down his forehead and face.

Take it, Molly said, smiling broadly now behind his visor. I said take it, Nick.

Nick obeyed. The shovel resembled a beach toy in his hand as he went to scoop the kits up, halting only when Molly seized him by the wrist and lifted one of his helmet's mufflers.

Fuck you playing at?

Getting 'em ... so I can put 'em somewhere safe.

The kits were motionless, having crawled from the drey. Still Molly said nothing and again that was enough.

You're not serious? said Nick.

Am I not?

What if the mum comes back?

She won't, Molly said. They never do.

Down went the mufflers. Nick shut his eyes and raised the shovel. The rain had slowed and in a few minutes the sawdust would be blowing again. There would be a din amid these trees and their bark runnels, and beyond all that would be silence, the kind of silence everything reaches in the end.

Field Mouse

———

A SIX-FOOT WALL OF IVY separates the new house from next door. It's a protracted stretch of scraggy green divided by a row of towering poplars, and Jim can honestly say he's not given it much thought until today. The thing is, there's a man on the other side of it speaking in a voice that's as bitty and dense as wet mortar, and he says, You know what the problem is, don't you?

Locked out and waiting to be let in, Jim leans out of the porch doorway but he already knows there's no one about, he's been knocking-on for ages. All there is, is rain. It's really chucking it down. Fishing lines of water catch in the tangle of poplars and slug the red convertible Mercedes belonging to Mum's boyfriend Paul, which is parked in front of the garage at the top of the drive. A grimy basketball hoop belonging to the house's previous owners is fixed to the wall above the garage door. It has no net and the backboard has rotted away. The hoop drips steadily.

Jim peers across the drive until the voice comes again. The problem's the bloody Irish, it says, the words punctuated by a wooden staff that pushes through the ivy, sweeping a break in the leaf and overlay. They're taking all the good weather, I'm telling you, lad.

The gap reveals a swarthy man with a substantial beard. I'm Gos, he says, tapping his temple with one finger. From next door.

Jim doesn't know how to react. Gos is wearing metal-framed aviator spectacles, he has a nose you could grab easily and hair that's slicked back, tight. He's holding a large golf umbrella that shields his cigarette from the rain.

I *said*, lad ...

Jim tries to smile. He's eleven years old.

You're not deaf then, Gos says, his entire beard seeming to emit smoke.

Not deaf, no. Jim's actually a big talker on his day. He's just home from his friend Lenny's house and although he's avoided the worst of the downpour, his face is glassy with sweat having jogged the briar shortcut past the Lord Raglan – a whitewashed pub on the edge of the moor – and each of his hands is bleeding. Caught in Lenny's wake, the composed sequence of steps, their tympanic thud, Jim spooked a pheasant and it made him stumble over in the gravel-dirt. The shade of Gos's jumper reminds him of the incandescent bird: a surprise of autumnal colour that took flight, squawking above the heather and harebells.

Gos toots his deteriorating cigarette. He's leathered by the looks of him, he might even have been in the Raglan before. He goes, Ireland gets the good weather, so Lancashire gets the shit. You know what we wanna do, lad?

Definitely leathered.

Sink the place, an' all them micks ... Then we'll get the good weather, and Yorkshire can have the shit!

Gos's wooden staff retreats through the gap and as it slips from view, Jim notices the bone handle, a hint of brass visible where it's screwed into the wood.

See you, boy, Gos says.

Their first meeting.

The second comes by proxy. Jim sits in the kitchen a few days later, eating cinnamon toast, when Paul shows up and sets cold-as-clay hands on either side of his neck. Look at that nutter, Paul says. Your mum never thought to vet the neighbours before she came. She never bloody thinks.

Paul is a line manager at the debt recovery agency where Jim's mother Harriet works. He'll be coming to live with them soon, he claims, and now, watching Gos indignantly, his thumb presses the skin above Jim's collar. Paul kneads it, *once*, then stops.

Jim's father has moved away after getting the job at Bradford Royal Infirmary, and Jim's brother Callum has gone with him, sick of their interfering mother, or so he says. It's all Jim's fault. If he'd only refused when his mother asked him to pinch his dad's work mobile while she distracted him. If he'd only stood up for himself, then she'd never have seen the mysterious number that kept cropping up. Although he sees his dad and Callum every couple of weeks, there's no denying that there's a pair of male-sized vacancies in Jim's life, and the idea of Paul stepping into either role is terrifying. Those chilly hands are still on Jim's shoulders. Jim is careful not to react but he does see what Paul is chafing at: the new neighbour has no top on. Jim thinks that if a conker had somehow managed to assume human form, it would look a lot like Gos. A Cub Scout green shirt swaddles the man's head like a turban, and he's digging a hole in his front lawn, clean-shaven now. His jowly chops seem rubbery without the beard.

Realising he's being watched, Gos straightens up and runs a finger along his brow, sending a series of wet beads rolling down the edge of his hand. He aims to wipe the sweat on his cargo shorts but grazes a hip instead, then hawks a ball of phlegm out and spits it on the trees, where it dangles creamily from a leaf like an icicle.

The act draws Paul to the window. What you doing, you? he calls out.

Building a pond, Gos calls back, triumphantly. Do you consent, sir?

He mock-salutes Paul, and winks at Jim. An intricate four-point compass is tattooed to his forearm, a delicate jaunt playing around him. Jim wonders who wrote the music coming from Gos's radio, who played the jazz guitar that's floating across the pea gravel.

Their third meeting is down to Lenny, or Leanne, as her mum calls her. She and Jim perch with their legs dangling from two planks hammered into the beech tree at the back of Jim's garden. The wooden platform makes for a shoddy treehouse but it offers a perfect, private view of next door's garden, and it's also a fine place for them to stuff their faces with the sweet, sticky squares of orange jelly that Lenny's taken from her fridge at home. The topic of conversation is Frank Gosthorpe, who happens to be as new to this part of the valley as Jim. They've found out he's a former deck cadet from the merchant navy, and seemingly a lot else besides. Gos has people talking. He claims he's here to look after his father, who's bedridden with the shingles, but everyone knows he's only here to collect the disability allowance. Little bookie biros in his pockets and a patina of grime on his hands and under the nails as if he's spent the day foraging in the earth somewhere.

Not that this bothers Lenny, little does. She lives near the traffic lights with her mother in the rented cottage before the track leading uphill to the Lord Raglan. Although it's known that in her last house Lenny's dad jumped from the landing over the stairs with one end of the bedsheet knotted around his neck and the other tied to the top banister, no one knows why and Jim will never ask. He first met Lenny when she came to post business cards for the taxi rank where her mother works. Sitting on the porch step, hiding from Paul, Jim got chatting to Lenny and ended up showing off by saying he could drive. He climbed into Paul's Mercedes with the idea of demonstrating how it was done, and accidentally released the handbrake. When the convertible rolled down the driveway, colliding with the quartz rockery and puncturing a tyre, rather than laugh, Lenny made a sweet lie out of what happened, almost convincing Paul that *he* was the one who'd left the brake off. That's just the kind of person that she is.

Can you not hear him? she says, salving a recent nettle sting with a clump of dock leaves, the damp residue distinct upon her hand. Jim's sitting so close to Lenny that he can touch the line where the natural pantone of her skin meets the sheened area she's dabbing, just caught in shadow. It's like a line separating before from afterwards.

I dunno, he says. I don't think so.

They descend from the treehouse and wade through a pot-pourri of dead leaves and twigs towards the unruly hedge. Next door's clipped expanse of lawn is tinted with frost, and, sure enough, a man is singing ... *Catch a boat to England, baby, Maybe to Spain* ... Only the voice is too perfect. Jim spies Gos and his radio near the potting shed. Gos's head is clamped by a pair of earmuffs and he's pretending his spade is a microphone by miming into the blade. Eyes closed, he appears to be thoroughly enjoying himself.

Lenny thinks this is hilarious. She wants to film Gos's performance with her phone, so to please her Jim defies his instincts by forcing his way through the hedge. He scurries over next door's crunchy lawn until he's kneeling behind a rose bed forming an island about a yard away from Gos. Although Lenny doesn't know it, there's no way he could do a thing like this without her.

She soon joins him and together they film Gos through a veil of thorns, through rose flowers that have been shrivelled into little clumps of burnt cellophane by the winter. Gos talks to himself. Doddery as anything, he keeps scratching his head, which has a huge plaster matting his now-bushy hair. Jim strains to hear what's being said – something about owls – but one of Gos's flip-flops knocks the china ashtray in the grass and he can't make out the words. The scent of ash merges with that of some wood smoke emanating from a fire as yet unseen. Jim can see iced particles in the soil where the rose stems enter the earth.

And still Lenny isn't satisfied. She crawls around the flower bed with a view to pinching the large bottle of gin standing next to an empty glass tumbler, either that or Gos's trowel or his pipe, while Jim captures the entire thing. As Lenny's outstretched hand enters the frame, Jim sees, for the first time, a legion of welt-like score marks disfiguring her wrist.

He daren't zoom in on them.

Lenny has nearly grasped the bottle when Gos whirls around, sprightly for a man of his age, and roars at her like a lion. Jim can hear his neighbour's knees clicking, a rickety set of patellae that sound like wooden toys.

The gin bottle skittles and tolls against the tumbler and its contents deposit an ellipse of green on the frosted grass. Lenny collapses onto her rear and tries to scramble away, sending Gos into a huge bout of laughter, great belly-cackling like a pirate. Only it seems to hurt. He straightens, wincing. That's what you get for being a sneak, he says through gritted teeth. And you, Field Mouse. You're not invisible either.

Jim gets to his feet, a corkscrew of smoke purling in the sky.

Enjoying the show? says Gos, switching off the radio. Or did you just fancy trespassing on my property and you didn't mind the cold?

Everyone's breath is visible. Gos winces again and shuts his eyes, allowing Jim and Lenny to get a proper look at him. He's wearing a thick pair of blue walking socks stuffed into heeled leather sandals, and a striped grandad shirt ringed with sweat, just visible under a woollen tank top. The dressing held down on Gos's head with sticky plasters has a burgundy conduit running down its middle, the rest of it as yellow as the supply of Post-it Notes Paul always has in his briefcase. A bloom of dirty fingerprints, where Gos has been pawing at the dressing, is patched along the edges.

Barn owl, he moans. *Bastard* barn owl.

Lenny seems unafraid. She steps toward Gos.

Bastard, repeats Gos, sagging into his deckchair. He wears shorts in spite of the cold, his inner thighs spotted with pimples. There's also what looks like a code tattooed to one wrist. Below the compass is a set of numbers.

Don't ask me what the chances were ... he says, stopping as he notices the spilled gin. *Oh, bloody hell.*

He snatches the bottle up and slurps its dregs. He does the same with the tumbler and seems close to tears as he tugs the cardigan about himself, touching his head, again, as if for luck. Making his shuffling way back towards the house, Gos halts and faces the youngsters.

Are yous coming then or what?

The living room has an ornery smell. Its curtains are drawn, making it dark even on this crisp Saturday afternoon, and there's a fire living in the hearth fuelled by dried pine cones, a supply of which are heaped within a scuttle.

Gos apologises for the mess as habitually messy people always do, kicks off his sandals and belches. A cabinet of bad taxidermy makes for a coffee table between a couch and a chaise longue with a spring coiled in its seat like the sandcast of a worm at a beach. In the cabinet is a diorama: a weasel-type thing prowling a dead log with a dead bird in its dead mouth. On top of the cabinet is a rubber plant with dust-coated leaves. Some Victorian daguerreotypes of expressionless robed natives are mounted in frames up the opposite wall.

Dharamshala, Gos explains, gesticulating in the pictures' direction. Fucking monks. I did a silent retreat there a while back. Rode an Enfield up from Haridwar after the Kumbh Mela ... An' guess what? he says, eyes widening theatrically. I got kicked out for talking, one week in.

Pissing his sides laughing, he heads into the kitchen. Jim thinks Gos must easily be fifty, or maybe even ten or twenty years older than that. He's surprised there isn't a dog here, a wattle-and-daub substance plastering its arse and tail. It's gravy he thinks of. His nanna's gravy. There's a similar beefy smell in this house. Rising damp is foxed green in the corners of the room.

Lenny is nowhere near as apprehensive. When Jim signals with his eyes that he wants to leave, she pats him on the knee and says, What's he gonna do, stick us in a pie? and Jim feels like *such* a baby.

Gos rattles in from the pantry carrying a saucer of pink wafer biscuits and two glasses of milk. He sets the refreshments on a fold-out TV stand before Jim and Lenny, then slouches in an armchair at the other side of the room. He takes a sketchbook from a magazine rack by the chair, and after lighting a pipe with a taper ignited in the fire, he begins to draw, a wispy trail chimneying around his head. His knees are the most extraordinary things. Their skin is like the walls of a cave.

Come get warm, youths, Gos says, without breaking from his sketch. Get to fire.

Neither Jim nor Lenny move.

You live on your own? Lenny asks after a couple of minutes, toying with the cuffs of her long-sleeved stripy top. Each wrist is bangled with neon bands, and she wears clumpy skateboarding shoes. Jim has been saving his pocket money for a pair of his own. He sits by Lenny's side and sups his milk.

Wi' me dad, Gos answers. The old fruit's upstairs. Aren't you, Old Fruit!

He rises as if he's about to proffer a sermon, seizes the wooden staff and beats its rubber base against the roof, causing the sconces and scarlet tassels of the wall lights to shake. The racket makes Jim start.

Festering in his pit, Gos chuckles. I'm his son. Part-prisoner, part-warden, part-nurse.

Silence. Gos sits back down, clears his throat and mumbles something imperceptible as he selects one of many Cadbury's Creme Eggs piled in a hammered nickel bowl on the sideboard. With great relish he unwinds the chocolate egg's foil binding, bites it open then prods a little finger, knuckle-deep, into the fondant. He tugs the finger out and sucks it clean.

A weakness, he declares. One of many.

Jim can't take his eyes from the staff. It's varnished, giving it a rich coffee hue, with the odd cleat erupting from its length at an acute angle. With its bone handle, the staff looks almost occult.

Holly branch I let stay a year, Gos explains, passing it over. I screwed a hare's skull into the top, drilled a hole in the wood to fit the bastard first, mind you. And I had to boil the bone, he says. Cause of the germs. After a sanding it were ready for life as an 'andle. He turns to face Jim. How you finding it in the big place?

Gos's debauched features are as oddly familiar and as damaged-looking as the facade of a dilapidated building. Jim returns the staff to him, too nervous to speak. His fingers aren't clenched. They're active. They knead the palm of each hand, a habit that has begun to give him almighty calluses. Jim doesn't know when he started doing this. All he knows is that it has to do with the unbearably dissatisfied feeling he gets if he doesn't complete tasks in multiples of three before leaving the house. Opening and shutting bedroom windows. Turning all the plugs on and off. Locking and unlocking the front door. It also has to do with whatever it is that has him counting the steps of every staircase he comes to, counting to whatever age he is, then stepping on that *exact* step with his right foot, as flat and even as he can get the tread, before starting the count all over again. On the way downstairs Jim must stand on the age stair with his *left* foot, to make it even. Thirty steps there are, in the new place. Three floors. Four bedrooms. Two gardens and one living room. It's all thanks to the divorce settlement and his mum's promotion. The new house, Mum says, is her not-so-little present to herself. I really love it, she says to Jim in that ornate hallway that looks like it's made out of meringue. I think I'm *actually* in love with it.

Gos coughs. A son at home, he says, frowning at Jim. You're like me, you are. A couple of tributaries, us two. Tributaries to a greater flow. He nods at the ceiling conspiratorially, but Jim has no idea what a tributary is.

You've a mad house. Your dad, I mean, says Lenny.

Ah, most of the stuff here's mine, Gos replies. I filled it wi' a few things I collected over the years. Him upstairs weren't about to say owt. Practically empty, it were, when I come.

Dad'd gamble on two flies crawling up a window if he could. He gambled his whole life away. Would again if he could still move. Bloody miracle he kept the house.

He flinches at the obvious pain under his plaster, reaches into a pocket and produces a small plastic sheet of tablets. He contorts the sheet and snaps out, one after the other, what must be at least five pills, then snaffles the lot in one. Chewing with his mouth open, Gos has a gob full of anaemic cream paste.

What happened to your head? Lenny asks.

Gos swallows with difficulty. Already said.

Barn owl, offers Jim. Which ones are them?

Snowy bastards what don't belong in this realm, is what. Buggers what do this.

Gos peels away the plaster dressing to reveal a savage streak of red scab and crusted hair, a cloven slack from where a set of terrible natural weapons have apparently parted the skin on his scalp. The wound suppurates and it's visibly inflamed.

Lenny gasps. Oh, that's infected.

There's also a smell. Gos waves her away. T'other week after Lord Raglan, he come. Pitch dark, it were. An' I swear to Christ it were like being hit by an Accrington brick. Accrington brick is the best brick there is. Did you know it's Accrington brick what built the Empire State Building?

A pause for effect.

Well, this owl felt like that, says Gos, thumping his palm. *BAM!* Out of t'dark. Two screeches an' that were him.

Thankfully Lenny isn't shaken, or if she is, she makes a damn good job of faking it. The animals around here are all a bit tapped, she says. There's a horse at the livery where my dad used to take us that bucked about. It went in circles making dog noises. It'd have your fingers if you tried feeding it. Lenny stares at her tatty jeans as she picks a hole bigger in the knee.

I've tried getting on paper what happened, Gos says, lifting his sketchbook for the youths to see. The A3 page contains an exquisite charcoal drawing of a man in a woollen hat and a duffel coat. Down the scarp he goes, away from some trees, leaning on his staff while behind him is a bleached-white pub in the night's ink: a cuboid beacon with a car park. Above that is a broad, spectral mass, a feathery spread that's punctured by some evil-looking talons. The owl's enormous wings take up the high places. They distract from the sky and all that's in it.

That cut needs stitches, says Lenny. Disinfectant.

That's Accy, says Gos, ignoring Lenny and tapping the illustrated owl. I'll get him for this. An' you can do one wi' them stitches, lass. He turns to Jim. You havin' that, Field Mouse?

Jim has nothing to say.

Next time I go the hospital it'll be the last time any man sees us alive. And that's a promise, Gos says, and Jim believes him.

The next day Lenny calls round with a first-aid kit. She makes Jim knock-on at Gos's, and when there's no answer she barges indoors because, as it turns out, the house is unlocked. They find Gos flat out on the carpet: a fat old stick man. He looks naked without his glasses, old and vulnerable, and now Jim is tasked with waking him. All he can think to do is take the holly staff and prod Gos's stout chest with it. Gos flaps into being a moment later, rubbing rimes of sleep from his eyes and commencing an extensive lung-evacuation process. His taut belly reaches to a chest the colour of tanned hide. A tattooed set of eyes, a top hat and beard, have given one of his nipples the appearance of a doodled Abraham Lincoln.

Oh, piss off, he says, when Lenny holds aloft the first-aid kit, but she's serious, even to a relative stranger. It needs sorting, she says, and Gos reluctantly complies.

With utmost care, Lenny bathes Gos's wound with warm water and cotton pads, then, when Gos is at his most relaxed, she produces a bottle of Dettol, dabs some on a dry pad and firmly applies it to the raging head wound, running it lengthwise, laughing and apologising as she does so.

FUCKING COCK CUNT!

Gos leaps from the couch and flattens against the furthest wall, knocking the rubber plant over on his way, a gunpowder trail of soil spackling the floorboards. He's babbling, swearing blue murder. Lenny tells him to give over and chucks him a clean dressing from across the room.

Get out! Gos yells. Get out of my house!

They return a day later with a 35cl bottle of Napoleon brandy. Jim presents the amber tonic to Gos the moment he answers the door, while Lenny shows off the Dettol. Grudgingly, Gos nods for them to come inside.

They call around twice more to apply antiseptic until the wound is less garish and they can stitch it. On this day, Lenny boils the stove kettle and pours the contents over a needle. The needle's already been threaded with a suture, so after it's sterilised she heats its prick with a lighter, numbs Gos's wound with an ice cube and sets to work. She flesh-stitches with a steady hand. She's some years older than Jim and has done this before, she says, although she won't say where.

Meanwhile, Gos swears vengeance on the owl. He grips the couch's threadbare arm and, every now and again, pounds his thigh. Jim stands to one side. It's his job to wipe the pad soaked in Dettol down Gos's bristling new scar, and as he touches the weeping mark, he can't shake the feeling of recognition. It feels like more than déjà vu, like a premonition.

Jim doesn't see Lenny again until about a week later. She's been helping her mum, she says, and revising for her exams. Gos shows up almost as soon as she arrives. He tells them he wants to thank them. I'm giving you these, he says, producing from behind his back a shoebox wrapped in tinfoil. He plonks the box in Lenny's arms and grins as Lenny opens it on Jim's drive, finding inside, wrapped in a shredded *Valley Courier*, two shrunken human heads, painted and with polished skin. They look like a pair of coconuts.

Pair of *tsantsas*, Gos says proudly, informing Jim and Lenny that each head once belonged to a fallen Shuar warrior from the Peru–Ecuador border. Each *tsantsa* has eyelids and lips that have been sewn together with cotton string, their stiff faces blackened with vegetable dye. I've had 'em years, Gos says, scratching his huge, pored nose. They're a source of great power. A gift of souls is the least I can do after what yous did for me.

There is no denying the oddness of the gift, but Lenny seems pleased so Jim pretends to be. He studies the *tsantsas* and imagines his own head and Lenny's perched on a shelf in Gos's attic. Painted and preserved. Their hair bound in scuzzy little topknots.

Now listen, Gos says. Can I interest yous in a spot of adventure this evening?

The day ebbs and is lost. Mum is washing her hands at the sink. Thanks to the sunset draining through the window, Jim can really see the effect of the tanning injections she's been having. The melanin levels in her face have been amplified to the point where she looks caked in creosote. He wonders if she was always this quiet, or if it was the divorce that silenced her. She does work a lot – maybe that's why she can't be bothered to speak when she gets in. His mother *is* her work, that's what Jim's father used to say. Jim travels into school with her every morning on her way to the office, and he can't say she has much to say to him then either. Still, maybe it's not her fault. Maybe the fact that Callum and Dad have gone has highlighted every absence in Jim's life. Whether it's a flat conversation or an unremarkable day, a joke at his expense or an argument over what to watch on TV, he will feel it more keenly now, he understands that. Also, come to think of it, his mother *has* maintained an interest in his progress. She studies his school reports, she makes sure he does his homework and she's even been known to email a teacher if she doesn't agree with their feedback. This is the kind of stability, Jim overheard her telling his equally morose and distant Aunt Claire, that made the judge look favourably on her during the custody case. However, it might have helped if the judge had thought to ask Jim's mother about the art of conversation. Surely that should have come into the decision-making process. Tell me,

Mrs Tinker, do you have even the faintest idea of how to engage with an eleven-year-old boy?

Paul is reading the newspaper on his shining tablet. He ignores Jim, who can see the pasta boiling over on the hob. When Paul finally notices the pan and hurries to rescue it, he accidentally knocks Jim's knife off the table. It bounces on the tiles and begins to turn in a way that the compass tattooed to Gos's arm will never do. You blind as well as thick? Paul snaps. The kitchen smells of garlic bread, oregano.

An hour after sneaking out of bed, Jim, Lenny and Gos are making their way to Whitelow Cairn: a Bronze Age burial site located somewhere above the Lord Raglan. The moon is bold tonight, and studded underneath is an unusually bright star. *Jupiter*, Gos explains in an awed voice. And don't you think, youths, that it looks as if the moon has dropped his pocket watch?

Jim sticks close to Lenny. With her mother directing taxis until the morning, she's had no trouble slipping out either. Her hood has become a caul obscuring the snot green of her hair, her silver-hooped nose and spiked lip piercings. She's in a quiet mood, and Jim considers his own nervousness about what they're setting out to do. He supposes that when you've someone you confide in by not confiding in them at all, you begin to depend on the bond of their company to spare what's unsaid becoming deafening. You'll follow them anywhere.

They have one good torch. Three sets of strong boots. Here on the bridleway above the light pollution there's a bleakness to the atmosphere that must have been sensed before by centuries of people. Pilgrims. Druids. Roman soldiers.

This is Whitelow Cairn.

There's the coppice, says Gos. He's referring to a mob of trees gathered as if in conversation. They're alders planted by foresters in an experiment to see how high they could get a wood to grow. The trees are stunted, Gos says, but they're tall enough to hide in if you have to.

At the foot of the first alder Gos attempts to set Jim at ease by pointing out the ranging apexes of the deciduous larches in the valley beyond. Then, with his torch, he illuminates the star rot on some grass and a nearby branch. Gos tells Jim that star rot is a galactic jelly, a gooey essence deposited on earth by meteor showers. He dips a finger in one of the clear, gelatinous blobs and holds it under Jim's nose. It smells awful. The secretions of space, Gos says, and Lenny laughs.

They're here for gold. No, really. Gos says that amid these experimental alders is hidden treasure. What if I said there were a man who burgled the jewellers when he were a kid? What if he got caught but managed to hide the stash before the cops arrived, carving an X into the tree it were buried under?

Gos shines a torch on his wrist, those coordinates.

But by the time he were released the tree had grown so tall he couldn't tell which one his shit were buried under ... Such is *life*, youths! Gos cries joyously. Such is life!

As for the barn owl, well, Gos has the air rifle in case *he* turns up. Lenny finds the whole thing hilarious. She and Jim take spades to help excavate this ancient burial ground, Jim attempting to dig twice as fast as Lenny, feeling at first as if he's proving himself, then worrying that his muscles might seize up, an abysmal tension beginning to settle upon him with each strike of the blade. The feeling reminds him, oddly, of boarding the plane to Cyprus on holiday with Mum and Paul last year. The moment he said goodbye to the ground, totally convinced there would be a crash.

As they dig holes at the foot of well over a quarter of the trees, the feeling needles Jim and it won't go away. He watches Gos prodding each pit with the holly staff. He watches him find nothing there. Clouds have begun to creep across the amethyst sky. They are animate, inviting, and as Jim stares at them, he thinks about all the people this barrow has been sacred to over time, and he's about to ask Gos if he can please, *please*, just go home, when a dreadful screeching tears the night in two.

KRRRREEEEE!

It's the owl. There's a flood of cold. Lenny follows the noise with the torch as a second call erupts, a pitched and awful sound that seems to come from everywhere all at once.

KRRRRAAAAA!

Gos fires the air rifle and halloos like a Native American. There's a photo on the wall of his bathroom of one such man: Geronimo, solemn, expectant, *proud*, although perhaps in that defeated Apache's mind as he sat for his portrait all those years ago was the very thing that Jim can sense all around him: an invisible perception of dread that seems to hang over everything like a debt. Jim listens for more birdcall but there's only the sound of the wind moaning through the Lord Raglan's carpark gates. Perhaps this is what makes him decide to run for it, fleeing not so much the threat of attack, rather the feeling that he's sure will overpower him one day. *Moloch*, dry and hot. Gos is calling his name but Jim won't answer. He's away beneath the clouds, knowing that there will come a time when he has to stop running, knowing that he will have to turn back.

Black Ice

IT HAD BEEN THE LEAD STORY in the *Valley Courier* over the last couple of weeks: a local man had been dragged into one of the machines at the paper mill. Chunky Deakin, reduced to an article in the news: a dead man staring blindly at the living from a Perspex tub in a petrol-station forecourt.

Benj hadn't known Chunky that well, and what he had known of him he hadn't liked. Still, nobody deserves a death like that. After the machine's workings were finished with him Chunky's remains had to be extracted from a 120-foot silo, along with the colleague he'd died trying to save. It was certainly a brave way to go, but Benj knew Chunky was no hero. He was the kind of guy who'd take you to one side and whisper to you about what he'd like to do to the eighteen-year-old behind the bar if he got her on her own, the kind of guy who'd clout you between the shoulder blades if you were at his side during the crescendo of any story. Whether he knew you or not, any moment worth sharing required a salvo. That was Chunky. You couldn't show it hurt or you'd get another.

Although Benj could only imagine how Chunky's family must be feeling after the accident, they could have been a little more selective when choosing the images for the media.

Was *this* how they wanted their son to be remembered? The Deakins had opted for a simple yet intense close-up of Chunky that emphasised one of those taut 'big-lad' faces that Benj knew Chunky had been self-conscious of. In the photo, Chunky's hair wasn't as tamed as he usually kept it either, and the pupils of his eyes were kindled by the camera flash, making him look possessed, uncomfortable with having his picture taken, his attention snagged by something out of shot.

Benj wondered what Chunky had been looking at. Judging by the tobacco-yellow walls behind him – *Tarshell*, you might call it – he'd been in the Woolpack where the majority of valley booze-hounds congregated every weekend. Perhaps it had been Christmas Eve, anorexic tinsel stapled to the beams above the bar, the beer pumps never slowing and the staff growing progressively rattier with the drunken patrons. Unlike a lot of the local pubs the Woolpack was still in business, although Benj hadn't visited the place in years.

Although he was overdue for sign-in at the halfway house, Benj went into the petrol station to buy a copy of the paper for the latest update on the story. Across pages two and three the heavy particulars had been spread – the mill's scrabble to avoid liability, the firing of the ageing shift manager who'd put the youngster on the job with Chunky when he was nowhere near ready, the date of the inquest and the developments of the Deakins' compensation claim. Finally there was a gooey paean from Chunky's sister positioned above a colour photo of Chunky's widow, Danielle, and their son, Scott, who gripped yet another unflattering photo of his father in a fat-fingered hand. Dani had barely changed. There was that blistering of freckles, and that coy expression Benj remembered so well – as always, most visible in her eyes – that was there too. Dani was an optician now. She ran her own practice. Benj whistled to himself, rolled the paper up and stuffed it in his back pocket.

A few days later Benj was perched on a leather chair in Dani's examination room, waiting for his eye test to begin. Neither of his hands reached the lip of the armrests and his trainers tapped an ungainly rhythm on the metal step.

Engrossed by her computer screen, Dani hadn't bothered with a greeting. When Benj entered the room she simply spoke at him over her shoulder in that dismissive way some medical people have, and told him to take a seat, remove his spectacles and study the lightbox reflected in the mirror.

To the sound of fingers ticking across a keyboard, Benj did as he was told. He could make out twin rectangles on the light-box, one violent red and the other a livid green, black targets at either end for him to stare at, and if he squinted at the blurred capitals spelled out on the chart in increasingly small rows, he could read them too. To his left was a refractor head. Fixed to a gleaming steel derrick, the device was suspended, ready to bear down with a series of portals through which Chunky's widow could examine Benj's eyes and deduce, if not his soul or his intention, at least his prescription.

Benj was surprised by how prickly and hoarse his voice was as he at last thought of something to say. You've cut your hair, he croaked.

Dani swivelled in her chair and made a funny noise. *Uh.*

It's Alan, said Benj. Alan Benjamin.

God, Benj, replied Dani. What you doing here?

Been ages.

Yeah. Dani laughed incredulously. It really has. You just back?

Kind of, said Benj. This is nice.

Dani looked confused.

Benj gestured around the poky little examination room. Your business?

… Right.

Sorry, do you not run the place?

Dani shook her head.

But I thought …

Dunno where you got that from.

Fucking papers. Benj began to play with his watch.

Unfastening it, refastening it, tightening it. It's still good to see you, he eventually said.

Dani shrugged. Or maybe it was a roll of the shoulders. No, it was a shrug. Benj was sure of it. He supposed he had it coming. Before she met Chunky and her name became alliterative, Dani had been Dani Swann, and attended the same grammar school and sixth form as Benj. In many ways Dani had been a good girl. She didn't do drugs, she didn't really drink. She wore flares and crop tops and had bright orange hair for a while; she even drove a scuzzy Fiat Panda around that had a rubber James Brown figurine dangling by elastic from its rear-view mirror, and a lot of people thought that was all there was to her. The thing was, Dani hung about in the lower common room: the domain of the unfashionable cliques, sarcastic teens and overt self-doubters whose every relationship was rooted in esoteric movies, heavy metal and shared sympathy over the latest hopeless crush. According to youthful hearsay the downstairs girls were all slightly touched, and they'd go with you into the woods if you asked them the right way. This lent supposedly pure girls with a rock-chick edge like Dani a certain credo within the upper common room, which was itself a nasty hall of flippant girls and cocksure boys destined to become atrophied versions of their teenage selves. Back then, the upper common room said, you could go with a girl like Dani Swann, but developing any kind of meaningful relationship? That amounted to a serious breach of social protocol.

Benj had found this out for himself when he and Dani kissed at a house party one night when they were seventeen. After exchanging texts and arranging to attend a NOFX gig together, the upstairs common room got wind of the arrangement and Benj was shamed into crying off. Dani didn't reply to the cancellation text and within a month she was going out with someone else. Benj salved his disappointment by spreading a rumour about Dani having BO that didn't take, and not long after that they finished their A levels, Dani leaving home for university in Lancaster. Two boyfriends later she moved home like valley folk always do, and met Dennis Deakin. Chunky to his friends.

And how you finding it all? Dani asked, messing about with a wooden tray of lenses on her desk. I guess it's all been pretty weird ...

It's okay, said Benj.

That's good.

Yeah.

Yeah, right. Dani obviously knew. The whole valley knew. After all, like Chunky, Benj had made the news once. The reports had left out very few details. Benj had been twenty-one, off his head behind the wheel, bombing it from the rave on the fells off Scout Moor to the after-party at Tim Ashworth's house. One thing the papers didn't report was that Benj was in fancy dress, a tiger suit, of all things. Nor did they report the windscreen wipers' broken locus, the placid warmth of his car's interior, the spearmint chewing gum that had given his mouth something to do amid the rush of Ecstasy. The minty wad he'd spat onto himself after his bloodied car came to a stop, smoking, fucked, the cow he'd struck even more so. The cow had escaped its field. Benj had slammed into it, spun around and hit a tree. The countryside was silent save the pounding car stereo and the dreadful lowing of the animal lying on its side, its ribcage decimated. Benj had coughed his gum out while Al Pinder, Tez and Pete gasped in the back. Pete held a nose broken so badly that he looked like a different person. Holly Lomax wept against the airbag in the front seat. As the youngest member of the party, Tim had been in the boot. *Our Kid* the flowers decreed up the interior window of the hearse in its corsage, two weeks later.

Dani looped a strand of hair about her finger. Like everybody else she probably wanted to ask Benj what prison was like. The answer was that prison was like spending several years in a doctor's waiting room, or at the funeral of someone you barely knew, or at a bus stop at night, or any other place where the tyrannies of emptiness and boredom ran riot. Except for Benj every day inside had been veined with fear, immense fear, and a sinking feeling he hadn't been able to shake since.

He'd moved south immediately after his release. He'd married a woman he didn't understand, their union preceding three years of peeling themselves from the floorboards. Three years of the needle and the pipe. When Benj and Kizzy first met on London Fields neither of them had slept since the night before. Perhaps this was what made things appear so magical. To Benj, Kizzy's Caribbean heritage had been impossibly exotic, and in a way it still was. His own forebears all hailed from the valley: generation after generation of broad-talking, fair-skinned, brown-haired Jacks and Michaels, Davids, Matthews and Toms, stretching back to the Industrial Revolution that had made the valley, and beyond. To this day Benj still thought of the acute loop-the-loops of Kizzy's hair, the thin stripe of glitter she'd daubed across her dove-grey eyes that morning. The two of them got so drunk at their wedding a month later – the ceremony cost just fifty quid – that Benj could remember almost nothing about it. The whole thing had been one more instant to be boxed off like any other, hours, afternoons, whole weeks sectioned into simple units of time that made the mire of his existence a little easier to wade through. What was another forgotten day in a life spent trying to get lost?

Well, no more. Dani wheeled towards him, her chair's castors struggling over a rick in the thin, olive-coloured carpet. Benj could smell her, her otherness. He decided to just come out with it.

I was sorry to hear about Dennis.

Dani practically winced. No need to apologise.

I know, but—

Uh.

I am sorry.

Dani cleared her throat. Well, we all were. *Are.*

Back at work now though.

Just trying to keep busy.

Has to be done, said Benj.

Dani angled her head.

How much compensation are you getting? Benj wanted to ask. *How often have you thought about me?*

When the test was complete Dani typed the case notes up, selected the appropriate contacts from a cupboard, parted Benj's eyelids then suckered each lens onto a cornea. The transgressive intimacy of the act made Benj want to get up and walk around the room.

Now he could really see. One lapel of Dani's business suit was frayed and her sandy hair was centre-parted, reaching her neck in soft, dissonant layers. Time had added creases from her nostrils to the limits of her mouth, but to Benj she was still attractive. Maybe it was the idea of her. The nostalgic age she would always be associated with.

What you up to these days? asked Dani. And how do they feel?

Benj blinked. Fine. What do I do?

Since coming home.

He started to say something, then shut his mouth. How could he explain that he was unemployed: that returning to work had been a nightmare? It was funny, Benj still felt misled. When he was sent to prison it should have been the judge's responsibility to explain that the unwritten part of any sentence was that after your release your card would be marked; that prison stink would always linger about your person. Visas, jobs, credit cards. Good luck. Just because you weren't using didn't mean you weren't an addict, and just because you weren't in prison didn't mean you were no longer a convict. Even after the charge was spent. Even then.

Dani was smiling at him politely. After an awkward silence she said, Well, good luck with it all.

Yeah, thanks, Benj replied, accepting Dani's hand, even though such formality with someone he had groped felt inane. You too, he said.

He was outside a moment later, his head bowed beneath

shreds of leaves that tickered to the ground, collecting in riotous shades of amber and plastering the road. Ahead was the churchyard bench, and Dani's shift would be finishing in an hour, or thereabouts.

E-cig. Phone. Keys. Wallet. Benj stood outside Brooklyn's Wine Lodge a while later, a bar that had a cold wet stone smell, like a graveyard, and echoed all week when it was empty. Only tonight was a Friday, post-work drinks time, so the place was filling by increments.

Benj used to drink here all the time, he and his friends popping in and out of the toilets in ones and twos, high on baggies of whizzy coke and wraps of gunky MDMA, egging each other on to crack onto the ugliest girls they could find, ending up alone, for the most part, as alone as now, so perhaps little had changed.

The evening felt gravid with rain. Solidified bird shit decorated the ground by the drainpipe and a discarded condom lay in a patch of moss curled around a drain. Paddy Morgan, head of the valley family you wanted to mess with least, was working the door tonight. Paddy, an old friend of Chunky's, raised his arm at Dani Deakin, who was by now tottering up the road, her brash lipstick visible from yards away.

Paddy stamped the cold from his feet. *Here she is.*

Hey up, Pat.

How you doing, love?

Oh, not so great.

Having a drink, I take it.

Uh.

Course she is.

Paddy slid a lump of fifties from his pocket and peeled one loose. As Dani reached for the note, Paddy scrunched it out of reach.

Come here, he said, pointing at his cheek.

Dani went on tiptoes, planted a kiss on Paddy and was dragged into an immersive cuddle. Hiya, Pat.

It's good to see you, Dan.

Yeah, you too.

I mean that, babe.

I know you do. Ta.

Benj tooted his e-cig and exhaled a huge flume of strawberry-infused vapour that drifted into the road. Noticing the cloud, Dani smiled at him over Paddy's arm. You following me? she asked.

Benj didn't answer.

At the bar, Dani got the round in. Tonight Scott was at football training, then staying at a mate's, so she at last had some time to herself. She was drunk, Benj realised, and, like all drunks she conversed by acting as if she was listening when really she was waiting until it was her turn to speak. Benj's father had been like that too, but fuck him.

It was Scott, said Dani. He suspected her of trying to replace Chunky. He was on a crusade about it and now she felt taped off, like a crime scene. She was also finding it extremely difficult to forgive her son for walking in on her when she first heard about Chunky's accident, interrupting a vital moment of catharsis.

I was in my room, said Dani, touching Benj's arm. We'd just heard what happened – I needed a minute. And without a word, in swans Scott ...

She spread her shoulders, lifting each arm at the elbow and setting her chin against her chest in an uncanny imitation of a fourteen-year-old.

... He's *staring* at me, like, while I'm lying there, crying into Dennis's shirt, do you know what I mean? Staring. What'd you do if you saw your mum like that?

I dunno. See if she were okay?

Scott doesn't even speak. He knew what he were doing as well. I had to pull myself together when the one thing I needed were to let go. Have you ever had to stop them kinds of tears, Benj?

There was a time when ... Benj caught Dani's eye. No, never.

So I said, Do you want a minute? I don't know why but I thought he'd say no. Scott just goes, *Yeah*. He comes over and takes Dennis's shirt off me ... I left him to it.

She wouldn't say any more.

The bar filling, they found a small circular table that was sticky to the touch and already covered with empty shot and pint glasses, coloured bottles with flashes of alcopops going flat in the bottom. After a while, fetching another round in, Benj caught sight of Tim Ashworth's mother Elaine pushing through the crowd towards him. He swore and tried to turn away but it was too late. As Elaine arrived, he noticed she was dressed in an ancient shearling jacket and a familiar cabbage-cream T-shirt badly stained by a continent of red wine and what looked like cooking oil. Elaine was of Romany stock, aged maybe sixty-five, someone for whom the sullen imprint of 1950s Catholicism, with all its grandiose, miasmic language, had been firmly imprinted.

You've got to be *joking*, she said, prodding Benj in the chest.

All right, Elaine.

When the hell did you get back?

Oh, not long now, I suppose.

And already on the lash.

Last time I checked, it weren't illegal.

Elaine curled her lip but didn't speak. She couldn't really, she in that glass house of hers. Benj had made relentless apology to this woman over the years, efforts grand and small. Time after time she wasn't having it. While the wynds and closes of mourning traced a nebulous route to every heart, within Elaine Ashworth they had digressed into a complex knot of rancorous tunnels. Elaine had glutted upon her grief, suing the farmer responsible for the stray cow, ruining the man. She'd had Al Pinder arrested for possession of Class A's with intent to supply, and been the one to press the charges against Benj – death by dangerous driving. She swayed at his side, glaring at him, ignorant of the pathetic figure her vast pissed sorrow had reduced her to, the deep pall she had cast over so many lives.

What do you want? Benj said, keeping an eye on Dani, who was by now standing at the door, smoking, while Paddy Morgan stared at her backside.

Just my wee boy back, Elaine replied tearfully. *Is that so much to ask?*

The glacial exterior of Benj's pint. The singular tune of the quizzer to his right. I was just a kid, he said quietly.

And that makes it okay, does it?

How many times do you expect me to apologise, Elaine?

Oh, we're past that. You've a hex on you now, *wastrel*. See how that fits.

Elaine clutched Benj's arm, tugging his sleeve until it felt like she'd tear it at the shoulder. Her nails dug into his skin. Her eyes slit, she murmured something, a scarified pentagram sigil visible on her wrist.

Benj yanked his arm free. Are you wearing Tim's—

I've a mind to speak to the Morgans about you, *Benjamin*. Don't worry. The way you traipse about. Lord of his mews. *King Fuck.*

Benj glanced at Paddy Morgan. That huge, cropped face, in the doorway.

Look, can I not get you a drink, Elaine?

For a moment compliance was visible on Elaine's purple-stained, chewed and sore-looking lips, then gone.

No.

Oh, come on.

I said *no.*

You obviously want one.

Elaine was too short to reach anywhere near Benj's height, but she made a valiant attempt at getting nose to nose with him. *Not from you I don't*, she said. I'll swill a little more of meself away without the help of some *darky-lover* like you, Benjamin, thanks very much.

Oh, for God's sakes, Benj said, bumping Elaine's shoulder roughly on his way to the door. He'd just made eye contact with Dani when he felt a set of talons sinking into his arm.

69

How's about I get *you* a drink! Elaine yelled. She raised her pint glass and emptied it all over Benj's head.

Dani was sorting the drinks, a tenebrous outline behind the frosted glass dividing her kitchen from the lounge. A Nickelback album played on the stereo while *Star Wars* and *Predator* figurines were posed on the lintel. A blown-up Deakin family portrait watched over everything, the image stretched across a canvas, one of those filtered-to-the-point-of-white-out jobs that are commissioned and carried out in a studio. Dani and Scott grinned manically in Chunky's crushing arms.

Dani entered the room carrying two plastic cups of Jack Daniels and Coke, no ice. She handed one to Benj then flopped onto the couch, dust blooming from the cushions. The mix in Benj's drink was overwhelmingly in favour of the whiskey, and the Coke was very flat. He assumed a secretly alert position by the fireplace and ran a finger along the mantel, clearing a trail in the grime.

Er, Dani? he said after a couple of minutes.

What?

Benj tugged the hem of his drenched shirt.

Shit, Dani said. Shit, yeah.

He watched her buttocks move as he followed her upstairs. From the landing Benj could see the asthma nebuliser on a shelf in Scott's room, which was adjacent to Dani's. Out of Dani's window, past the unruly welcome of the unmade bed, a grizzled dusk had fallen upon the valley. Benj could see the curve of a hazy moon glowing through the branches of a sick conifer that had malted needles all over the patchy lawn.

Dani, with what was surely intended as an air of mystery, beckoned Benj towards a third door with a broken slide lock on the outside. Dennis's man cave, she slurred, leading the way into a room rich with the furring stink of sour laundry. Benj wrinkled his nose. Chunky's stuff was everywhere. Some of it lay under dust sheets, some of it was piled around an overflowing basket of washing, the rest stored in towers of boxes.

From an ironing board full of empty glasses and plates, Dani removed one of Chunky's rugby shirts. It would be massive on Benj, but he took it anyway. Incorrectly washed, the red and white stripes had distorted into one another, leaving spectrums of blurry pink.

Want another drink? asked Dani, peeling away a bedsheet.

Is that a fridge?

All sorts in here.

No shit.

Dani shifted a box of VHS cassettes so she could sit on the couch, then nodded at different points of the room. Exercise bike. Rowing machine. PlayStation. I don't use any of it and Scott won't come in here.

There was a bean bag that had an arse print in it, Benj noticed. Unmistakably Chunky's.

From the fridge by the couch Dani removed a beer and tossed it Benj's way. You tell me, I'll tell you, she said, her bottle fizzing as she cracked the lid off with her teeth.

About what?

You know what.

Why was she so interested? Benj had been incarcerated in HMP Durham, one of 196 inmates on a scabrous wing martialled by only a handful of underpaid screws. In the neighbouring cell had been a guy named Tony Ritchie. Tony had been caught running a car-valeting business as a front for his cocaine-smuggling operation. Get your lips around this burner, mate, he'd said to Benj on his first day inside, handing over a cigarette that turned out to be packed with Spice. The last thing Benj remembered before *going over*, was bare-chested Tony stooping above him. *You'll smash jail, you, son. Fucking smash it.*

Tony's Geordie brogue would become all too familiar as the months dragged on, floating as it did through the pipe that connected their two cells together, delivering the latest instructions as to what contraband Benj was expected to stow under his mattress or up his rectum this time. Phones. Kinder Eggs full of pills and, plenty of times, a knife. Benj had spent many a day in segregation on Tony Ritchie's behalf. Once he took a pan of boiling water to the lap after his cell was spun and Tony's hooch was confiscated. Another time Benj was forced to pin a fellow prisoner down who'd refused to take a charge for one of Tony's friends. He'd seen that poor bastard cut cheek to cheek.

Try to imagine the least intimate place in the world, Benj said, moving closer to Dani. That's what it's like.

Dani rested her head on his shoulder. Dennis and the young lad were chosen to fix the silo, she said. The conveyor belt was supposed to have been disabled.

What about the inquest? Benj replied. You must have a fortune coming your way.

It's in hand, replied Dani, eyeing him curiously.

One of the contact lenses had become bothersome. Benj removed it. Money changes everything, he said.

They did it right there in the man cave, Dani gripping the handles of the exercise bike, having to stop at one point because she'd stood on one of the pedals and lost her footing. Her phone rang in the other room almost as soon as Benj came and pulled free. He was left alone while she disappeared to answer it, his attention drawn to a humming canvas cubicle with a flex of aluminium ducting protruding from the roof, attached by gaffer tape to a vent in the ceiling. Benj knew a hydroponic tent when he saw one. He found six marijuana plants wilted inside.

He always kept it hidden when I came in, Dani said from the doorway. She approached Benj in her blouse and knickers, her tears glistening under the buttery glow of the grow tent's lamps. All them years married and I never knew. Check that tin, she said. If you think this is mad.

Benj had been wearing Chunky's rugby shirt the whole time. He pulled his boxer shorts and trousers on then opened the biscuit tin next to the PlayStation. Inside was a wrap of cocaine that must have weighed half an ounce, a zip-lock baggie containing hundreds of pills with the Mitsubishi logo, and two mini Tupperwares, one holding magic mushrooms and the other a great many blotting tabs, pudgy Buddhas illustrating each. Benj's stomach flipped when he saw an ochre block of what he was certain was heroin.

Dani said, You'd never think Dennis was so—

Avidly in pursuit of his sensations?

Dani nodded.

I've known a lot of people like that, Benj said.

Dani held up her phone. Scott's to come back, she said. Little shit's got impetigo and he's not told me. They've only just found out. Can you give us a lift? she said. I'm over the limit.

I don't drive.

You can use my car.

I said I don't drive.

You're gonna get me pissed then make me pay for a taxi. *Is that it?*

The all-weather pitch was a floodlit plain backing onto an endless spread of farmland. Hail began to fall as Dani and Benj walked downhill from the school under the protection of an umbrella. It fell so thickly that the teenagers playing in their bibs had to stop their game altogether. The players sank to their knees, hunched and cowering as hail bulleted the Astro-Turf, coating the ground with a trillion polystyrene-like balls. A buzzing pylon towered in the next field. A herd of cattle stood beneath it, chewing cud in the latticed shadows.

Every footballer was soon huddled like a snail, except one. This player sprinted onto the pitch from the side-line, controlled the loose ball and dribbled it around his clustered teammates and opponents until he reached the waiting goal mouth, where he stopped and smashed the ball into the open net from a yard away.

This was Scott.

The kid stopped celebrating at the sight of Dani and jogged over. As Scott approached, Benj felt in his coat pocket for the coke, pills and heroin he'd lifted from Chunky's tin, and recalled the cow's final euphoric bellow, the clunk of the car boot as the fireman popped it to reveal Tim's body. The feeling Benj had when the boot clicked might have been similar to the one Chunky had when he felt that conveyor belt jolting into action.

Scott had a red blister on the tip of his nose that looked like a scrap of confetti, and his kit was nylon and too tight. The boy was overweight, much like his father, his hair cropped in the exact same way that Chunky wore his. Scott Deakin even had that same cruelty in his eyes, as if he might be about to pull your trousers down in front of everyone you knew.

He looks like Dennis, said Benj.

It's like living with different versions of the same dead person, replied Dani. Except they're both in the one body.

I scored, Mum, said Scott. He had a lisp. *Thcored.*

Well done, said Dani. I'd hug you but you're infectious.

The hail ceased, as hail does. Scott stared at Benj. Who's this?

A friend, love. This is Alan.

Your mum and me went to school together, Benj said, offering his hand.

Scott didn't take it. He looks like a fucking mage, he said, nodding at Benj's shoulder-length hair, the buttoned raincoat.

Don't be so rude, Scott.

Scott plugged a nostril with a thumb and expelled a florid jet of mucus into the grass, the snot flashing a centimetre from Benj's shoe.

I'll meet you at the car in a minute, Mum.

The kid insisted on sitting up front while Benj drove, struggling to make out the road with only one contact lens in. At first he thought Dani was asleep, but her snuffling betrayed her. She was making the most perfect sobbing noises behind him, each as delicate and unique as a snowflake.

The car crawled over a swell of ice that led into the night, future's horizon. They were on the high road where Tim had died. Benj kept an eye out for the killing tree, but it was difficult. What had once been festooned with bouquets and broadly lettered condolences was now empty save a cow carved into the rippled bark, save a black sign staked into the earth with a red flower crying a blood teardrop. It was useless. The woods sped by, simple trees: rough columns growing road-side, branching out and disappearing into nothing.

Benj was sweating in spite of the cold. He unbuttoned his raincoat and opened it, but as he did so he realised Scott was staring at him.

That's a nice shirt you've got on.

I'm sorry?

I said that's a nice shirt you've got on.

Benj attempted to pull the coat about himself. Thanks, he said.

It weren't a compliment.

Scott, said Dani, leaning forward until Benj could see her in the rear-view mirror.

No, Mum.

Scotty, love.

That's Dad's shirt!

It's not, said Benj. It's definitely not.

It is, Scott insisted, pawing at Benj's sleeve. *That's Dad's shirt.*

Benj shook the kid off, the car veering wildly to the left and nearly leaving the road. He fought to straighten the wheel and stepped on the accelerator pedal. This is my shirt, he said. Okay? I've been wearing the bloody thing all day.

Scott wound the window down, strident air filling the car. It was hailing again. Benj leaned forward. Struggling to make out the road, he glimpsed his own reflection in the windscreen and did not like what he saw. He was on the black ice now, speeding, and the steering felt almost weightless in his hands.

Phantoms

―――

CHARLOTTE USED TO SAY it was like a pepper grinder was turning somewhere in the sky, and I always thought that was a nice way of putting it. She was on about all the ash, the monochrome flakes that floated onto your head and collected in pockets on the windscreens of local cars. God, that summer was bonfires. It was smoky silhouettes standing like the ghosts of pagans from the olden times, great mounds of carcasses with hoofed legs poking clean out of the blazes. Everyone blamed the Marshalls. They lived on the farm next to ours, my family's neighbours for the only year and a half I ever spent away from the valley. The Marshalls were the cause of all the hair: the matted clumps that clagged external walls and garden furniture, the tempting smell of roast meat that floated down every lane. It was because of them that my family moved home, so that makes it their fault that my dad ended up taking the job at the abattoir that finally broke him, and that makes it their fault that whenever I stepped outdoors in the summer of 2001, I had to ignore the creeping sense that something terrible and unnatural was occurring not more than a mile away.

The Marshalls had sons, and Roo and Burn were their names. Burn was really called Brendan but everyone knew him as

Burn because he'd once torched a dead tree, the fire spreading to the Marshalls' old barn where the family's Swaledales were spending the night ahead of shearing the next morning. The Marshalls were useless farmers. Their yard was ramshackle and potholed, a car ready for scrapping in a corner, loose chickens, sludge pits and hay bales, but to this day I can't get over how they decided to keep their herd in that tinderbox. I also can't help thinking that Burn knew what he was doing. Maybe he started the blaze because fire creates light and light creates visions, and he wanted to see something amazing. How must it have felt seeing those eaves become a fuse, watching dying livestock escape into the night with their coats ablaze, an outbreak of flames picked out against the distant flanks, gullies and savage daleheads of the Kentmere Horseshoe? Whatever Burn's reasons, his brother Roo, the eldest and therefore most corrupt son, was blamed for the fire, and although it was a while before the truth came out, when it did Brendan had himself a nickname.

Burn was on my mind back then. If he hadn't have set that tree alight then the Marshalls would never have turned to imported cattle, and foot-and-mouth wouldn't have come to Staveley. I'll never forget him. He had moles on his face and pissy little eyes, weather-blasted skin and spaced-out teeth. His brother was quite a bit taller, and seemed scuffed around the edges like a pencil sketch. Roo Marshall was always lurking around Burn's periphery, almost as if he'd asked his brother a question and was following him around until he got an answer. Even after the outbreak I was envious of the Marshalls. I didn't have the nerve to think like they did. I didn't carry a penknife or make dens or ask for cigarettes from strangers. I couldn't talk to girls. At school I watched them always and at home I spied on their farm from my bedroom window. I never told anyone I did this. I was embarrassed to be so fascinated.

After the outbreak Roo and Burn were home-schooled. Their parents were scared of what would happen after the windows of their farmhouse were put through and a cow's tongue and a set of hooves left on the doorstep in a bloodied shopping bag. Dad laughed when I told him about that. He actually rubbed his hands, the brackish surfaces of his palms coated in O'Keeffe's Working Hand cream, his coarse face turning my way when he thought I wasn't looking. Them bastards ruined a lot of lives, he said, and I remember thinking to myself that he could as easily have been referring to the lives of the slaughtered animals as those of the affected farmers.

Our name is Glove, and there's only a year and a half between me and my sister Charlotte. Charlotte's always been the more outgoing one, but when she was sixteen you wouldn't have thought it to look at her. She wore thick tortoiseshell glasses, and she never had her shirt untucked, and while everyone used to say how reserved she was, I knew different. The truth was that around her neck my sister wore a fool's gold chain that spelled her name, she smoked and drank as soon as she could get away with it, lied readily and with ease and went out of her way to teach me about things that had never occurred to me before. What it meant to be gay, for example. What a Siamese twin was. That vodka was made out of potatoes. Charlotte loved knowing what I didn't and all the time I was growing up she made me feel like I was missing out on the world's secret truths because I was younger than her. She made me feel like I'd slipped and fallen in a race and could never dream of catching her up.

The Marshalls were in the years above us at school. Roo was in the lower sets, prone to these mad bursts of energy where he'd carve the desks up with his compass, or start booting the lockers at the back of his form room. Charlotte told me about that. She also said Roo had brought a BB gun in once and shot it in a lesson, and although the teacher didn't notice, someone else told on Roo and that was why he was suspended. When I heard this story for some reason I thought of Burn. He was a lot cleverer than his brother, you could just tell. Grassing on Roo to see what would happen seemed like something he might do.

After the outbreak everyone lost money. Not small amounts, but thousands. They announced a quarantine and we were encouraged to stay in the village, public footpaths were closed and throughout Cumbria where the A roads became B roads and on the lanes running to every farm, huge mats were laid, doused with disinfectant to prevent the virus from spreading. There was fire and there was heartbreak and it bled into everything, and that summer I swear I could hear the cattle screaming whenever I shut my eyes. *Them Marshalls*, people said, and maybe they were right to. I think the Marshalls' guilt was what made Charlotte seek them out to begin with.

I discovered what she was up to almost straight away, and I wish I'd made more of an effort to stop her. We used to catch the school bus together then walk home between dense hedgerows that grew taller than me, along narrow tarmac roads that bent brazenly through the country. But when Charlotte told me to go on without her one day, I knew something was up.

Where you going? I asked.

None of your business where I'm goin'.

It is when I've to explain where you are to Mum.

Mum won't say owt, Charlotte scoffed.

Course she will!

Oh, you're proper fuckin' naive, John.

How do you mean?

'Cause nothin'll happen!

I ended up letting her go. I hated that Charlotte could do what she wanted, and I hated how right she was about everything. Not a word was said that evening. I spent the whole of a canned macaroni-cheese dinner waiting for a question that never came. Mum sat near the window waiting for Dad whilst a cherry sun lit the mismatched table and chairs and her badger streak of grey that ran in a line along the top of her head. Not that her silence was anything unusual. We'd left the valley that summer, putting a failed farm and the brown frontier of Pendle behind us. With hardly any friends and a new direction to focus on, the move north wasn't that bad for

Dad and me, but for Mum and Charlotte it was difficult. The gossipy ties of our Lancashire communities and the crammed towns built within spitting distance of one another, people soaked in a quiet cabal lore that you could trace back to the days of the witch covens, had been replaced by occasional farms that looked like they'd been dropped out of the sky, miles of country rising into brooding fells or ending in yawning stretches of windy beach.

Mum ... I remember saying that night, but the words caught in my throat. Better to let her think I didn't know how fucked we were than pat her on the shoulder and tell her things would be okay. My silence was the greater kindness, the far sincerer gift.

After dinner I had a bath, my hair washing gently from my head, my spine occasionally catching the gritty bottom of the tub. I imagined I'd drowned. I imagined someone had found me, breaking apart the bubbles like they were hunks of coral and coming face to face with my clear open eyes, my rubbery lips pulled back to show the edges of my teeth. Afterwards I went to find Charlotte. Staveley's outskirts are typical of the lakes: fertile dells and denes, open copses ripe for hanging around in if you've a mind to. It didn't take long for me to spot my sister's school blazer flashing redly through the trees not far from our house, but as I got closer I was horrified to see that Charlotte was with the Marshalls.

The brothers seemed taller than usual. Burn had a massive branch he was stamping on while Roo stood a fair way off, pouring a fat bottle of cider into Charlotte's mouth. Just beyond the three of them I could see a pitched tent, its yellow roof winking at me.

That tent was mine.

I don't think clearly when sudden things happen – I always seem to do the wrong thing. For example, if an old person topples over in the street, or if I spot someone I haven't seen in ages coming towards me, I tend to quail and pretend I haven't noticed them. I still do this now but I was especially bad for it then, so in that same unsure way I found myself walking towards Charlotte pretending I hadn't seen my stolen tent with those bringers of disease. I did this until I was hovering uncertainly before all three of them with what felt like an apple lodged in the middle of my chest.

What you doin' here? said Charlotte.

What the hell do you think? I said back.

My sister's cheeks flushed, but before she could say anything Roo came over and Charlotte let him lean on her in a way that made me feel ashamed. *Glove*, he said, drunkenly imitating my unbroken voice. How's school, kid – you started your joined-up writing yet?

Ignoring Roo, I glanced at Burn. He was keeping his distance. Pulling his broken stick apart like a chicken bone was more important than interacting with the likes of me.

Mum wants you home, Chaz, I said.

Already said I'm staying out.

Not in my tent you're not.

That got Burn's attention. I'd been doing double physics that afternoon, and as Burn approached me I saw it: his huge reserves of Potential Energy. He was all chemical, nuclear, gravitational, whereas Roo was Kinetic. He was current, crackling voltage. Burn's piggy eyes were emphasised by fatigue-bags that I thought could easily have been ash circles, and they seemed to widen as he dragged the stick behind him until he was a couple of inches from me, going, What's up with you, mate? He was so close that I could feel the heat of his breath spreading across my cheek.

Nothin's up, I said.

Burn had noticeable BO and it made me conscious of my damp hair, the ringlets carrying the perfumed scent of shampoo from the bath I'd had before coming here.

You don't mind us using it, do you? he said. We need it case we fancy a sleepover.

Charlotte couldn't hold my accusatory stare. The knot of her school tie was as broad as my fist, its tip stopping short to become an arrow that pointed at her breasts, and although I noticed she'd taken her glasses off, I didn't say anything. I just shrugged Burn's hand from my shoulder and frowned.

You could 'ave asked, I said.

For your sister or your tent? replied Roo, jamming his greasy cap onto my head and tweaking it so it came over my eyes.

I tore the hat off and threw it at him, feeling my eyes swell against my will. Both the Marshalls laughed.

Brendan, said Charlotte. Will you leave him?

Burn reached for the cider bottle and took a long pull on it. I could see a liquid film on his teeth: white spirit that might ignite if you held a match there.

I'm not sure what's up with old Glove here.

He don't like that we've borrowed his tent, said Roo.

Reckon you're right.

Well, shall we give it back, if he's getting all upset?

Suppose we could, said Burn. But only if he can fuckin' down all this.

The murky plastic bottle swung towards me like a wrecking ball, and as I caught it, I thought of the day's departed moments: the goal I'd scored at lunchtime, making my new mates cheer, the liquorice-coloured road and the steam rising from my naked body when I rose from the filthy bathwater. It all seemed very far away.

Yeah, down the rest of this bottle and you can have your tent back, said Burn.

John...

Nah, I'll do it, Chaz, I snapped, warm cider dribbling down my chin and T-shirt as I put the bottle to my lips. The sickly smell stole up my nose. It was cheap, thin, acrid stuff: the kind of booze only kids and homeless people buy. I began to drink, gulping as much down as I could, managing about fifteen seconds before my body betrayed me yet again and I had to splutter and choke, fighting the urge to vomit while the Marshall cheers poisoned the air around me.

Glove fails! Burn cried, snatching the bottle from me as Roo reached vainly for my sister's hand. Glove stacks it!

I wanted to tell Charlotte she was coming with me anyway, but all I could do was stagger off into the woods, pushing through a midge cloud as the last of the evening's light faded. I could hear Marshall laughter and my sister's scolding voice as I bent into the rhododendrons to be sick, but the groan of my own embarrassment was far louder. It sounded in my head all the way back to our failing farm.

My parents argued that night. I heard them downstairs as I played on my computer. I didn't intervene. I just turned up the volume, fought an interstellar war and waited for it all to be over.

Charlotte returned after Mum and Dad had tired themselves out and gone to bed, the click of her latch never coming because she'd fallen asleep on top of the duvet with the door open. I didn't need to hear that familiar sound to know she was home. I could smell the cider and cigarettes from across the landing.

She began to spend almost every evening out. I never asked where she was. I didn't want to know. I'd have to lie to our parents if I was asked – not that I ever was – and I couldn't be bothered with the risk. I was spending a lot of time training with the football team by then anyway, and helping with our remaining cattle: mucking the sheds and forking bales into the feeding rings. I had no energy to think about anything else, then later on Mum left, which was another distraction.

She's gone back to the valley, staying with her friend Rosie, Dad explained, sitting me down one evening before heading to the pub, to clear his head, he said, leaving me to think about Mum's kiss and the tenner she'd pressed into my hand, a gift that hadn't made much sense at the time. I used to lie in bed thinking of my mum's knackered face. Dad said she'd promised to call regularly, and as time passed, she did; she called the house every Friday. The thing was, neither of us had much to say to one another what with the distance her defection had put between us. I used to stand there, the phone going hot against my ear, doodling on the notepad and staring at my reflection in the glass table, pretending I didn't know Dad was leaning against the banister with his hands in his pockets as if trying to remember something he'd forgotten. Mum would always ask me how school was and I would always tell her it was fine.

Sometime after Mum left I was in the cattle shed sweeping up, scouring broom over concrete, dragging scrags of hay and flakes of dead animals' cowpats about, when a white plastic stick grabbed my attention. It was a device with a digital reader on it, half-hidden where it had been discarded amid the scurf. I picked it up and saw a blue cross on the display. Moments later I was pelting into the house where I found Dad in the lounge watching TV.

Is it back?

Is what back?

Are they all right, Dad?

The white stick clattered onto the coffee table between us.

Have you been testing 'em? I'm not doing another of them fuckin' bonfires!

Dad set his beer down and picked up the device. He spent a long time staring at it, ale as foamy as horse piss fizzing out of his can and leaking over the table in a funny-shaped pool.

What's up? I said.

No answer.

Dad?

Dad rose. He was a big unit, my dad. He rubbed his beard and stood, his breathing heavy, apparently unsure what to do with his hands. The next thing I knew, he was stomping upstairs while a magpie spluttered on the muddy yard outside. The sound of splitting wood filled the house. Charlotte's door was exploding, the panels crunching as they succumbed to the impact of Dad's hobnail boot.

What the fucking hell is this, Char? What've you been doing?

I was confused. I couldn't understand what anything I'd said had to do with my sister.

When Dad stomped back downstairs, he snatched his coat from the kitchen hook then brought me out to the barn. After we'd got tooled up, we set off in the Land Rover for the Marshalls'. Charlotte was too hysterical to confirm which brother was the father, but Roo was the eldest so we wasted no time in putting two and two together.

I rode in the back with my cricket bat, a pitchfork, sledge-hammer and a scythe at my feet. We collected Dad's mates along the way. It was a Saturday so Don, Fraser and Kev had been in the pub all day. They shared their whiskey with Dad, the four of them swigging straight from the bottle.

Once we screeched into the Marshalls' yard I stayed in the Land Rover while Dad and the others attacked the farmhouse door. When they couldn't get inside, they put the house's windows through and did the tractor, smashing its windscreen and headlights and doing the radiator, side panelling and roof, baying for Roo and shouting the odds about the outbreak.

Seeing it through the window was like watching it on TV, the lead actor my father, wax jacket tight across his back, roaring, having to be restrained by some paunchy twats from the pub, spittle flying from his mouth and comb-over floppily erect like he'd laid his hands on one of the Van der Graaf generators at school. That night I thought of him being shoved into the police car as I pushed my dinner into the microwave and slammed the door. I wasn't even hungry – I left the tray of bolognese to go cold, my heart going like the clappers as I slid a sock over the mouthpiece of our phone to disguise my voice.

Ruben Marshall's dead! I screeched, leaving a message on the Marshalls' answering machine. *He's a fuckin' dead man from now on in!*

I never told my dad what I'd done, even though I know he'd have approved. At the time admitting to any similarity in our characters seemed like confessing to a crime, some kind of terrible atrocity.

*

The pyres and ash clouds around Staveley eventually died out, but notices on lamp posts, telegraph poles and shop windows appeared to sour the brightening mood. They were appealing for information about Roo. He'd disappeared, and although people speculated as to his whereabouts, no search parties were arranged because no one would lift a finger for a Marshall.

You'd see his brother about from time to time, but whether Burn was searching for Roo or just wandering aimlessly, I never knew. Me and Dad drove past him once. He was on his crosser motorbike with no helmet, a cigarette trapped between his lips, framed by many stacked clouds: gables of bright powdery feathers that were skylit tremendously above the hedges. Another time Burn showed up in the Eagle and Child, climbed onto a bar stool he'd parked in the middle of the room and demanded people let Roo come home. I'd been allowed to drink that year so I booed with the rest of them and made cow noises. Burn soon stumbled outside, where he was lost to the silken dimness of the lanes. I don't know what he was expecting, who the hell he thought he was talking to.

By the time Roo eventually surfaced, Charlotte's belly had swollen like a tumour. She'd been a subdued presence since deciding to keep the kid, eating constantly, occasionally whispering on the phone – to Mum, I wrongly presumed – and catching up on her coursework while Dad and I secretly painted the spare room. She hardly spoke to either of us but always said thanks when I brought her a cup of tea. One day she even asked if I thought she'd been stupid. Course I do, I said. But it doesn't matter now, does it.

I was at the attic window when Roo finally surfaced. I spotted him sneaking up to our house: a fugitive in a baseball cap covered by a hood, dressed in blue jeans and mucky trainers. When he knocked-on, I poked my head into Charlotte's room, but she was fast asleep. No way was I disturbing her for a Marshall.

All right, Glove, Roo said when I stuck my head around the door. His eyebrows were raised as if we were mates, and he had a ratty beard, prominent blackheads peppering his nose and a sleeper earring dangling so explicitly from his ear that I found it offensive.

What do you want? I said.

Give her a message, would you?

You serious?

Wouldn't be here if I weren't.

What fuckin' message?

Tell her Burn wants to meet. Tomorrow night.

Burn?

Down station, said Roo, walking backwards.

In her condition? I called as he reached the corner, but Roo didn't turn around.

He was gone.

That night I patrolled the fields in my waders, sloshing beneath the troubled light of a weak gibbous moon until I arrived at the walled quicklime pit where the remains of our cattle had been buried. The prematurely slaughtered beasts of the north had mostly been interred in enormous trenches at Great Orton Airfield. Our animals, however, had deserved to be buried respectfully where they'd lived, so me and Dad did it ourselves in secret. By then the grass had returned but the patched area had formed a pale circle of growth that made it look as if a spotlight was shining on the land. I stood on the circle's edge and remembered our livestock, their massive rolling eyes, the drool suspended from their mouths, their outraged roars. I thought of the smoke trailing lucidly towards the ceiling from Mum's cigarette, the fizz of cider bubbles and Charlotte's voice. *Brendan*, she'd said. It was then that I decided to go see the Marshalls myself.

When the time came I walked it to the station, savouring the brittle tang of the air and kicking at the crunchy leaves flung loose by the roadside. The station was a small building built into the hill. You reached the ticket windows by climbing a set of stairs, then to a platform by heading along an open-air gangway built over the tracks. As I approached the building I spotted an orange dot rising and falling in the dark: the ember of a cigarette heading from a shadow's face to its hip.

Burn? I said.

Glove?

That you, Roo?

Where's Charlotte?

In bed, why isn't Burn here?

Where the fuck is she?

She's busy.

There was a long pause, a scratch of feet. I thought she might turn up, said Roo. If she thought Burn was here.

How come? I asked.

He didn't answer.

I deliberated whether to go home, but something was urging me to stay. Although I was afraid of the Marshalls, I'd turned up that night with a mind to threaten Roo or even get violent, but those feelings drained away the moment I saw that washed-out face of his, because when I looked at him – I mean, *properly* looked at him – I realised that even if I did have it in me to hurt someone, I'd never have been able to do anything because in front of me was nothing more than a forlorn and broken-hearted little boy.

Where've you been, mate?

Potter Fell.

Serious?

Knew no one'd look for us up there.

Where you been sleeping?

Remember your tent?

Shit man.

Roo laughed. Was gonna get my head kicked in if I hung around here.

I said nothing. The solitary station lamp cleared a neat path of woody light through the darkness.

Least's not winter, I said eventually. Would have been cold.

Been cold enough, but it ain't been so bad, cookin' and

sleepin' and the stars. Burn brings me food. Then again he owes me one, doesn't he?

Roo stubbed out his cigarette, a dazzle of sparks cascading down the wall. In the light his face was almost featureless, and I had to stop myself from staring at it. Although I think he noticed, he never said anything. He just produced a bottle of cider from his pack and said, Peace offering. I could tell from his voice that he was smiling.

I took the bottle. Ta.

She really not say nothing?

Afraid not.

Not never?

What was I supposed to say? Not since the pregnancy had Roo's name been mentioned. In fact, when I brought him up with her once, Charlotte actually laughed.

Sorry, mate, I replied.

Roo cleared his throat in a thin way. I've tried calling but she won't answer. I love her, man. Will you tell her that?

Course I will, I lied.

We slid down to our haunches with our backs to the wall and lit cigarettes, the first and only time I ever smoked. After a long while I tried to leave, but Roo implored me to stay and I ended up letting him persuade me into climbing over the station gates and heading up to the gangway overlooking the train tracks. We were young and we were drunk and it was raining, the water crackling the electric wires that slung like a washing line into the distance behind and in front. I listened to the weather pestering the charge, the current's hum and the droplets clattering against the bridge's walkway. I could see Roo. His hood was up and he clung to the metal handrail, not a patch of skin visible except for a pair of bone-white hands. Something about his body language hinted at a closing of something inside. A part of him was disappearing.

She never said nothing?

I'm sorry, mate, I—

Not even about Burn?

Look, I've no idea, all right?

A shock of thunder.

We never meant it, Glove. Dad never knew there were summat up with them cattle.

I know.

Too late now though.

Yep.

We finished the cider and listened to the power lines and eventually Roo turned to me. I had my hood up by then, but, too small for my head, it stopped at my hairline and dribbled brooks of rain into my eyes. Roo was becoming a blur: a Marshall swaying sombrely in the darkness.

See them cars? Reckon we could jump on them from 'ere.

I looked down. No way.

We fuckin' could.

Over the rail, some ten or eleven feet below, was a row of articulated haulage carriages: a set of gloomy boxes stationed on the tracks and waiting to be towed out in the morning. As I squinted through the downpour I sensed Roo observing me with that same dreamy, half-cut expression he'd had in the bonfire summer, only this time that goofiness was gone, replaced by an odd kind of serenity.

He started climbing on the rail. Scared?

Fuck off.

Well come on then.

Although I was with someone, I was as alone as I'd ever been. There was no one to make us stop and no way of letting the matter slide, and so I joined Roo on the rail, almost crouching with one hand on the metal bar.

On three, Roo said ... *One* ...

Fuck waiting, I jumped. The wet air blustered past me as I hurdled the fizzing wires, a nipping wind breaking around me, its whistle the only sound, right up until the point when my feet rocked on the carriage roof with a resounding metallic thud. It hurt, but I was fine, and so I whooped, Roo landing with a clang at my side.

Glove! he cried, leaping into the air. *Glove!*

There isn't a day that goes by that I don't feel bad about what happened next. I think about it at home, I think about it at work, and after I make love to my wife, it's there. Even when I'm holding my daughter's hand on our way to nursery, taking in the patchwork of fields pushing against the valley's limits, it's in the back of my mind: Roo's exalted face, his arms lifting through the rain in celebration, my silence, my open mouth as I saw his fingers approaching the electric wire, the awful moment when he grazed it, the explosion of him jolting off the carriage, landing on the shingle by the train tracks as heavy as a dropped bag of wet cement.

But believe it or not, that's not what haunts me. What plays on my mind instead is that after Roo lay there, his clothes in smoking tatters, rather than jump down or call an ambulance, I knelt on the carriage and stared at him, thinking to myself that one of those untouchable and unknowable people that I'd always been so embarrassed of admiring was lying beneath me. They were just as defenceless as I was. It took what happened to Roo Marshall to make me realise that those who intoxicate you are really just phantoms, totems built by folks like me with an empty slot in their heads where their confidence is supposed to be. I didn't regret not warning Roo. I didn't think about whether or not he was okay. I just watched his silhouette smouldering, a loose smile pasted across my face. I felt enlightened, like I'd learned something.

I still have a hard time dealing with that.

Waddington

———

THE RIBBLE COMES THROUGH WADDINGTON as a brook, and you can fish with your hands in it. Lowry and me used to do this back in the day before graduating to drop lines, the cane pole and then tackle, car batteries when we were shit-faced. In those days we were supervised by Lowry's dad, who I only ever knew as Mr Lowry. Mr Lowry was curious for a lot of reasons but mainly because he only had the one arm. Yes, I found it weird.

Mr Lowry was older than most dads. He would have been about sixty by the time Lowry and me were ten. You wouldn't have known it other than for his white eyebrows and the tufts of hair that sprouted in clutches from his ears, as sharp-looking as those hairs you get on insects' legs.

Mr Lowry used to stand in the water a few feet away, or up on the road spinning his boot heels on the tarmac, clasping the railings overlooking the river with that lonely hand of his. Meanwhile us boys would sift pebbles and corner Stone Loach. Then we'd spool them up and plop them in our jam jars. Lowry never seemed bothered by the empty sleeve of his dad's fleece, so while I often found myself fantasising about touching his dad's stump, my friend would get on with the business at hand, his ponytail a plaited segment of skipping rope that would drop over one shoulder, grazing the rock gunk and sometimes the river, swaying always.

Lowry usually caught more fish than I did. He had a knack for reading nature's patterns, its habits, and after earning his diploma in horticulture he went on to become the groundsman at the local golf course, where he lived for many years in a bungalow overlooking the lake. Maybe three years into the job Lowry got married, and after that it was just him and his pretty wife and a trio of doomed pet rabbits that neither of them ever stopped talking about. Egg, I called Lowry's missus, Egg.

On this particular occasion all three of us had the day off. Egg drove so me and Lowry could drink and we travelled in Lowry's car, which funnily enough was a Golf, with me and Lowry sat in the back. Although they weren't the longest rods it was always a pain in the arse taking them apart, meaning that whenever we went on these trips we kept them whole and propped between us, creating a divide down the car's interior with me and Egg on one side and Lowry on the other. That morning the rods tickled the front window and once or twice slid over the dashboard so Egg had to shove them away and go, Can you not hold 'em, one of you? *Fuck's sakes.*

Lowry pinched my arm when I tried to apologise. As the boot was full of crap from his work, the front passenger seat had my tackle box and the butty boxes, with room for not much else, whilst in the footwell was the crate of Guinness Draught put there so Lowry couldn't get to it until we arrived. On the way to the river he kept tapping my knee whenever we drove past any woman under the age of forty, going, What about her? Though in his accent it sounded more like, *Wah bow terr.* I suppose he thought Egg couldn't hear him over the radio.

Cracking day for it. The sun blazed and the grass could have been fake it was so vivid. J. R. R. Tolkien taught down Stonyhurst College, which isn't far. They say the Ribble Valley was his inspiration for Middle Earth, which might explain why Lowry and me were always so obsessed with *Lord of the Rings* growing up. Whenever we had more than one person in tow we'd call ourselves 'a fellowship', and I suppose that's what we were that day, with me ferrying the fishing stuff to the river bank while Lowry and Egg got intimate against the Golf's sun-kissed bonnet.

My thoughts went as loose as they often do when I'm in open country. There was loads of colour fighting through the short grass: meadow yellows, rowanberry reds and cotton whites. All kinds of qualities if you took the time to notice them. I remember a gun-grey heron loping in flight directly over me.

It was my job to set the bivvy up in case the weather flipped as it was forever at risk of doing. Then I began to thread and weight the fishing lines. Downriver was Waddow Hall, which made me wonder what Peg O'Neil was up to. Peg is the ghost of a girl who was tricked into drowning in a well many centuries ago. There's a statue of her in Waddow's grounds that was beheaded in the misconception that it would stop Peg's ghost from getting up to I-don't-know-what. I have always believed in spirits. I must have got it from my nan who held no truck with mummery but did teach me in her gravelly manner that there are ancient spirit guides for each of us. Apparently hers was a Benedictine monk. Daft, isn't it? But there you go.

Are you on wi' that or what, Buzz? Lowry went. He'd been rolling a fag while I got everything ready. At this rate it'll be solstice by the time you've done.

Matt, can you not call him by his actual name for once? said Egg, not looking up from her John Grisham.

Lowry chuckled, although as usual I wasn't sure he found it funny. He said, He's Buzz Lightweight to me and he always will be. Right, Buzz?

True story, I said to Egg, while the sharp ridges of the Ribble's flow caught the light.

We settled down on the blanket for a smoke and a couple more beers. Egg didn't partake in that sort of thing having not touched so much as a drop since I first took her down Planet Ice when we were fifteen, the night Lowry got her to do all that whizz. At the time Egg was new to the valley. She'd moved four doors down from where I was living with my nan, and because I was an Ice Card holder and Egg didn't know anyone just yet, I invited her to come with me one day.

Although I can be a nervous person, it was easy asking Egg out because I'd already had a vision of her saying yes, the same kind of dream I'd have years later when I foresaw the violent deaths of her pet rabbits long before that fox ever slunk into her garden. In my dream the trip to Planet Ice went well, but then, because not all of what the spirits know can be revealed to us, things got misty. I wasn't put off. I knew I'd made the right decision when I saw how impressed Egg was with my Dayrover bus pass trick. The Dayrover was a flat-fare ticket where you could ride as many buses as you wanted in one day. What I did was get on first, show my Dayrover to the driver then ask what time the last bus was. Whilst the driver fannied about with the timetable, which was usually stowed down the side of their seat, I passed the Dayrover back to Egg. She flashed it when I sat down and got a free journey.

I began to understand what the last part of my dream was about when I saw that Lowry was on shift that day. He only ever had a part-time job at Planet Ice, his illustrious career as an ambassador for ice skating ending when the management realised the scale of his contempt for the general public. They'd stuck him on the desk where you swap your shoes for skates when me and Egg showed up together, and you should have seen his nostrils go when he saw us. Like a pair of blowholes, they were. Lowry's nose always does that when he's trying to hide something. The top lip stiffens and there you have it.

After I introduced him to Egg, Lowry asked me what skates I wanted even though he knew full well what size I was. He thought it was well funny dumping a pair that were too small for me on the counter. We don't have any that'll fit you, he said.

Oh right, no worries, I replied, then, glancing at Egg, I insisted that I could skate in pretty much anything.

As it turned out, I couldn't show Egg any of my tricks and the blisters were that bad that I had to sit in the café when Lowry snuck us back in after the rink had shut for the day. I remember watching him and Egg pair up on the empty plain of ice. The resurfacing machine appeared as they glided off in tandem. It scraped up loose pieces of the day's ravaged surface and resprayed water that would freeze in its wake. Egg and Lowry were soon lost to me, shielded by a pale arcing screen of textured mist.

Soon we were on the bank lip. I took the broken stool which I had come to regard as my own so often was it forced upon me, while Lowry struggled to find the maggots. When his back was turned I held up my phone, pretending I was after signal, the cracked screen offering me a superb view of the gentle boundary of Egg in her leggings. She was reading her book and turning the page, plucking absently at the grass with her toes. Each toenail was painted black and together they looked as round and shiny as ten dogs' noses. Egg wore sunglasses and I did wonder, and so I did.

When Lowry failed to locate the maggots I made a show of fetching them, triumphantly lifting the twenty-ounce bait management container from the tackle box, then flicking open the lid, only for a confusing mist to lift into the air, rising from the box as if it had been sprayed from an aerosol. A dreadful amount of flies hummed around us. They split in the direction of the field opposite, became dots and then nothing under the ragged-edged sun.

Lowry took it better than I thought he would. That all of them? he said.

I nodded.

Makes things more interesting, I suppose.

Lucky it was hot. The two of us returned to the splash of buttercups outside the bivvy to eat our sandwiches and drink yet more Guinness. It was another boozy Saturday, and when we were well oiled with treacly stout we decided to make a fire. If there's one thing I know, it's fire. I soon had an old pallet going. The bottom half was grass damp, the wood hissing and loads of woodlice crawling out, but with a light breeze around us the fumes weren't too bad. The smoke billowed and pulsed behind Lowry, trailing in such a way that it looked like noxious thoughts were sifting out of his head. All the while Egg played music off her phone, making a sound-system by setting the mobile upside down in her empty Thermos lid. I always said she was wasted working the till at the supermarket. I said it there and then, shyly, but she didn't thank me.

Once our beers were finished I suggested we fish like we used to do when we were lads, as it would be a shame to come all this way and not have a go. Lowry agreed that this was a great idea, so the two of us removed our socks, trackies and trainers, then splashed out into the river, the water, straight away, reaching up to our waists.

Freezing it was. I gasped downstream to where it was shallow and the flow was less busy and I could see properly into the water. Through the cloudy green my legs looked paler than normal. They were these truculent lengths of bone that struck out at odd angles from my knees. My shin hair had disappeared. I could have been walking on fucking stilts.

A lovely day. I dipped my hands into the lazy water and waited, thinking to myself how this must have reminded Lowry of fetching the balls from the shallows of the lake outside his house on the golf course, wading out in search of dimpled pearls swung into the silt by blokes who lived in patchy states of crisis, driving five-door saloons home to stare at the insides of their garage while the wife clatters plates on the breakfast bar and tries not to cry.

Typically, Lowry caught a fish nearly straight away. He brought it to his eye and checked its flank, then he tossed it onto the bank's knoll where it arched its spine and gulped at nothing. He grinned at me as the fish died, probably to make sure I knew he was tallying his catch. I know Lowry. How he thinks.

I kept at it. River water is obviously unlike the sea yet it is not without its superstitions. I called upon the water sprites, song filling me like it always does – people like me thanks to my fine singing voice – and I began to sing under my breath until a fish came.

Roach. Rust-coloured dorsal and fins. I found it upstream because rivers are quickest where they're narrow and deep. I had left such an enclave, arriving at a broad bend by the undergrowth of the meander.

Egg's yolk-coloured hair was visible above the reeds. I listened to her telling someone over the phone about what one of the rabbits had done the other day: digging its way out of the run Lowry had built it, shitting all over the strawberries before escaping onto the putting green of hole ten.

The roach was drifting my way. I let him come, gliding straight into my hands until I could cup him from the water, which I did. Cold. My fish was deeper-bodied than your chub or dace, about the size of a school ruler. I plucked the bastard from the gloom. Best one I ever caught by hand.

And then I called her.

Egg!

She didn't come.

Lowry answered instead, sloshing over to me and clapping me on the shoulder. Belter, he said. Get in, Buzz.

This was good of him, I know that. Still, because he couldn't be trusted with my excitement I tried not to let him see it. I hadn't trusted Lowry in this way since we first went lamping up Cowpe when we were about twenty years old. What we did was sneak into a farmer's field and wait outside a rabbit warren, shining our torches at whatever came out. Great do. The rabbits freeze as soon as the light hits them and make easy pickings. Yet the next Friday when me and him were in the beer garden of the Woolpack, Lowry took the experience away by making out to everyone that I'd been the scared one, patrolling the foggy glen at nearly midnight. I never did get the chance to protest because Egg was there. She said, You're so daft, Barry, which was enough to make me go along with the whole thing. She shook her head fondly. How I miss her.

Where was I? Me with a fish. Me willing Egg to come and see it. I was the flicker and sheen of a dragonfly's wings, the sporadic thrust of a water boatman, the dense lamb kofta of a bulrush head. I couldn't see Egg. There was only my river, my fish, the distant road sounding unfastened and plangent, almost as if the traffic was aquaplaning across puddles a hundred miles in radius.

The sound made my thoughts wander as they often tend to. I had a vision of Mr Lowry standing in the water nearby, fifteen years dead yet watching over me with his terrible stump arm revealed. The arm suffered 'heterotopic ossification', bone growing where bone shouldn't be, the stump looking like it had been dipped in cold rice pudding. Ossification can be caused by a blast wave passing through the body, altering its genetic codes. There are different kinds of blast wave. Death is one. Love is another.

Lowry must have read my mind or seen me slipping into another of my muddles, because he snapped me out of it by shouting, Fuck's sake ... Emma! Come see this tiddler Buzz's found, will you?

That drew her. The reeds skittered as I presented my bounty to Egg: a weak fish with lidless eyes, pupils like single drops of balsamic vinegar paralysed in cups of olive oil.

Egg smiled at me with both rows of teeth. What you gonna do with that then, Barry? she said. And all I could do was shrug, conscious, of a sudden, of my boxers and T-shirt, the tideline of damp around my middle.

Lowry read it all. Oh, give over, Buzz, he said, shoulder-barging me and making me stumble, my knees striking the rocks. Trying to keep hold of my fish, I couldn't put my hands out to save myself. My head slooshed underwater and I lost my cap. The river looked like diluted Cola, except it was stark-tasting, empty, dank. But I held my fish. I kept him true.

Egg must have said something to Lowry whilst I was flapping about in the water because by the time I managed to resurface and get to my feet, Lowry's nostrils were flared and he had a strained expression that cracked his face apart. With his lank hair and fake smile, he reminded me of them pictures the two of us used to make when we were little by glueing dried up bits of pasta onto the insides of cut-up cereal boxes.

Check him for a rainbow, Lowry said. That's what me dad used to say. If you see a rainbow up your fish's side, chuck it back as that's a sign God's touched it. If you see no colour then you've dinner. Though coarse fish tastes like mud so it'll need salting.

Tomorrow's dinner, said Egg.

Tomorrow's dinner, I agreed.

And so I brought the fish to my eye and looked down its length like an archer might look at an arrow. There it was: a wonderful prism of colour formed along the fish's scales. Light's spectrum, glistening in shiny June.

That was it decided. I took in the glorious rainbow once more, kissed the fish's body and then its lips, then into the water it went. It spiralled in the air before sloshing a few feet away, coming to a stop where it floated against some dull yellow foam at the base of the reeds, bobbing loosely.

Lowry started to laugh. His whole manner opened.

Egg, too. She was laughing at me.

The floating fish reminded me of a sickle moon caught in an evening sky. Egg and Lowry left me to it. I had to listen to them making their way back to the bivvy, and in that moment all that was left of me was what's inside, the part that glints loneliest, that waits the longest.

After a long while I waded over to my fish because I owed it more than the death I'd given it. I raised its body above my head and begged the water sprites for one more favour. There was no denying the comfort in the simplicity of the water against my legs.

I brought the fish to my chin and begun to sing to it, gently, and eventually I was rewarded by the feeling of movement against my beard. The fish was flexing. I dipped it in the water, smiling at the gentle tremor of bubbles emerging from its delicate gills. Slowly, my fish rippled. It breathed in the shallows of my hand for a second, an hour, a lifetime, before bolting away, a quick-flash slipping silver into shadow. I could hear Egg sat somewhere above. She was chatting on her phone by then, and there, on the opposite side of the Ribble, was another girl. She had two badly bruised eyes, her hands hung loose at her sides and she had a dandelion in her mouth, a passionate yellow. It was Old Peg. And I said her name aloud as she entered the water and waded towards me.

Some Rivers Meet

———

TWO OF US HAVE BEEN WATCHING TELLY and as of last minute I'm the one heading to the shop. A game of rock paper scissors is usually what it takes for me and my housemate Hannah to decide who's doing what between us, and now I've lost the best of three rounds I've to peel myself from our duvet nest and get going. You enjoy it, I say. Hannah says she will, her head dunking back into the covers, her phone a periscope that's snapping a picture of my defeat. Post that and you're dead, I tell her. I'm in my comfiest clothes, greasy hair balled into a bread roll shape on top of my head, and no one needs to see that. I slide into our other housemate Smurf's bubble jacket that I know he won't mind me borrowing, then I take the angora scarf from the peg in Hannah's room. I won't, Hannah calls out. She's such a liar.

It's gonna piss it down, you know when the atmosphere gets thick? I hurry along the secret way behind the row of beaming takeaways that are always busy at this time of night. The secret way T-bones the road where the petrol station is, the petrol station being the only place that's open: home of the six-quid bottle of plonk and the gummy sweets I've been sent in search of. It's just about light and it's absolutely freezing, and because

I don't fancy running into Buzz tonight, I sink into my hood as I pass the Embassy, the back yard of which is the arena for more fag breaks than Buzz's allowed, impromptu vomitings and the odd knee trembler between the bar manager, Lorraine, and Jack, the owner, who Smurf sells coke to. Buzz's one of those suggestive guys who doesn't have the guts to ask you anything outright. After making me privy to the staff discount last night – which resulted in an unforeseen kiss that he probably foresaw all along – I can't say I'm that fussed about hearing what he has to suggest to me this time. It's not that Buzz isn't nice and everything. It's more that he's missing that combination of cynicism and vulnerability that really gets to me. What I'm saying is the guy's got no fucking edge.

The alleyway's dingy, rape city. I dig my key out, get the jagged bit sticking between my index and middle fingers and walk as quickly as I can. The cobbles remind me of toads: several thousand toads packed in filmy rows. There's a broken TV stand as well, propped against some bins. Above that's a cat, a haggard thing that looks like a living twist of rope. I've been wary of cats ever since I watched an episode of this TV programme where the main characters are this dweeby yet kind of cool group who investigate paranormal goings-on in apple-pie America. One of the cagey, business-suited guys the gang are always hunting said, as they cornered him in an alleyway, his voice verging on the manic, that the Devil is always in the background and his favoured messengers take many forms. Then he lifted this cat from behind a metal bin, and the cat had an *awful* goblin face, gold eyes with no pupils and a forked tongue. This one's mewling. I hiss at the bloody thing, watching it bristle and flow along the wall before pausing to stare back at me, unknowable. When I hiss again the cat scarpers, and I'm on my way.

At the bottom of the alleyway shines a taxi, an old man struggling out of it. You can't miss confusion like that. The way the guy's hands are going for the wall at his hip, it's as if he's a live current in need of earthing. Even from here I can see his bottom lip going, *Buh Buh Buh*, the taxi leaving him to grope his way along the bricks. He's at least sixty, his posture's a total nightmare and his hair's marshmallow-grey at the temples and darker, slicked up top. Honestly, does anyone who's not a pensioner still use a comb?

I've a roll-up on the go so I finish that while I decide what to do. A few tokes and the smoke's crushed against a toad and I'm heading over, asking the guy if he's all right.

His *I* sounds like an *E* and he doesn't pronounce his *H*'s. 'Ave you got et? he says.

Got what?

He's gazing, no idea what at.

You lost, mate? I say. You need a hand?

Oh, he says, obviously trying to say, *Oh no*, except not getting to the *no* part. And although I can't really be doing with this any more, I say, Here y'are, where you off to? Which entrance: A, B, C or D? Then I point at the doors of a carroty-coloured block of flats about ten metres away from where we're stood.

Matey-boy's eyes bulge: cloudy discs of colour on either side of a nose mangled by what has no doubt been a lifetime on the sauce. His expression makes me wonder if I've done the right thing going over like this, because you worry, don't you. You've got to worry, what with men being the way they are. This old guy's studying the flats harmlessly enough and I know I shouldn't be nervous because I can stick up for myself, I've had to, but it's something to think about, isn't it? Because let's face it, a man can grab you if he wants, or say something, and a lot will do and there's potentially nothing we can do about it. I mean whether it's the shortcut down the secret way that I just took or anywhere in a place like the valley where you can easily find yourself on your own, there's a chance you're going to spot someone coming the other way at some point, some strange bloke, and no one could blame you for being on your guard. That's why even with this confused pensioner standing in front of me the doubt still seeps in. I become the spun coin. What I do now is look him in the eye and ask which door he's after. Which door's yours, mate? I say. This feels important because you should always try to do what people think you can't do, and you should always go out of your way to shake the worry off and go *where* you want, *when* you want. In this way putting fear out of your head can become a feminist act. A vital rebellion.

This one, the man replies before dawdling in the direction of door B, checking over his shoulder to see if I'm still there, which I am. It takes him ages to get to the door. It takes him forever with the fob, as well, and no word of a lie, he's dead chuffed when the receiver bleeps green and the lock snaps open.

Click.

He enters the foyer, I don't. We're at the brink of some concrete stairs and I can smell stale hash. Shit, the smell's coming from Smurf's coat. I check the inner pocket and there's a joint docked-out there prematurely, which is another thing this old boy hasn't a clue about.

His hand is on the banister. Please.

Please what, mate?

Oh. He's staring, not seeing. A colourless flap of chewing gum sits on his tongue.

Go on then, I say, pointing at the cavernous stairwell. Go on, off you go.

He doesn't move. He just stares. I ask him what's up again, laughing to myself when his mouth opens like he wants something chucking in it. I notice a cut on his chin from where he's had a clumsy shave, and I'm becoming conscious of the time, because it's a Sunday and I haven't got all night. I've to be at Tatt's Haulage tomorrow for five or Sharon will go spare and give my shift to someone else.

Look, I can't help you if you don't tell me what's up, man.

I—

Go on. Time to get yourself home.

Oh.

Bollocks to this. I step out onto the street and the door nearly shuts behind me, and that's when the man speaks up, his voice taking on a real heartbreaking note of frustration.

I just don't know where I am, he says.

I search that raddled face for lies and turn nothing up. Every wall of this lower stairwell has been tagged with marker pen. CRUSTYMAN, the walls say, next to a scraggy picture of a beardy face that could be a drawing of the great outdoors in human form. It's mental seeing a thing like that on concrete. It's almost like it belongs to another era, another mindset entirely, and it can see right through me: the face of a God that we might have forgotten, but who still remembers us. If the face's eyes were coloured they'd definitely be green. My mouth's gone well dry and the lights have timed out. I step in front of the sensor and bring brightness back to the stairwell, revealing a blue rubbery handrail that if you were to fall against would hurt easily as much as the steps. It'd be just my luck for this guy to fall and hurt himself. I take the poor bastard by the elbow.

We go upstairs, me assuring the guy that blah blah blah, and so on, then we're outside of what I guess must be the place. A plasticky door leads into a wall. Hey presto, the guy's key fits the lock and the door opens directly into a sitting room that smells like mouldy bread.

Now, this flat, well, bear with me here, but let's just imagine for a minute that every person's life's a river, right? You've your streams, rills and becks, and say that's some people. Then you've got great sunny winders like the River Nile, choppy rapids, *sewers*, even, or them ice rivers you get off the telly, the ones that go through glaciers that are pretty much the bluest things you've ever seen. Now imagine that these rivers are other people's lives, then remember that they come together, you get confluences, *then* remember that they sometimes split apart again like nothing ever happened. Either that or they keep flowing until there's no real difference between them. Now these rivers flood into the sea. Every fucking one. Some might take a while, head wherever. Others might stretch further, go slower, but at the end of the day they all end up in the one place. Well, I take one look at this guy's flat and I can tell straight away that he's come to the end of his course. This guy's about five minutes from becoming one with the salt. I step indoors and scour my feet on the heavy twill rug. Our two rivers have crossed tonight and now I'm going to have to get on with it.

There's a couch and a coffee table, a booth of an adjoining room with a single bed, a kitchen and a pisser and nowt on the walls. No signs of a life save the telly. Everything's as plain as a block of Cheddar cheese.

On the coffee table though is what looks like one of them barrels you fetch raffle tickets or bingo balls out of. So there's that as well. Look, it's for medication. There's a note sellotaped to the table with a smiley face on it; in gangling biro letters it's reminding the poor bastard to cheer up.

I give the dispenser a spin. Nothing comes out. That's when I notice the digital panel. Ah, so when the timer goes, the machine gives the guy what's necessary. Who needs a wife, eh? Forget companions.

I help him out of his coat. He's shaped like a bloody Easter egg. Sitting on the couch like he doesn't know what it is.

You all right, mate?

Oh.

Fucking *oh.* The guy takes it in. He takes me in: the skinny pants, cream, which Hannah says suit my complexion, and Smurf's coat: a puffer jacket. Purple, massive and warm.

I'll make him a drink then do one. Tea?

The man nods.

Yeah, man. A brew, yeah? You want one?

The man smiles. I suppose people will never forget tea.

What's your name? I ask on my way to the kitchen. I'm Samirah.

I?

Your name, mate? I say, turning around.

The man wrings his spotted hands. He's forgotten the question.

Through the kitchen window above the sink I can see the

petrol station. The bright banded sign makes a picture of the drizzle. Below it are empty streets, steep potholed roads and the occasional pollarded tree. Cheap rent and a council that handed out hackney cab licences then didn't check whether you operated in the borough brought my parents to the valley. Although Mam and Dad's marriage was arranged by their families before I was born, they were lucky because they ended up loving each other. Skids moved in next door, one neighbour said, talking on his phone the day we arrived, going into himself when he realised I'd overheard him. I remember the cardboard box sagging in my arms. It had sat on the pavement for ages, its base soaked through, my stuff trying to escape out the bottom. I stared the neighbour out but I never actually said anything. You don't, do you. Or at least I never used to. At that moment I knew my dad had been right when he'd told my mum that I'd get a good education if we moved to the valley, although what I learned wasn't exactly what he had in mind. Dad's old school. He can't appreciate that you can class yourself as having been taught something if you know not to take things too seriously. Considering how bothered he was about coming here and how demanding he was when it came to me doing well in school, Dad never once took the time off from his taxi to come to parents' evening, and he even had the nerve to go into a week-long sulk when he found out I'd been eating hotdogs from the ice-cream van at lunchtimes.

There was fuck all he could do about that. He'd wanted this life for me, that's what he got. You might want things on your terms, I said to him. That's not how it works. Course I'm a veggie now – those poor pigs! – but as a teenager school was hotdogs. It was Mars bars and Panda Lemonade, a fumble in the basement cloakrooms with any older lad who was up for it. It was Lambert & Butler in smokers' corner behind the sixth form common rooms, my initials bound up with my mate Charlotte's in a love heart on the fence. Charlotte moved away and had a kid at sixteen, while I sacked school off altogether. I haven't seen her since – it would only be weird now. Mad how things go. The way people neglect each other.

Mildew on the sill. Pure grime. Outside, a mile or so past this middling strip of civilisation, the countryside begins, rising out of the night like a killer whale, stone terraces tucked here and there with people in them. Man, you should see this place in summer. Not that we're anywhere near that time of year. The window opens enough for me to lean out of, so I spark Smurf's joint up using the hob and have a smoke from two storeys up while the kettle boils. Course there's no milk. There's no mugs either. Just mouse shit sprinkled all over the cupboard shelf and a pair of glass tumblers. I wash the tumblers under the tap then dry them with a bit of tissue from my pocket as the wind chucks itself against the building. What a thing it must be to lose your marbles on your own, with not even enough milk in the fridge for a proper brew.

In the living room I set the man's tumbler of black tea in front of him then ask if there's anybody I can call. When he instinctively grabs for the drink, I try to stop him before he burns his fingers on the hot glass, but I mistime my swipe and we both end up getting scalded. The tea slops onto the table and leaks into the smiley face, staining it brown. As the man gawks at me like I fucking did that on purpose. I point at my burnt hand and ask if there's anyone who can come and help him instead of me. Or will he be all right on his own now?

He's dead confused, fuck's sake. Daughter, he says, while I'm towelling the spilled tea dry with a minging rag from the radiator.

I've—

Is she local, mate?

Joanne—

I look at him.

Joanne ... She lives in ... Reading.

Reading. You got a number? I reply, making a goofy 'phone' signal with my pinkie and thumb. I sound like a nurse. I remember waking up in casualty once after necking a bladder of sangria around the back of the spiritualist church when I was about thirteen. One of them talked to me the same way. I know she meant well, I still swung for her.

The phone trills. I'm that edgy after the spliff that I jump. Old boy does too. His head jerks as if his skull's tethered to a bungee cord. The ringing fills the whole flat – it's a horrible sound, the sound of the years trilling by, crashing to a halt when you least expect it.

Will you answer the phone, please?

I'm not answering your phone, man.

Oh, please.

No.

PLEASE, will you just answer the phone?

Distress is enough to make me do anything. I've not used a house phone in years. Hello? I say, shaking my head when an American voice answers me, male.

Hi there.

I've never chatted to a real Yank before. I imagine him with his gun and Bible. I suppose he's picturing me with my wonky teeth, thinking life owes me a living.

Wow, he says, once I've explained the situation. That's good of you. Thank you for stopping.

You're all right, I say, picking at a stain embossed on the wall. It comes off, taking a patch of wallpaper with it.

He's my uncle, the Yank clarifies. My mom and I have a weekly phone call arranged. He's not doing so good ...

Well, duh.

Excuse me?

I twiddle the spiral cord flex. Look, is there no one you can call, mate? No one who can come sit with this guy? I've things to do.

The American exhales. There's his daughter and whatnot. She's—

Joanne's in Reading.

Of course, you're right. Wait, hold on a second ...

A conversation I can't decipher twitters from thousands of

miles away. Then this woman comes on the line. Like my host, with his shop dummy expression, peering at nothing in particular, each hand clamped upon each knee, the woman is the owner of a mixed-up accent. She thanks me: *Thank yew*, and calls me sweetheart. *Such* a kind thing you're doing, helping my brother.

Bruth-er. Maybe she's right. I weigh this act against the things I've done, the things I will do. I suppose it'll be one to stack in my favour when the time comes. And that's something, isn't it. I'll take that. Every single one of us, we take what we can get.

No worries, love, I say.

The woman promises to find help. I ask if she wants to speak to her fuddled sibling but she doesn't hear me, and that's when it occurs to me that not only do I not know this man's name, the family haven't thought to tell it me. How often do they think of their brother? How important is he to them? Are they getting on with their lives already, moving on before he's even gone?

I offer him the phone. Your sister.

My?

Your fucking sister in America.

The man tears the phone from my hand and slams it in the cradle.

Hey!

Bathroom.

What you on about?

Bathroom.

No.

BATHroom.

He's already on his way to the pisser, which has no door. He's unbuttoning his trousers, or at least trying to, stopping midway, *Oh*, fumbling, getting all agitated, and he might be about to wet himself here and then where will we be?

Come here, I say, holding my breath as I help the guy get his trouser button undone. The icy burnish of the naked pisser bulb sets me alight as I'm helping this lost codger pull down his trousers. When the deed's done I shudder into the sitting

112

room, anxious to leave the man with some shred of, I want to say dignity, then I retreat to the kitchen where I sit at the table and picture a river shrieking into the ocean, into a sea bigger and colder than any other.

Enough's enough. I'm about to leave when I spot a keyring attached to some keys in the empty fruit bowl. It says, *If you find this man lost, please call this number*. Like a stray dog, I can't help but think, pressing in the digits on my phone.

It's another old boy in the end, a puny guy with mole-eyes and wrinkles that spread outward as if his nose is a stone dropped into the pond of his face. He hesitates at the sight of me and I can tell what he's thinking, but no way am I giving him a reaction.

All right, I say. He's in there. I point at the toilet. Just in there.

Right. The man slips off his coat as he enters the flat.

Just in the toilet.

Okay. Yes. Fine.

The man glances past me, unwilling to make eye contact.

I'll be on my way then.

What?

I said I'll be on my way.

Finally the man looks at me. I'm at the door by this point. By the way, he says. You've done a good thing, helping my pal.

You're all right. I nod. He's just a bit lost, isn't he.

Aye, the man agrees. He is that.

The way it goes though, at his age.

The man runs a hand down his face. Do this often, do you?

I … How do you mean?

I'm just surprised. Your lot. You never normally get involved, do you?

I don't reply.

I mean, most of the time you keep yourselves to yourselves. I wouldn't have thought you'd have stopped when you saw him like this. Most of you wouldn't bother.

I think I say yeah. I think I agree. I've grasped the door handle when the man asks me what's wrong.

Nothing, I say. I'm all good.

The guy starts apologising. He starts saying he's sorry if I'm offended and he didn't mean what I think he meant and yeah, yeah, fucking whatever, mate.

He comes over and touches my arm. He has this magnified expression on his face. Timid, yes, and yet hate is there.

I can't move. I can't speak. My head's gone fizzy and there's this hysterical feeling that reminds me in a way of when a microphone gets too near a speaker. For a terrible moment I'm completely exposed and it takes a hell of a lot of willpower to pull myself together, but when I do, I rip my arm free and tell the man it's fine. I've gotta go, I say. I need to get out of here.

Really, I—

You're all right, pal. I wipe his clamminess on Smurf's coat. He's gone all quiet. Fuck's sake. Now I'm feeling guilty. He's making *me* feel like *I've* made *him* feel weird. Have I gone mad or something? Am I being mental?

He's a stubborn old bastard, the man says as I get the door open. He nods at our mutual friend, who has by now hiked his trousers up and is pottering into the living room as if his ankles are shackled together. He knows not to drink, he does it anyway. Every day he's out, boozing alone.

Can't say I blame him.

The man goes to the window. Suppose.

Right.

The man hesitates. Well.

What?

You know …

What?

Nothing.

I flick my hood up. Sound, mate.

Wait, the man says. He looks so lost. I was just going to say that, well … you're a sweet little thing and you really remind me of—

I walk out. The first one, the dying one, he is climbing slowly into bed.

A bitter darkness has descended upon the valley. I loosen Hannah's scarf and face the rain. It's almost as if a giant diamond has broken into smithereens up there, and now the most brilliant shards of neon are floating all over the show. No way can I be bothered with the garage now. I head back the secret way, treading on petrified toads until I come to the broken TV stand, which makes me stop, because in the stand's cracked glass the street lamp on the corner is madly reflected. It's a crazy thing to see in this frame of mind. It makes me imagine that a bomb's gone off in a parallel universe and somehow the explosion's been caught in a time lapse in the glass. It's pretty beautiful, so lovely in fact that maybe it's more than an explosion. Maybe it's a comet captured as it sears its route through deep space. Yeah, that's what it is. It's a fading star and I've never noticed it before tonight, and the only place I or anyone else will ever be able to see it is here in this lonely valley where the countryside has begun to reclaim what the town took. There's no doubt about it. I can hear the ocean heaving as I crouch in front of the cracked pane in the TV stand. I'm wishing the light was warm, but it's not, it's cold. It's the simple chill of a mossy sheet of glass. A noise makes me jump. It's that cat. It's staring at me from the wall with this *look* on its face. Now I can hear footsteps. They're heavy. Getting closer. And I can hear waves, the sea.

Rosco of the Pineys

———

WHEN ME AND MY FRIENDS started at the paper mill the other guys who worked there said we'd get used to the stink, but I was the only one never did. I suppose I always saw the job as temporary, so why should I bother trying to come to terms with it? Other than me and Sean White it was Tom Kirklees and Marcus '*Aurelius*' Towne, and the four of us drank every day in the Woolpack after our shifts. I can't speak for the others because we don't talk any more, but if you want to know what it was like grafting in a stench that's come to characterise my youth, then I'll tell you: it was thirsty work.

That mill has a lot to answer for. To this day if you put so much as an omelette in front of me, I go all funny. The eggy mill funk was an unfortunate byproduct of dropping the wood-chip into the liquor so it could be digested into pulp and later bleached, processed into paper. The process released sulphur, which, as any self-respecting chemist or evil genius will tell you, can be used to make stink bombs, so imagine the reek of a paper town. The mill where I worked was in Stubbins, Lancashire, so naturally the place was nicknamed Scrubbins and the people who worked at the mill were known as Scrubbers, as was anybody unfortunate enough to live nearby.

These days they've brought in ways of masking the fugitive emissions, but back then us scrubbers car-shared from the mill with the windows down. With it being a few miles to the Woolpack our hair would be all over the show by the time we arrived, four bog-brush-haired blokes in work togs, diving straight into a pint of lager each capped with blackcurrant, usually drinking until about eight, except on Friday nights when no one would drive and we'd down a shot of Jager every other round until closing time. We smoked screws of tobacco rolled in liquorice-flavoured Rizlas, and often only had one lighter between us that would never come home with its owner. I remember going round Sean's one Friday after the pub and finding his stash: dozens of coloured lighters that belonged to the rest of us, wrapped by an elastic band and stowed in a cupboard. The efficiency of his operation astounded me – it had taken resolve. If any of us had tried that Sean would never have let it go. Then again that's him all over.

We've known each other since we were eleven, four average students from a state school: a group of braying, cartwheeling lads who lived on the same bus route, our houses a few miles apart. There's not much to do in the valley other than drink, and you've eighteen years to get through before you can do that legally, so growing up us four spent loads of time playing football down at the rec, or hanging out in the pineys: a local wood.

Our friendship was whelped amongst those eerie towers of flaking bark. Hidden from the nosey occupants of a row of cottages banding the lane leading to the trees, we used to get stoned on teenths of weed that Sean bought off a woman on his street. Of the numerous methods we devised for getting high, the pipes fashioned from empty Coke cans were probably the dirtiest. What you did was unwrap your weed lump from its cling film, put the flame to it then crumble a load up along with some torn cigarettes, the outsides of which had been toasted first to give the tobacco a better taste. A pinch of this mix was sprinkled over some holes we punched in the can with a safety pin. Light the bastard up and suck the fumes out of the drink-hole. *Always Coca-Cola.*

Each boy was another's alibi to his parents. We even slept in the pineys, cosy in our sleeping bags like a row of pupates. Or when the pineys were riddled with the valley's frequent showers, we retreated to an abandoned furniture warehouse on the Burnley Road. To get into the warehouse we used a skip around the side of the building, which gave us access to a scaly tree that looked like it had thrashed out of the dirt fully grown. Usually drunk, always stoned, we'd step from the tree's upper branches onto a twelve-foot-high stockyard wall, tightrope our way along that then duck into a smashed section of roof onto the ceiling beams so we could clamber to the ground. How none of us broke our necks, I'll never know. The warehouse stank of mouldering carpet and cat piss, and by the end of an Ecstasy-fuelled summer where we set a junior world to rights, every window was smashed, the place covered in marker pen. BEST MATEZ, we wrote on the walls.

THUG LYFE.

None of us bothered with college. We had the sacrament of the pool table and the dart board to be getting on with. We were the order of the benches in the beer garden. I loved the Woolpack, still do. In this very cubbyhole I met my wife, Sara. At that time she was taking a break from studying for her geography PGCE, a red-haired girl who didn't know she was sat in my seat. Sara's the only person who's ever taken my writing seriously. I think meeting her made me acknowledge for the first time how little Sean and the others understood who I am, which only compounded my own revulsion at how willing I'd been to follow their lead by sacrificing myself on the blood-drenched altar of the nine to five. I still drink in the Woolpack and I suppose one day Sean will carry out his threat to knock me out. He was easily the most raging when I quit the mill and eventually the group. I tell myself that kicking-off is his way of admitting he misses me.

It's Friday night and I suppose I could be drinking elsewhere, but the bar staff all know my name here and, if you ask me, that's something worth holding onto. Sara's caught the bus into Manchester tonight with a few mates. I've been painting the wainscoting all day at the flat with her dad, Oliver, who booked the afternoon off work to help. By now I should be chilling with him and the boys but I've ducked out before I end up throttling him. The old prick's worked at the mill all his life but has never risen above the level of shift manager. Oliver had Sara too young and became aware of himself far too late. I've often overheard him telling my wife that she's to put her foot down and force me to go back to that stinking nightmare, or at least to go full-time at the removal company that took me on. *Full-time.* I'd like to see Oliver sneezing up cat hair and hodding couches around three days a week, let alone five. It's not like I'm sat on my arse all day when I'm not working either. Raising twins and supporting an overworked teacher is a dear do, emotionally as well as spiritually, as for that matter is writing a book at the kitchen table till the early hours nearly every night. Life expects that much sometimes that it really needs telling where to go.

I've said I'm fetching tea: a pitta filled with doner meat, full salad and yoghurt sauce for Oliver, a lamb shawarma kebab for me and a cone of chips with red salt each for the lads. The order's pencilled on the back of a receipt that's collecting table-damp this very second, while in my hand's a golden sleeve of bubbling lager. I'd stay all night if I could. If I'm quick I might even squeeze in another pint.

The past, however, is always lurking. This time it's waiting for me at the other end of the bar in the shape of Aurelius Towne. One of the old cohort's always here, avoiding eye contact, making me wonder whether or not I should try and salvage something from the rubble of our friendship, but I can never decide if I should go over.

Thankfully Aurelius hasn't seen me. The Woolpack's an odd-shaped pub with recesses that can hide you from the main sections of the room, and the roof's low, the walls populated by framed black-and-white photographs of unsmiling workers from the long-defunct textile mills, plus there's a sort of padded wallpaper that absorbs the occasional thrust of unwelcome voices like mine. I concentrate on my book and the story of old Stephen Dedalus, and take a long draft of Chestnut Mild. Another advantage of knowing Gerry the landlord is you can get your drinks on the tick, slip out unseen then come back another day to settle the tab.

Still, part of me wishes I could speak to Aurelius. He always found me funny so was someone I liked having around, even though he had a habit of borrowing money and not paying it back, which caused predictable tensions. The abuse Sean used to give him you wouldn't believe.

A coarse, hacking cheer fills the bottom end of the pub. I can't hear what's been said but the Woolpack's only pool cue is sticking out of Aurelius's fist, and two youngsters are facing him. One's wearing those thick specs you used to get on the NHS that cost a bomb now. The other's face is obscured by a hair-straightened curtain of bleached-blond hair. The blond one, him in the red denim jacket and green Converse trainers, has something about him that's familiar. Fuck it, I've time for another pint. From my new position at the bar I can see a pair of sticker-pocked guitar cases propped against the windowsill, while around the corner is Aurelius, just hidden from my line of sight.

That were a lucky shot, he says in that natural baritone.

Luck? the youth in glasses replies. Yeah right, mate.

Peeking round the corner, I've to smother my laughter at the sight of Aurelius, who's flapping his hands like they're camp little T-rex arms. *Yeah, right, mate,* he's going. *Yeah, right.*

Well, that's pool, Glasses replies stuffily, looking to his blond friend for assurance and not getting it.

Pool. Aurelius jerks a thumb at the youths, summoning more stock laughter from a set of blokes I don't recognise, all of them bald or balding, the kind of jocular disdain I've seen meted out by suggestible men throughout my life.

The youngsters huddle around the jukebox, unaware that

not only have the Woolpack's tunes not been changed in years, us regulars come here to escape our lives in silence. Aurelius strides over and switches the jukebox off at the mains. The screen's gaudy animation winks to black.

Boys—

Hey, we just put money in that!

Ah, selection's shite anyway.

Come on, you know that's not the point.

Have a day off, says Aurelius, producing two silver coins from his pocket. Take this fifty to cover it and stick this one in the fuckin' table.

The youths exchange exasperated expressions. I can't put my finger on who the blond one reminds me of. He's got diamanté earrings that do him no favours whatsoever, meanwhile his pal Glasses is soft and dun-skinned and as slight as Scrubbins paper.

I emerge from behind the corner with my toes clenching and unclenching, pausing behind Aurelius, whose head is as freshly shaven as it was the day we first met, his shoulders far broader. Now I'm leaning against the bandit, near the door, my elbow jarring against the flashing, sharp-edged buttons.

I thought it was winner stays on, says Glasses, indicating the row of change regimented along the wooden edge of the pool table. You said it yourself. You have to put a knock down and then wait your turn.

Aurelius knows the rules, he's been bending them since the nineties. He doesn't answer the boy though because he's making a point of ignoring me. Yet my presence *does* something. I can see it in the way Aurelius sets the pool cue on the table, rolling it towards the rich green of the parallel cushion. Two against one, he says, friendlier now. Twenty quid to the winner.

He smooths a purple twenty flat on the table, and as he does, I assess the youngsters, their closeness. You didn't used to get kids like this around here: your students, your smashed-avocado-for-breakfasts. Most of them wouldn't have dared set foot in a pub like the Woolpack when I was a kid, and when I was old enough to drink, a place like this wouldn't have been cool enough, certainly not for any metropolitan just home from uni who'd been lucky enough to have the world pried open for them rather than having to work things out for themselves. These days I suppose youngsters come to the Woolpack in search of what they see as an authentic experience. They come here in a tongue-in-cheek sort of way, while the rest of us just come here. Here they are conferring at my side of the table. I take a step in the opposite direction because whilst Aurelius might think I want to count myself among these strangers – I know Sean, Tom and Oliver definitely do – I want to give him the idea that at best that's only half right. That, if anything, mine's a simple case of envy, because these boys will never have to break from everything they know in order to be who they're sure they are.

What do you think? says Glasses to his friend. The blond one answers with a firm shake of the head, then, ignoring Aurelius, he takes a fresh knock and glibly places it in the table's coin mechanism, popping it to release the balls into the portal by his knee.

Aurelius's mouth shrinks to the size of a dog's arse but the triangle is full and the lads begin playing without him. The pack is smashed apart, a perfect geometry of colour diffusing noisily across the baize.

Carrying his beer back to his seat, Aurelius has to come past me. I whistle at him gently, inflating my cheeks and crossing both eyes when I have his attention. The way he halts, my heart skips, but that amiable grin I remember so well finds my old friend's face and he goes cross-eyed too.

Good old Aurelius.

I've just received a salutary second pint when a name I haven't heard in ages is uttered.

Rosco.

I should have known. Perhaps I did know. I take a big swig of my beer and say *Reight, boys*, because Sean and Tom are by the brass cask pumps to my left. They must be off out this evening because, unlike Aurelius, they're not in mill togs. Their noses are rosy from the outdoors and both seem amused to see me. Tom in particular, I'm startled by. They used to say he and I looked alike.

Nice sideburns, he says.

Sara likes them.

Neither of them mention my hair.

Tom scouts for Gerry's eye. She not out tonight?

I shrug. Gone town. You?

Off Embassy.

Embassy, man. Imagine a flotilla of lights on full whack above a dance floor, girls gyrating in huddles and various lads circling them like a bad mood. Every weekend there's fisticuffs in Embassy's car park, hordes crammed into the adjacent take-away. Trays of chips with cheese and mayonnaise. The worst fucking music you've ever heard.

Summat up? says Sean, surveying me like I'm surveying him. Sean's got this narrow, rugby-ball-shaped head and deceptively mild, open-mannered eyes. He also wears silver-link chains strung around his neck and a wrist. When he was fourteen Sean took the short-term decision of not having braces fitted, and now he has to live with the long-term issue of having a gob overcrowded with teeth, especially on the top row.

I don't make a face or shake my head. I don't do anything except say, Just can't believe you're still at it. And *still* Sean seems pissed off. He sticks his tongue behind his bottom lip and nods at Gerry, who prepares two Jagers, two beers.

Still facing forward, he says, Nowt wrong wi' Embassy.

Aye, if you don't mind having the same night over and again, yeah.

Sean widens both eyes, *slowly*, which makes me feel like the most hideous snob.

Suppose there's nowhere else though, I add, around here.

Tom gestures at the galaxy of paint speckles on my hands and clothes. Been doing your nails, Rosco?

I attempt a laugh. *Huh*. Me in paint scruffs while Tom's got crow's feet and wears a silk turquoise shirt with a white collar and cuffs. In the glare of the spotlight I can see the wet-look hair gel coating his scalp. It's as slick and opaque as pork-pie jelly.

Sara's been wanting the flat doing, I explain. Me and her dad been on wi' it.

Sean and Tom instantly recoil at the mention of Oliver.

He at it again? I ask.

He never stopped, Sean says, and although we're all smiling now, our mutual glee is painful because the three of us were once so united by taking the piss out of things, and this is a reminder that, like most people, I really miss being young.

Who's the latest victim?

Our Dec.

Shit. No way. Sorry, Tom.

Since when was Little Dec a Scrubber? My mind casts back to an eight-year-old with a fixed frown whenever we wouldn't let him come up to the pineys with us. A jutting jaw, hooded eyes and silence.

Olly's got him on the top conveyor tomorrow, Tom adds. Fucking Deakin with him, of all people. There's been a fault in the silo feed.

Little Deccy Kirklees, I reply disbelievingly. Not so little any more.

You're telling me, says Tom. Fucking Olly ... He stops himself. No offence ...

No, you're all right, I say. I hear you, man.

Sean, who has managed to sink three quarters of his drink whilst Tom and I have been talking, nods. What about them stories of yours? he says. Paying you a wage yet, are they, Rosco?

I could mention the thing I had in the magazine last year, but I don't bother. They're going all right, I reply.

Well, least you're looking the part.

The beer is actually weak and overpriced, and I'm thinking of Oliver, of how much time I've got before he'll have the right to start moaning at me when I get back in. My book's still in the alcove, the seat going cold. I dream of a blue plaque screwed into the wall there when I'm gone. A marker of a life drunk, a life lived.

G. G. *Ross*, Sean says, grinning.

So he did read my story!

What's the other G. stand for?

It doesn't have to stand for anything, I reply, shrivelling inside. What you doing for work these days?

You know where.

An' where you living now?

Sean's silence is answer enough. If that flat were a noise it would be the sound of someone clearing their throat. It's a one-bed above a pet shop that made the news a few years ago when the owners realised one of their fish had markings on its scales that said Allah in Arabic script down one side, and Muhammad down the other. Part of me was hoping Sean would have moved. Another part of me wants to click its heels at the thought of him spending every night alone there, just him and his Pot Noodles.

I don't have to say anything.

What? says Sean.

Nowt.

No, go on, Gaz. Enlighten me.

I didn't say a word.

Typical fucking Rosco.

How do you mean?

Fuck off, mate, how do *you* mean?

Even Tom looks awkward. He knows as well as I do that the utilitarian dump Sean calls home wants tearing down. How can a guy get so defensive over a place littered with betting slips, duct tape mending all the splits in the cheapo flooring? There's a picture of Sean's kid who he doesn't see drawing-pinned to the wall. Last time I was there some new potatoes had been left by the sink for that long that they'd begun to sprout wan, green-budding tentacles.

I just hope you're wiping your feet when you go in, mate, I say, chuckling.

Yeah, calm down, Sean-o, adds Tom.

Shut it, T! Least I pay my own way, Gaz. Last I heard it were your missus ...

I snatch my beer and walk away. Just like that. But on my way to the alcove I take a sip and realise I've picked the wrong drink up. It's the wrong bloody one and now I'll have to make do. Grabbing my book and coat, I gulp most of the tepid bitter down but the chemical flatness makes me gag and I have to stop at the door. That's when I catch sight of Aurelius. He's talked himself into another game with those youngsters, and it looks like he's not giving the cue ball up.

I can't help it. I go over, happening to fall in behind Sean and Tom in our old formation.

Aurelius stares at us. The Three Musky-rears, he says, aiming the cue at me like a rifle.

Marcus Aurelius.

Don't you start, Sean.

Has the emperor gone and had it? Has his luck finally finished?

And losing to Lord and Lady Tarquin here an' all, says Tom, raising his pint cheerily at the youngsters.

The jury of bald guys crack up at that, and Sean's gaze flicks my way, probably to see if I'll get involved like I might have done in the past, but I'm studying the two lads. I've realised what it is about the blond one that's bothering me. He's the absolute spit of Shelley Mullins, a girl Sean once fell for. There's only three people in the world who know that when Sean White asked Shelley Mullins for her number, she gave him the details for Rollo's Pizza, then, when he confronted her about it the following weekend, she called him Jaws and said she wouldn't touch him with a ten-foot barge pole. Shelley and me saw one another for a while after that, and she made me promise to keep it from Sean. I was true to my word, although it would have been *easy* to break it, necessary, even, after the way Sean became around women. I guess that's how it was in our group: the slightest thing could become a currency between us that opened up a class divide it was easy to find yourself on the wrong side of. After his failure with Shelley the only option Sean had was to come out swinging. That holiday to Magaluf I still think about to this day.

I doubt he's noticed how much the kid looks like Shelley. Never mind the fact the resemblance runs right through the youngster, from his posture to those jeans that look painted-on. I consider his mother's slender thighs, how I used to run my hands up them. I wonder how Shelley's getting on. She ended things between us abruptly and now she lives in the pineys in two cottages that have been knocked through to become one. I see her driving her Range Rover about sometimes. It's got a private number plate.

This is in the bag, mate, her son says, lining up his next shot, grinning at Sean and Tom. Check this out.

Sean just sneers. Get your hair cut, love.

And Aurelius laughs.

The lad still pots, he can really play. Two shots still, he says, which makes Aurelius practically cough up his beer.

It's not two-shot carry!

Hang on, you fouled and I potted … I've still—

You've the one!

Oh, come on, Marco, I blurt. Give the kid a break.

Who asked you, G.G.? Sean says, drawing the attention of Shelley's son, whose eyes widen at the sight of me before hardening pointedly. The kid looks away.

For some reason that dismissal hurt. When the kid misses his next shot, I cock my head at him. Just another barbarian, am I?

Aurelius takes the cue, chalks it and crouches, his eye above the corner pocket of the table. The thing about games like these, he says, is they're a marathon not a sprint. He squints at a quadrangle of yellow balls.

Whack.

Played, Marco, Tom says.

Well in, pal, I want to add. That was a lovely development on the next shot.

Aurelius pots a second ball, then a third. Meanwhile the lad in glasses checks how many cigarettes he's got left. Ever alert, Sean can barely keep the anticipation from his voice as he demands one. Here, send us one of them, pal, he says, beckoning the lad with every finger.

Glasses does as he's told, just the one smoke remaining in his packet. Not that this is a problem for Sean, who passes the cigarette to Tom – Tom pops it behind his ear – then eyeballs the youngster again.

Sorry, it's my last one, says Glasses.

You what?

I said it's my—

Mate...

A loud crack. Aurelius has struck the pool table with the thin end of the cue. *Bastard.*

The cue nearly bops me in the nose on its way past. Glasses seizes it by the tip and hurries to the table, ignoring Sean, who reflexively hides those crammed teeth with his lips.

Glasses has just bent over the table when Shelley's son pipes up.

Come on, Sam!

Everyone cracks up at that, even me. The kid sounds like Mary fucking Poppins! He retreats behind his torrent of fringe, and I'm sure he's staring at me. Come to think of it, I *know* he is. Right through his hair. Was I laughing louder than the others or something? I finish my flat beer and fake a cough.

Glasses bends over the table. It takes him a minute to overthink his shot though and ultimately he slices it. A sarcastic cheer fills the room and once the beery surge and sluice of laughter has subsided, Tom calls out. Here, *Where's Wally*, he says, indicating Glasses's thick, black spectacles. You might wanna get them bloody looked at.

Glasses plays along. Ah, fuck off, he says good-naturedly, and although the room knows how that was meant, it still goes quiet. The silence feels almost *velvety*. Offence is the order of service and Sean White is its incumbent spokesman.

You what, lad? he says, stepping towards Glasses.

I'm sorry? the kid replies.

You said summat.

No, I didn't ...

I heard you, mate.

Honestly, man, I didn't say anything!

Come here a sec, will you? I wanna talk to you.

Glasses focuses on his drink, as well he should. For a second he shifts his feet and straightens, and this has me worried, but thank fuck he keeps his mouth shut, and thank fuck he stays where he is, because the room isn't silent any more, not in the slightest.

You little *shit*, Sean says, so everyone can hear.

The game is nearly over. Everyone is amused by Aurelius's rash play, everyone except me. I'm more interested in Sean. His curls creep out of his head like a thousand twisting ampersands. Whispering in Tom's ear. Whispering, with so much to say.

Shelley's son is up next. He has to come this side of the table to reach the cue ball, and that's when I spot Sean's hand move.

Oi!

I lunge forward to try and stop Sean, accidentally knocking the blond youngster's elbow and making him miscue his shot. The white cannons into the black match ball and sends it plummeting down a pocket. Everyone goes fucking mad. Aurelius dives onto the table, his cycling feet catching the lamp and sending an oblong of pukey light rocking up the stucco wall. Sean and Tom fall about laughing and Tom even shakes my hand.

Get in, Rosco, he says. Fucking legend, man.

Now Shelley's son is pointing at me and we look so alike in the moment that it could be me standing there, humiliated. And it shits me up. *Jesus*, it does.

The boys are forced to hand over the money, and Aurelius uses it to get a round in. He buys pints for Sean and Tom and, to my surprise, hands one to me as I reach the door. When Aurelius claps me on the shoulder I can see the hurt in his eyes at the distaste I've been unable to keep from my face.

So in a way I'm glad when Sean makes his move. He strides

up to Glasses and pretends to deliver a savage one-shot to the nose. Glasses dodges, trips on the pool table and falls into the radiator. His specs have come off and one arm is askew when he picks them up again, gingerly touching his head. Blood. He has to be helped up by Shelley's son, who says something visceral to Sean that I can't make out, then barges out of the back door with Glasses following him. No one else sees the bereft look on Sean's face. No one else cares. I shove past him, grabbing the boys' guitars on my way into the beer garden.

Lads! I shout. *Lads, wait!*

There's no sign of them. I wonder if it's worth fetching the car. I'll find them easily enough. Maybe I'll run them up to the pineys where Shelley lives, chatting to them about music and books and films, telling them life won't always be like this, even though that won't be true. I set down the instruments. The Woolpack door's ajar and I can hear the jolly rumpus bustling inside. I think I must be the only person who finds laughter like that sad. Maybe it's because it never seems to include me. Maybe it's because I can't help suspecting that it's at my expense. Above me is a litany of movement in huge trees I don't know the names of. I head to the nearest one. Each bough's this crazy track, a wooden route to a silver hermitage in the sky, perhaps. Oh, that's nice. I make a note in the jotter Sara bought me. It might fit this story I've been working on about a girl who takes a trip on a yacht with some mates. Their boat capsizes in a squall and they all have to swim for it. The girl almost makes it to shore when she realises some of her group are still in trouble. She swims back to help, and that's when she finds, struggling, this lad she's always had a thing for. I haven't decided what happens next. Either the lad's so wild with panic that when the girl gets to him he clambers all over her until she has to kick him away. Or he's not drowning. He wasn't even drowning in the first place and the girl gets so tired swimming back to shore that she passes out and sinks to the bottom of the sea. I'm not sure if there could be another ending for my story. If a different outcome for these people could exist.

One Fixed Point

———

THESE MORNINGS MADE THE EARLY STARTS more bearable. The valley looked like a Rothko painting, thought Nessa, colour transferring from uneasy blue to red. She had her route down pat, this same hike every day. Up the ancient packhorse trail, following the gravel snake until she was up on top: overlooking Calf Hey Reservoir and what was left of the eighteenth-century spinners' cottages. From her vantage point the ruins resembled the beginnings of a misspelled word, or a series of runes, as if someone had used the stone to write on the hill, vainly trying to remind the world they still exist.

There was never anyone here at this time. This was Lancashire, a couple of hours' drive from the Lakes' tourist trap, west of the Peaks' stonescapes and occasionally bordering Yorkshire's intersecting wolds. Come the weekend you could count the passers-by you got here on one hand, sometimes less. In fact, commingling was so rare on the valley's hills that to see another rambler was to have something sacrosanct interfered with, your meditations halted. Whenever Nessa saw another person on these baldly intimate heights, she tended not to greet them. She would steel herself like a gunslinger then hurry on staring at the ground. There was no other way to overcome such challenges to her thoughts. The rest of her walks were spent pretending nothing had happened.

This is why she was surprised by the figure patrolling the crumbled cottages below. Nessa didn't need binoculars to recognise the metal detector, nor that it was a man carrying the device, for who else but a man would be out grubbing for treasure at this hour? Nessa's shift started at ten but she headed down-track anyway, able to hear the chopping reservoir in its embankments, the guinea-pig squeal of the detector and the metallic *un-click* of the micro-shovel as it extended in the man's hand. She watched him remove his backpack. She watched him force the tiny shovel into the grass.

She unhooped the binoculars from her neck. By dividing her view into quarters, she located the man. He knelt on the grass a fair distance above twin pats of sand on the reservoir path, a fixed point between discarded tresses of builders' netting and a United Utilities sign that bulged outwardly on its posts. There you are, she said. His rippling turquoise anorak caught the eye like a fisherman's float against the water of the hill. And he wore his curly, Atlantic-grey hair shaved up the sides, almost militantly, thought Nessa, as the guy turned around to face her.

Jesus.

She dropped her binoculars.

Bloody hell.

It was Sean. Nessa dusted the binoculars on her jeans and hurried away as fast as she could without running. Already she knew that for the rest of the walk she'd be unable to shake the feeling that it hadn't been her that had seen Sean. Rather he had seen her.

She arrived at Steve Biko House about an hour later. Biko was a pebbledash care home with a scale-tarnished billboard on its side that advertised supermarket milk. It was owned by Ferry UK, a private company that ran domiciliary care homes for forgotten pensioners, semi-assisted living for neglected youths approaching their eighteenth birthdays: kids without a family who were about as ready for society as it was legally required they be, and, in the case of Steve Biko House, supported residencies for the children of failed parents.

A sharp lawn of bicycle-savaged grass sloped in front of the property, and opposite that were more houses and a green roadside cabinet where, in Nessa's day, local kids would have congregated. The window grille rattled when Nessa went through the back door of the building into the office: a converted garage with a bedroom built into it. Marion, the resident house manager, sat at the desk with Bryn, her unofficial deputy, ploughing through the usual slew of paperwork in a tract of coruscating light. The light entered the office once a day if it was sunny. Never if it was gloomy. Rarely in winter.

Now then, said Bryn. What prospects from the dale today, Miss Gooding?

Oh, the usual, replied Nessa. Kids out of their pits yet?

What do you reckon? Marion said.

Nessa rolled her eyes, clicked on the kettle.

But what can you do? continued Marion obliviously.

I dunno, wake 'em? said Nessa.

Funny.

It's well past time.

Marion waggled her head in faux offence, casting an odd shadow on the flocked wallpaper. Elbow-deep into her sixties, she had a neck-length bush of irregularly dyed hair. She also wore sunglasses, a prescription set she'd taken to after one of the kids snapped her spectacles in three. There was no point buying replacements, Marion said, seeming to prefer the sepia detachment the shades afforded her outlook, although Nessa wagered she was just a tight-arse. Marion had recently started seeing Bryn, their relationship glimpsed in chaste pecks on the cheek before the journey home to update social media with documents of their happiness. Pictures of them steering Bryn's remote-controlled model yacht on a boating lake; playing fetch in Lytham with his spaniel. Sunset-selfies in the back garden. Cheese-heavy trips to the South of France.

Nessa stuffed her walking gear into a locker. Since Bryn's local bus service had been cancelled, he'd been forced to cycle into work, and now his wet socks were always draped over the office radiator, making the room smell. Nessa tried not to breathe through her nose. You've not tried then, I take it? she asked.

You get some daft buggers, don't you? Marion said to Bryn, setting her pen down in order to address Nessa properly. I've all this to get through. She pointed at a wad of beige folders. Oh do us one of them, would you, Ness?

Nessa prepared another tea whilst Marion said something to Bryn about how lazy the kids were. Milk, no sugar, she said, placing a hot mug with the bag floating in it in front of her boss. You've a fine stack to be getting on with.

What's new, said Bryn, arching an eyebrow.

Nessa laughed. She liked Bryn, and he was dead right. With the constant threat of Ofsted inspection and a culture of blame to operate in, everything at Biko House had to be logged. Log, log, log was the way of it here. House logs to chronicle the daily activities of the place, individual logs for every resident, a weekly summary corroborating feeding, watering and hygiene practices, and a sheet the kids signed to prove they'd received their pocket money. Finally, there was a mighty incident log for tracking the relentless meltdowns.

Nessa grabbed her copy of the house log and began to leaf through it. Last night sounded like fun. Paolo had kicked a hole in the wall in his room and Big Andy, one of the other carers, had lost his wallet in suspicious circumstances. The remaining account was uneventful. Jordan goes to the toilet, two fifteen. Jordan leaves the toilet, two thirty. Jordan requests a glass of cordial right fucking now.

Nessa entered the lounge, empty save the screwed-down seating and a cabinet in which the TV, the unsung staff member, was confined by padlock. The stucco-coated walls were of easily replaced MDF, there was nothing free that could be used as a weapon – no pictures and no ornaments – there were no doors and the windows were enforced and had cages on them. The Wi-Fi router was locked away too, as were the fuse boxes. It had been a fine day when *they* were left open by one of the agency temps.

Upstairs, Nessa crept around Big Andy, who'd been on the night shift and was asleep on the fusty orange armchair in the corridor. She stopped outside a door speckled with Pokémon stickers. This room belonged to Jordan, the spider monkey of the house who required two-to-one care at all times. An awful childhood had been his. A sexually abusive father, imprisoned. A prostitute and crack-addict mother, dead. Jordan's mother used to accommodate the rowdy whims of her customers in the family home, leaving her eldest son to source meals for his younger brothers and sisters, a task he wasn't up to. Now Jordan had rage issues that separated him from his four siblings, who were cosseted in a foster home several miles away. Meanwhile Jordan couldn't be left alone with female members of staff. He was twelve years old.

Nessa could make out dubstep music dimly aching through the door as she spoke at the hinges. Jordan? she said. It's time to get up.

Silence. Memories of the past meant Jordan often refused to sleep at night. He tended to crash out in the early hours once the exhausted staff had given up trying to get him to bed.

Jordan? said Nessa, knocking on the door. Jordan, chick, you up yet?

The door flew open to reveal a full-featured boy built like a bedside set of drawers. Clad only in boxer shorts smitten with forks of lightning, Jordan's arms and legs were linked by a con-joined helix of spiralling blue marker pen.

He stepped towards Nessa. *What do you want?*

Nessa swallowed. It's gone eleven.

I know what time it is.

Well, you need to be up and at 'em, please.

I am up, you *div*.

Well, have you slept?

Fucking do one, you slag!

The door slammed shut in Nessa's face.

Nessa's thoughts drifted to Aidan, as they often did at times like this. She was so proud of him, making a go of it with his maths, keeping at his studies, unlike her. A fine life she'd made for herself, she thought, entering the kitchen, where she planned to crack on with breakfast in the hope the smell would tempt Jordan and the others downstairs. Still, her lad was a diamond, no kidding. And she'd gotten him into uni, she'd done that much. Nearly every last penny of Aidan's living costs Nessa took care of because the enormous tuition fees had engulfed his student loan. He'd signed up for part-time hospitality work with a recruitment agency. They minibussed their staff around the north-west, had them working the bar at racecourses, flogging pies at football matches, pouring wine at huge Jewish weddings and serving turkey in a bow-tied train of waiters at office Christmas parties. But between lectures, seminars and coursework, Aidan was barely available for shifts. Of course, coming from a single-parent family meant he was entitled to income support, but seventy-odd quid a week didn't go far. As far as Nessa could tell, her son was stuffed without the money she earned working Biko House's crazy sleep shifts, where you dealt with whatever torrid insults came your way, where you relied on stronger colleagues to subdue your teenage aggressors, your patience stretched like a wodge of plasticine, yanked and pulled until— *No.* Nessa was glad to give the money to Aidan. Put to good use, it was. She earned it to spend it.

She opened the cupboard and dodged a pack of flour that tipped towards her, emptying a chalky cloud onto the linoleum floor. Nessa cursed. The weekly shop needed doing so today's breakfast would be a paltry effort: a vacuum pack of bacon, the last of the sliced bread for toast and a tin of spaghetti. She was soon stirring a dust of white pepper into the tomato pasta, and thinking about Sean. They'd been at school together, and the first time she could remember being aware of him was when he'd sat across from her in French. He wasn't the best-looking – he'd some extra teeth – but there was allure to him, bags of it. He had a bludgeoning innocence that Nessa found charming, pursuing life like a kid chases a ball. And he was easily magnetised by things: rap music, TV catchphrases, Teletext, it all obsessed Sean; he could do a wicked imper-sonation of John Major and he had a genuine six-pack, one of the main lads in school for a good body. Also, he never men-tioned Nessa's spots or the patches of dry skin she often got on her back, which some of the other girls had ensured became common knowledge around the school. And his awful pro-nunciation in class absolutely cracked Nessa up. *Je m'appelle Sean. J'habite à Haslingden. Je voudrais une patate s'il vous plaît.*

What you laughing at, you? said a voice.

It was Alysha, a sour face on her as she peered at the loaf's heels crisping in the toaster. Paolo stood in the doorway behind her, reeking of weed. His face was swollen with sleep, an immature sixteen-year-old with learning difficulties and all the hallmarks of foetal alcohol syndrome: a thin top lip with almost no philtrum, a large forehead and little eyes. Nessa flashed the youths her most chipper smile but felt such an overwhelming stab of sadness that she almost gasped. She turned to face the cooker and the slivers of frying pork flesh as they emptied jiggling cream lumps into the pan.

Oh, nothing, she said, I were miles away.

The Biko residents could accrue pocket money by going to bed on time and attending a daily hour at the Pupil Referral Unit, and today Alysha wanted to spend some of what she'd earned by visiting the local sports centre. Because Nessa was one of the only staff members who could drive, she was always lum-bered with jobs like this. Pearlescent seeds of rain blew about as she fetched the house car – a Vauxhall Corsa that had to be parked streets away where the kids couldn't get to it – and kerbed it badly when reversing up to the house because the rear-view mirror hadn't been replaced since being ripped off the windscreen. Nessa beeped the horn so Big Andy knew to bring Alysha out – she was a major flight risk and had to be escorted everywhere – then removed her tea-cosy beanie as the girl slumped in the front passenger seat next to her and said, *Go on then. Fucking go.*

Fourteen and new to Biko, Alysha came from Blackpool, land of the mobility scooter. She'd involved herself with a twenty-five-year-old friend of her mother's, who was herself a party girl of fifty-three with two other kids in care. After her relationship came to light, Alysha was whisked into Ferry UK's arms by Social Services. Her boyfriend had been landed with a restraining order and a spot on the sex offenders' register, while her impenitent mother had been granted contact but hadn't bothered to visit. The woman had missed every scheduled call, broken every promise.

It was amazing to see what a paucity of love could do to someone, especially at a young age. The lip came thick from the off: comments about Nessa's weight, her looks, her skin. What was she doing with her life? And check her clothes, that perfume. Rank, she was.

You absolute minger.

The first few weeks were always the roughest, as the kids got used to the imposed routines, having no phone. Still, as far as Nessa could tell, it would be like this as long as the care industry was privatised, because the more difficult wards were currently the lucrative ones, the seriously troubled worth serious money to companies like Ferry UK. Jordan, for example, was worth a hundred and seventy grand a year to the company in government subsidy – so cases like his were prioritised. This was bad news for workers like Nessa, and even worse news for any better-balanced youth languishing in a foster home or a B and B until a residency could be found for them.

Nessa blamed that rude caseworker for putting her in this situation. It felt like she'd stepped into that murmuring, open-plan Job Centre with its wide colourful chairs and condescending posters, blinked, then when she'd opened her eyes again, twelve months had passed and she'd spent the whole time working in care. She'd only been planning to sign on for a month or so, just until she got back on her feet after the Booze Buster where she'd worked since Aidan went to college shut down, but the benefits system had changed and there that skittish cow had been, playing with her wooden bangle whilst bullying Nessa with blaring remonstrations and threats of sanction until she found a job, *any job*, because, frankly, there was so much work going. *Just a huge amount of work out there.*

When Nessa applied for the role at Steve Biko House, she had no idea that care work was so low paid and demanding that companies like Ferry UK couldn't afford to be scrupulous when it came to hiring, so generally only took on people who were unable to find work elsewhere, with predictable results. All Nessa had needed was a DBS check – it hadn't taken long – and although she knew the job was important, that it could even be enjoyable – she'd enjoyed taking the kids wild swimming, to the cinemas, and watching Jordan show off on the Xbox was a laugh – she felt badly out of her depth. She'd been planning her escape when Aidan got into uni, and now she was stuck supporting him.

It was funny, sometimes she found herself wishing she was from her parents' generation. The fifties and sixties wasn't an easy era, she knew that. Still, things seemed simpler back then. Nessa's father held a well-paid position as the foreman at a brickyard for nearly thirty years. Her mother had regular work on the production line of one of the valley's many shoe factories, a job she could slot in around looking after the family. In their jobs they'd made friends for life, her parents. They hadn't needed a degree, just the wherewithal to work their way up if they chose to. Nessa's life on the other hand had come to feel so precarious. She'd pinballed from waitressing job to reception work to retail. The hours and wages were usually crap, her colleagues were nearly always younger than her and to top that, the days were dull as ditchwater and the work felt absolutely bloody pointless most of the time. Office work wasn't much better. Data entry, customer service, telesales: Nessa had done it all. Before starting at the Booze Buster she'd spent three years as a temp doing admin at a debt-recovery agency, earning a weekly wage rather than a monthly one like her colleagues, offered only statutory sick pay and no proper holidays. She'd only got the job permanently after submitting a formal complaint, the irony being that the moment she'd signed her contract the job had felt all too real. Was this to be her lot? Was she signing away her true potential? All that she could be, as well as what she was?

She'd lasted a further six months before handing in her notice. She'd felt awful for quitting until Aidan, bless him, told her he didn't mind getting his head down and making do with less if it meant she could find something that didn't drive her up the wall for once. The Booze Buster wasn't exactly glamorous and if you wanted to look at it this way, it took from people rather than giving anything back to them, but the weekly rotas were super flexible and the work was a doddle, plus Nessa found a kind of autonomy there that was preferable to sitting in an office all day. Sometimes she'd be sat behind the counter with her magazine in the over-lit shop with its narrow interior alley, the red-framed panels protecting bottles of stock, and she'd remember administering the bailiff's case notes, unable to chat with her colleagues because they worked with their headphones in, sending group emails labelled 'low priority' to ask if anyone wanted to come for a drink after work, and she'd shudder. She also vividly recalled sitting in the meeting room every Monday morning, scribbling miscellaneous guff down in her notebook whilst her pervy line manager Paul Chaplow dialled into the Milton Keynes office using the conference phone, then got the spreadsheets up on the projector so he could go over how everyone could increase their productivity. The distant hills had been massive to Nessa then. An all-encompassing presence that spread on the other side of the reinforced windows.

But what could you do? What could anyone do? Nessa sped through the valley. The road had an uneven camber as she passed a newsagent with outdated circulars in the windows, a builder's merchant with chained gates and a garden centre next to a patch of ring-fenced wasteland where a washing machine had been abandoned on the scrub: its barrel torn out and used as a brazier.

Sitting in traffic, Nessa caught sight of Alysha's hand straying towards the door handle. She acted quickly, clicking the central locking on and winding the window down a touch. You can crack some air if you want, she said.

Fuck you.

It doesn't always have to be like this, you know.

Like what?

You know what I mean.

I wanna go home.

Not every time.

Look at you, fucking state of you, Alysha said as the car set off. She tugged the ashtray from the dash and emptied its packed contents out of the window, cigarette dimps and granulated cloud streaming behind the Corsa like a windsock, and dispersing across the windscreen of the van behind, which flashed its lights. Giggling, Alysha tossed the empty ashtray out of the window and cranked the radio up.

Some wistful nineties guitar music was playing. Slowdive. No, Galaxie 500, and it brought Nessa straight back to Sean and the time he came to visit her when she was an English fresher at Sheffield Hallam, free of the valley and flush with a grant, her future rainbowing ahead. They'd tried to make it work after she went away. They thought they owed it to themselves: a couple from the age of sixteen, winners of *The Most Likely to Stay Together* award at the leavers' assembly at school. Sean made it difficult for them by not bothering with college. He went straight into a job at the paper mill, never mind Nessa's suggestion that he had a brain for better things. Art, she said. You were always good at art. But where was that going to get him? It's a waste of money, Sean said, and maybe he was right. After all, Nessa had to admit that plenty of her student mates struggled to find work after graduating, and even more settled into jobs that had nothing to do with their degrees. Nessa dreaded to think of Aidan struggling after university. Slipping through the cracks the way she had done.

Sean, meanwhile, had cash to spare. He easily ingratiated himself with Nessa's housemates by turning up that first weekend with enough beer and E's to send everyone into outer space. That was where they all went, sofa-slumped with electric stars interfering with their vision, awake till the early hours a day and a half later, this very Galaxie 500 tune twinkling from the speakers. The room smelt of poppers and drained cans of lager with cigs docked in them. Ever since Nessa told him she was leaving the valley Sean had been awful, bedwise, but that evening things started frosting over between them for good when Nessa caught him eyeing up her housemate Gwen. In hindsight Nessa supposed she could hardly blame Sean. The upstairs bathroom door wouldn't shut properly, so from her bed you had an unavoidable view of whoever stepped out into the corridor, in this case a confident girl with a flat stomach and fulsome blonde hair that teemed past her exposed shoulders. Maybe that was why Nessa reacted like she did. With the shock of fending for herself for the first time and the stress of all the reading she was doing for her course, her own skin, in certain areas, had become an atlas of dry fissures, and she had sovereign-shaped scabs here and there, from all the itching and scratching.

Enjoying the show?

Eh?

I can see you staring, Sean.

What you on about?

Don't give me that.

I'm not!

You're pathetic.

The next time he visited, Nessa was onto him. She was listening in when, at another party, Sean described some poor girl as having a good face but a wide-load. A six out of ten. Maybe that was how he talked about *her*. His every fault was amplified after that. His gluttony, the way he catcalled the TV, commenting on people's appearances, never saying anything pleasant, his hostility to those he couldn't fathom, an attitude that had him labelled a famous arsehole by some back home, and his almost aggressive, condescendingly genial manner. *Come on, I'm getting you a drink. I'll get this. Come here. I'll sort it.* Nessa started not being in when Sean phoned, until he stopped phoning altogether. Aidan was conceived a few months after that. She didn't even know who the dad was. She told people he'd run out on her, the selfish prick, and, no, she couldn't track him down. God knows, Nessa found herself wishing Aidan was Sean's. She'd at least had the chance to fancy, adore, pity then dislike Sean – it had been organic. The father of her son was anything but that. He was anonymous. A throb in the dark. And for that shadow Nessa had dropped out of university and into motherhood.

The neighbouring cars beeped their horns. The Corsa was angling from its lane.

Jesus! yelled Alysha.

Sorry, chick, said Nessa, directing the car into the correct lane. I'm away again.

Away? Alysha gripped the handle above her door. The sleeves of her Man United hoodie, the elastic chewed loose at either wrist, slipped down to reveal ice white skin. Can't you watch where you're going?

Aye, it's just—

What you on about?

Nowt.

Fuck you doing?

Now Nessa knew Sean's haunt, she went back the next morning to watch him dig. He found very little today, certainly nothing that had him excited, although it wasn't really about that, she supposed. She squatted on a raft of heather while the climbing sun made the reservoir come alive, the Gaussian curve of the hill reminding her of readings plotted on one of Aidan's graphs. A buzzard glided above the valley, more machine than creature in flight. Nessa tugged the binoculars from her pack and watched the creature for a while, eventually training her sights on Sean. She was pleased to see him shielding his face, watching the bird like she was. Neither of them had left the valley. A youth spent wanting to leave a place, an adulthood spent getting used to how all right it was.

The wind snapped the hood of her windbreaker across her head. Nessa pulled it back and tightened the elasticated drawstrings, then smoothed her fringe from her eyes. She'd brought tomato soup. She poured some into her cup and took a brief, enriching sip. She wasn't working till later because Bryn, Marion and the new agency guy, Liam, were taking Paolo and Jordan out for the day. The boys had requested a visit to the Sea Life Centre in Blackpool, which meant Alysha couldn't go with them, and although this was tough on her, the boys would get a lot out of the trip. Nessa pictured them in the ocean tunnel, transfixed by an indolent shark flattened against the transparent roof. She pictured them in the rockpool zone, their tentative curiosity as they held strange, carapaced creatures. Bryn would have the logbook out. *Jordan handled crab, twelve thirty. Paolo asked about starfish, twelve forty-five. They have no brains or blood. Paolo was pleased and wanted to know more.*

When Sean was finished, Nessa followed him as he walked back into town. He was living in the Circuit, she was pleased to see. She knew he'd become the shift manager at the mill after his predecessor lost his job following that dreadful accident with those two men. Leaving the poky flat above the pet shop must have been the top priority for Sean once that first improved wage came in. Although his muddy garden was barbed with bramble and nettle, and the wooden furniture had gone dark and sagged into itself with rot, Sean had laid a welcome mat and hung brightly striped curtains. The front door looked newly painted lichen yellow.

Nessa hung back at a safe distance. She considered knocking-on ... Oh, who was she kidding? She took her phone out to dissociate herself from the moment, but immediately began browsing Sean's Facebook page. He was dressed snappily in his profile picture, which was framed with poppies to suggest his support for the armed forces. In the picture Sean had opted for a simple navy-blue crew-neck sweater rather than the deep V-neck of old, and he wore olive-green cords rather than those sand-blasted jeans with paint splats and pre-ripped holes that he used to wear.

So many pictures of him lined up with his mates. At the races. At a club. Someone's wedding. And there, holding a baby: his kid. Sean had fathered a little girl. The further back Nessa went, the more familiar Sean became, until it was the Sean *she* knew. Her Sean. And there *she* was: Sean's Nessa. They were cuddling after a Hard House night at Wigan Pier. Nessa's cheeks were pasted with glitter. Sean was trying to hide his teeth but, as usual, he wasn't quite managing it. Both of them sweating. Pie-eyed, free. As she walked away, Nessa revisited the photo and clicked *Like*.

Biko House, 6 p.m. Nessa arrived for her shift to find Jordan standing on the kitchen counter with no top on, the marker-pen helix now extended across his entire torso. He had somehow managed to get into the fridge, which was usually locked, and now spun a bag of apples above his head like a mace.

Liam held both hands out. Mate, we talked about this …

I didn't do nothing!

Come on, Jord.

Nah!

An apple rebounded off Liam's hunched back.

Nessa stepped properly into the room. Jordan, what's going on? she said.

Jordan headbutted the cupboard. It's them lot!

I need you to get down from there please, chick.

He headbutted the cupboard again. *No!*

Nessa turned to Liam. Why are you on your own with him? Where's Marion?

How should I know?

Well, what about Bryn?

Christ, love, *I dunno*. A second apple splattered against the wall an inch from Liam's head. This is way beyond my pay grade.

Nessa tried again. Please, Jordan—

I SAID NO!

Please, chick, what's up?

Jordan reached into the fridge and pelted Nessa with a tomato. As the juice seeped into her flannel shirt, he started rocking the refrigerator, trying to tip it over.

Jordan!

I didn't do nothing! This is bullshit!

He was mucking about on the way back, said Liam.

I weren't!

And we caught him smoking.

I'll do what I want!

Liam explained that Marion had taken away Jordan's one hour of unsupervised time a day, and to cap that, Paolo had been allowed out and he'd taken Alysha with him.

I'm getting Andy, said Nessa. You hear that, Jord? If you don't want to be restrained, I suggest you calm down.

Jordan thought about it for a moment, then hopped off the counter.

Right, said Nessa, surprised. Can we *please* now—

You should take away his Xbox, Liam interrupted, bending over Jordan. *You little shit.*

The boy launched himself at Liam. Kicking. Spitting. Butting. Nessa had to pull him off but as she did so Jordan nimbly snatched her mobile and the logbook from her back pocket. He leapt onto the counter again and opened the log, but he couldn't read it; he was illiterate. He tossed the book in the sink, then tried Nessa's phone, which was unlocked, the Messenger app open. Nessa caught Jordan's wrist and tried prising his fingers from the phone, but he was surprisingly strong. He started dialling random contacts.

Big Andy came to see what all the fuss was. He took one look at Jordan, yanked him off the counter and pinned him to the ground. The boy screamed and screamed and Sean White's face was illuminated on Nessa's phone. She hung up the call on her way to the office – no sign of Marion – and swept a coffee cup from the desk, a dark slash streaking mutely up the carpet.

Outside, she found Bryn standing in the middle of the road, hands on his hips, breathing hard. Nessa, he said.

What the hell's going on? she asked.

Bryn clutched his head. *I'm sorry.*

Jesus, chick, you okay?

Not really, no.

It's all right, Bryn, Jordan's sorted, he's—

Bryn was welling up. I didn't mean him.

Where's Marion?

We only took our eyes off them for a second.

Jordan was the only person Paolo ever confided in, and although it took a long time for Nessa to get through to him, he eventually calmed down enough to tell her about the bur-gundy-coloured house where triangles of broken glass were set in mortar along the garden wall, an outdoor trampoline dou-bling up as a bin. Paolo had an occasional habit of disappearing for a few hours when his spends ran out and he couldn't afford his weed, and none of the Biko staff ever knew where he went. Sometimes he returned with the money, sometimes not. Other times he'd return after being located on the streets by a staff member having broken curfew, and sometimes he came back with a police escort. It turned out that all along the burgundy house was where he'd been going, and this time he'd taken Alysha with him.

Nessa and Bryn knocked several times on the charcoal-coloured door, and eventually a balding, barefooted man in popper pants answered. Nessa told him who they were and asked if he'd seen Paolo, then, when he didn't answer, she moved past him into the corridor. At least a foot smaller than her, the man was like a tongue in shape and density. He wheezed to himself as Nessa covered her face at the reeking bathroom to their left, which was decorated with pages torn from a pop magazine, its toilet brimming with excrement.

Wait, said Bryn, Ness, we're not supposed to ...

Nessa left him standing at the door.

A TV blared a flashing pattern up the shadowy lounge walls, a smaze of weed smoke quilting everything. The kitchen window past the lounge thumped on its hinges, as Nessa examined a baseball cap left on the table.

It belonged to Paolo.

Upstairs, the master bedroom was empty. In the next room Nessa found Alysha perched on the edge of the bed dressed in jelly sandals, knickers and a vest, both her knees glistening, grazed red. Where's Paolo? Alysha asked tearfully. Nessa didn't know. A plastic cup of what looked like lemonade rested on the sill behind Alysha's head, an empty bottle of vodka and an indented mound of jaundiced powder railed along its side. At the sound of a toilet's flush, dazed Nessa stepped onto the stairwell where she was confronted by a wet-haired man emerging from the bathroom less than a yard away from her. Easily in his forties, the stranger had eyebrows conjoined at the bridge of his roman nose, and he wore a dressing gown and flip-flops, some silver dog tags strung around his neck. The moment he saw Nessa, his face twitched. He shrank back into the toilet and locked the door.

Nessa cut through town that same night, passing craft-ale pubs, an artisan butcher and a coffee shop, of all things. The isolated valley she had known was changing, becoming a spawning pool for Manchester, that horizon of thinning cranes and sky-scraper dreams.

She headed towards the retail park, long-delayed thanks to the recession but these days housing a Marks & Spencer food hall, an Aldi, an Iceland, a Costa Coffee, a Domino's Pizza, a TK Maxx and a B & M Bargains. Over the way where Nessa's college had once stood, was a huge McDonald's that had taken less than two weeks to build.

She pushed through the winter market. The fug of burger patties and baked samosas crept around the stalls, families guiding prams and sipping mulled wine. The town centre once held a boarded-up precinct of shops that you were scared to walk through. Now it was a car park where the Valley Major-ettes tubbed drums and twirled batons in a rendition of the hokey-cokey. A middle-aged man in an elf jumper jangled a bucket of change.

The outskirts were a far cry from all that. Nessa knew the way and after a long listing walk she arrived at the ruined Spinners' Cottages: a walled garden nestling below the buf-feted acres. She set a hand on low stone. Here was absence. Something felt. She was tapped into something huge and vital out here, a redemptive strangeness that was at the same time totally other, an all-consuming force that wasn't strictly eternal either. She wore her grandmother's silver necklace. Its weight was soothing, but that weight disappeared when she unfas-tened the link, wrapped the chain in a bus ticket with her name and number written on the back, and pushed the package into the earth. She opened the logbook and began to write. *Alysha found, six-thirty. Police arrive, seven p.m. Every resident taken away for good, nine-thirty to ten.* Biko House would never close. It was far too lucrative for that. Nessa thought of Sean, scanning the dirt and stumbling upon her love. She thought of them drunk again, sad again, their bodies weathered now, too much between them to ignore. It won't matter. They will become far more than ruins. They will become like the ice water that shirrs brilliantly from a foss.

Happening at Scoop Lake

—

MAYBE IT WAS THE NUMBER EIGHT, that big fella. Or one of those forwards – it could easily have been one of them. It was difficult to tell who'd done you when you were beneath this pile of thick, heaving bodies. Nurse's knee was bust. That was a certainty. Someone had clattered his thigh, spinning him one way. Someone else had simultaneously landed on his ankle, forcing the joint in two directions. He'd felt it go. That dizzying pop.

He tried to control his breathing. He tried to breathe. Usually rucks were to be savoured. Cradling your leather quarry, legs rising and falling around you like pistons, face pushed into the grass, or even better, the mud. There was no bleak pleasure this time. The players clambered apart and formed a ring around Nurse. Grimacing, Ossie removed his head guard while an away player with a mudpat for a face stuck two fingers in his mouth and split the air with a whistle.

This drew Manx from the touchline. It was a late kick-off and the coach was heading to a dinner straight from the game, so he'd changed from his tracksuit about fifteen minutes before final whistle and now picked his way across the pitch in a curry-brown suit and matching brogues. Attempting to dodge a puddle, Manx trod in a hidden bog and sank, ankle deep, in sludge. Cursing, he arrived at Nurse's side, the bridge of his nose concertinaed, capped teeth crudely revealed.

What's up now? he said.

Nothing, Boss, Nurse tried to reply, but the fat gumshield in his mouth jammed the words up. He spat the shield out and sat upright, the referee stepping towards him. Nurse shooed the guy away, hauled himself up under his own steam and gently applied some pressure to the leg.

Oh!

He landed heavily on his backside, shielded his face with the crook of his arm and yelped into his steaming jersey. When the blaze of pain had subsided to how it had been before, Nurse peeked over his elbow at Manx. The coach had already turned his back and was talking on his phone using his Bluetooth headset.

Stu, he was saying. Yeah, afraid it's not a good time, son …

Pause.

You what?

Nurse had earned his nickname way before Manx showed up. What else were the other lads going to call you when you drank your beer the way you did: taking your time with it, mothering it. *Nurse.* The nickname had started out as an endowment but under Manx's watch it had devolved into something shameful. Sad Nurse. Sloppy Nurse. Wearing a club tie and sipping away with the chuggers in the pavilion despite not getting as much as a minute on the pitch.

Manx had joined the Valley Harriers about three years ago, having eked out the last of an unfulfilling playing career as a lower-league amateur somewhere in Cheshire. According to him the game had become less gentlemanly, 'ruined' since turning professional. Manx claimed to have played against Lawrence Dallaglio as a schoolboy. *Do you know one of his middle names is Nero? Crunched the cunt. You should have seen it.* He was a powerful and handsome man who liked to stride about the changing room after everyone had showered, his broad, hairy cock swinging freely as he towel-whipped his teammates. Nurse had become a regular victim of Manx's thrashings. At first he'd been shocked and hurt to be singled out, but as time went by he'd found himself gravitating towards the tightly wound towel with a puzzling urgency welling up inside him.

It was hard to explain how being whipped made Nurse *feel*. He supposed it came down to a moment of surrender, of letting go and entering no place at all, a between place that surpassed the trivialities of work and play, town and country, women and men. It was a kind of bliss he was experiencing. That was it. An impeccable moment where his thoughts seemed to disappear completely. Nurse had become fascinated by this beautiful darkness, and time and again he found himself coming back in search of it. The other night he had even woken up having dreamt of Manx. In the hooting changing room of Nurse's lucid dream the naked coach's towel made a helicopter sound as it was wielded in slow motion, producing a glorious slicing echo, the dirty droplets of shower-water flecking through the steam. Nurse's skin tended to ripple whenever it was whipped, and he loved to feel the ribbed purple contusions when he got home, or at work, slipping away to the toilet to finger the cool raised stripes, thinking of Manx as he did so, remembering how the coach had talked to the others about him in the pavilion after training that time. *For a dreamer the big man's got buns of steel. Nurse's lighter on them flat feet than you might think.*

Oh Boss!

Naturally Manx played tighthead prop forward, the exact same position as Nurse. Even after Manx hung up his boots, going on to become the most studiously unimpressed of the Harriers' three volunteer coaches, Nurse had failed to regain his place back in the side. In his sadder moments he saw this relegation as going beyond sporting ability and coming down to an overall *lack* as a human being, because, at the end of the day, he was a clammy nightmare, he knew he was. He had never been able to make the others laugh in group situations, and he always got his handshakes wrong. He fucked them on the grip. He misread a fist-pump as a clasp and vice versa.

Since Manx took sole charge of the Harriers, the pavilion kitchen had been banned from serving chips, and if you missed a single training session, you weren't just automatically dropped, you got a bollocking. A bollocking, at this age. Nurse had to admit that results had improved since Manx took over – they were three points off the top spot of Division 3 North – although he personally had started playing rugby to have fun and make friends.

Thirteen he'd been, when he joined the club. The drinking hadn't mattered as much then. If Nurse's mother had known he was indulging in even a single beer she'd have been devastated, let alone the amount the other guys got through. Not one of Nurse's teammates had guessed the real reason he was slow with his drinks, and he wasn't going to shout about it because beyond the odd jokey comment, and of course his nickname, it was barely mentioned. Nurse worried they'd treat him differently if they knew he was Muslim. This was, after all, the valley. He clamped his teeth together and felt the grass soaking into his short brown hair. He felt sick, like his knee was on fire. Like it was angry with him. Today had been his first game back, restored to the starting line-up because his latest replacement, Del, was off on holiday. Things hadn't gone well. Fucking awful they'd gone. Fluffing that vital catch, gasping his way through proceedings then getting himself clattered. Things couldn't have gone much worse.

Squinting at the mild sun as the last wall of daylight filtered through the emaciated pineys beyond the touchline, Nurse tuned into Manx's imposing voice. For crying out loud, the coach was saying, Scoop Lake? What you doing there, lad, can your mam not …

Manx exhaled and swept his fringe back from his swarthy face with both hands. He'd grown his ash-coloured hair to a tumbling length, just shaggy enough to hide the blunt trauma of his cauliflower ears. Nurse, who had developed cauliflower ears of his own over the years, sometimes wondered if Manx had grown his hair out so the two of them wouldn't be mistaken as having something in common.

Okay, Manx was saying. I believe you. Listen, I'm on my way, Stu. Your dad's coming.

Manx pressed his phone's screen, rich curls of mud bursting over each brogue as he approached Nurse, pointing a finger.

Right, get this fat fucking lump in the back of my car then.

Sex was alive and well in the valley, it always would be. The rooms hadn't wanted for tenants in the three years since Ruth took over the parlour. Sienna rented the spot by the reception – it had the biggest bathroom – Tegan and Flo were in the middle because their opinions didn't count, and Christy was at the end because he liked the view out back. The play area in Stubbylee Park, he said, reminded him of the one near his mam's.

The CCTV screened the scabby-kneed urchins from next door, who thought they were getting away with leaping out of their top window onto the shagged-out mattresses Gavin had dragged into the back court the other day. Ruth chuckled at the grainy footage of the brothers plummeting past the camera like a pair of suicides, before bouncing off the mattresses back into shot.

The buzzer *buzzed*. Frowning, Ruth spoke into the intercom, instructing the caller to step left. She massaged her temples at the sight of Bobby Bonucci, who spread both arms at the camera positioned above the shuttered doors. Being careful of her bejewelled fingernails, which she'd just had done, Ruth clicked the button to let Bobby in.

Bobby and Ruth had known one another since Ruth, aged seventeen, made the deliveries from her father's greengrocer's to the Italian restaurant owned by Bobby's family back in the day. Five years older and with just enough swagger to detract from his immense, plain face (Tellyhead, people called him behind his back), Bobby had asked Ruth what her name was.

No, your full name, he'd said – then, when Ruth informed him that her family name was Stephen, he'd laughed at her. You can't trust people with first names for surnames, Bobby said.

Ruth usually gave as good as she got but even then she had a thing for older, callous men, so when Bobby asked her to go with him to the motorbike show on its annual visit to the valley, she said yes. It turned out Bobby had pasta for brains. He told Ruth he loved her on their second date, shortly after the third instance of being too nervous to get it up, then in the taxi on the way home, with the surge of the bike's engines still droning in their ears, he made a loaded comment to Ruth about how her father's business would probably collapse before the year was out. There were no more dates and the greengrocer's went under a year after the Bonuccis took their custom elsewhere. When the restaurant itself began to follow suit, Bobby managed to retain enough swagger to cajole two particularly gullible women into marrying him. Of the two ladies – Ruth couldn't remember which – one had given birth to a son, Reggie, who was apparently so introverted that it seemed unlikely he'd been fathered by Bobby. The youngster had recently come to live with his father. To hear Bobby talk you'd think Reggie was the most self-absorbed person on planet earth, which was what had finally convinced Ruth he was Bobby's. Undeterred by his renewed responsibilities as a father, Bobby still visited the parlour every day. He continued to fall for any valley girl who gave him the slightest *whiff* of attention. Sienna, who'd started at the parlour about a year ago, was Bobby's latest obsession.

He made the stair lino click with every step, then there was the sticky sound of the reception doors being propelled open. Before you ask, she's with someone, said Ruth without looking up.

Every time.

I've said for you to phone ahead.

Signal's shite. Can you not take a booking yourself for once?

Ruth ignored him. She didn't pimp or pander, as Bobby well knew. The parlour was a space where people who wanted to make their living a certain way could ply their trade as they saw fit. Although it could be said that paying for it left everybody involved done-in one way or the other, Ruth argued that this field was always going to be tilled by somebody, so it might as well be handled properly by her. Besides, this way her tenants didn't have to solicit on the street, illegally, or at home, legally, where people like Bobby could find them whenever they wanted. Renting your goods in safety is easily worth giving up that percentage, Ruth told her tenants. This was especially true when you considered that the scabby fuckers even got fed if Gavin was in the mood to cook. In Ruth's parlour everything was taken care of, which reminded her, dimmer switches and red light bulbs needed installing in the main corridor. She tapped another text to Gavin and pressed *Send*.

Bobby wore a black V-neck T-shirt with FCUK written across the chest, a maroon velour tracksuit jacket and blue jeans, the jagged teeth of his flies agape as if in preparation for his engagement with Sienna. He slumped on the rattan sofa, picked up a copy of GQ, leafed through it for a few seconds then slapped it on the coffee table. You'd think you were running a hairdresser's or summat.

I'm just trying to—

Any chance of a drink?

Ruth sighed. Tea?

Cordial, please.

Re-tying her long hair, Ruth entered the rear flat where she and Gavin lived. The TV jabbered the horse racing but her husband's gnarled feet were no longer visible sticking out behind the door on their customary position on the footstool. He'd have popped out. He did that. And one day, fingers crossed, Gavin might not come back.

Ruth dashed some cordial into a mug, diluted it to pink water then fixed herself a pod of coffee from the machine. Back in the reception, her drink, pungent as it was, failed to hide the perplexities in the air: the pervasive musk of sex.

These days Bobby ran a mobile disco, schlepping around the

valley doing birthdays, christenings, prom-nights and so on. Tattersall's Haulage tonight, he said to Ruth, proudly downing his drink and producing a stylus for a record player from his pocket. I've the annual do later.

Ruth smirked. We'll not be expecting Geoff Tatt this eve then.

Geoff?

Ruth shrugged.

Bobby nodded at his crotch, a grin sneaking across his face. Bet he likes it well weird.

You all like it weird.

Bobby sniggered.

Had one ask Flo to dye it blue the other week, said Ruth. Guess what he wanted her to call it?

Go on.

Her electricity.

Bobby smacked his leg. Plug yourself in!

Their laughter descended into silence. Bobby ventured to the window, finally noticed his flies and fastened them. Fuck have all them gypsies gone?

How do you mean?

Check it out.

Ruth joined him at the window. Usually the travellers were about, or at least a few were. Today there were none. A fair-sized community had descended on Stubbylee Park and the cash-strapped council hadn't done a thing about it. One night the travellers had cut the railings and guided their caravans onto the delicate grass. Now it was usual for the park to thrum with their generators, their aggressive yippy dogs and a menagerie of children that had colonised the play area. Other than these commotions and the occasional glut of evening fireworks, the park's new residents kept to themselves, although there'd been trouble the other night in the pub. The men tinkered with their fancy cars and there always seemed to be a woman crowing with laughter somewhere, a TV on the go. Today? Maybe they were finally leaving.

Ruth ventured downstairs. From the back court she could see the south side of the park where last week a batch of scrap had been fly-tipped: a decaying fridge, ripped-out cupboards, the charred remains of a scooter, portions of asphalt, furls of tarp. Before this mess gathered a clutch of people, one of whom broke free and sprinted in her direction.

It was a gingery teen with no top on. His nipples resembled coins of meat stuck to his spare, creamy body, and they jiggled with every step. He shoved into the caravan nearest the parlour and reappeared with a heavyset woman in her fifties who trailed after him whilst extracting her knickers from between her arse cheeks.

Ruth followed from a distance, sipping her coffee. More teenagers milled around the scrap, by the looks of it the usual mix of manipulators and the manipulated. The talkers were always the leaders. This one with tracksuit bottoms tucked into his socks had a badly split lip and a missing tooth. Another had a hillock yellowing on his forehead. A BMX lay behind them on the grass, its rear wheel slowly turning. The boys shifted uncomfortably before a burly, short-haired man who wore a polo shirt with the collar flicked up. He was the one doing the quizzing.

An' you let 'em have the run of yous? he was saying. Are yous fucking kidding me?

The injured youths seemed to be passing the silence among themselves. *You have it. No, you.* They jumped us, the one with the wounded mouth finally admitted. It weren't our fault ...

The man clipped him sharply round the head. Well what yous doing bringin' the kid to a ruck for?

Ruth turned to an onlooker standing on the same side of the railings as her, and asked what had happened. The woman was pushing a pram back and forth on the pavement with one hand. A blackcurrant lollipop was in the other. They've been attacked, she answered. Up Scoop Lake.

Ruth sniffed. So they say.

The lolly's soaked orb gleamed with spit. The woman licked it – *shlurp*. How do you mean? she said.

Well, Ruth began, her gaze shifting from one injured teen to the other, then taking in their collective audience. Come on.

The woman with the pram gave her a searching look. They've been feuding, she said. Youngest of them's not come back. She delved a hand into the leather bag suspended from the handles of her pram, took her phone out and started filming the scene. That's the father, she added.

Which one? Ruth asked.

I'll give you one guess.

The man in the polo shirt stormed out of the park towards the pineys and Scoop Lake, his steps resonating down the ginnel.

There he goes, the billy big dick, the woman said.

Ruth waited for the woman to stop filming, and at the same time checked to make sure no one else was listening in. What I mean, she said, is they're pikeys. *There*. She'd said it.

The woman faced her. You what?

Look at the mess they've made of the park.

Come on, that's not the kids' fault.

So?

So one's not come back!

Well where's he got to then?

Probably still at the lake, the woman said, her attention returning to her phone. Ruth craned to see the video she was about to post. Right next to a clip of the raging father heading off in search of his missing son, the woman had added a small animation of an abject cartoon girl pounding the ground in frustration. Above that, written in spinning purple capital letters, was the word *SCENES*.

The dumpy lady from the caravan had begun to snivel on the other side of the railings. State of her, thought Ruth. Padded jacket with pandas on it, earrings like Christmas baubles and laser-red hair muddied by earthen roots. The woman sunk to her knees on the grass, her hand extended regally for her friend to stroke the knuckles like a pet. An inexact sound emerged from her, emotion parping out like air from a foghorn.

That'll be the mum, the woman with the pram said, pocketing her phone and flicking her ravaged lolly stick through the railings.

She should look after her kids properly.

Apparently her kid's got the conniptions. Fits, like.

Well, there you go.

Jesus, love, he's ten years old. You do know that?

Ruth emptied the silt from her mug onto the tarmac, gave the travellers another once-over then stalked off through the park before the woman with the pram could say anything else. Along the way, her slippers damp-darkening with every step, Ruth snatched up an empty Hovis packet as it cartwheeled past, and shoved it in the bin next to the swathe of swollen black rubbish bags the travellers had dumped all over the grass. Turning for a final view of the scene, Ruth caught the yowling mother's eye and shook her head at her in disgust. Serves them right, she thought. The *way* they carry on.

Usually Gavin met Mr Dead in the Circuit, at the end of one of those back-to-backs where overgrown privet hedges blocked every downstairs window. The Circuit stood on an incline that gave it a welcome view of the valley, and the valley an unwelcome view of the Circuit. Gavin didn't know which dirty sandstone pile Mr Dead stayed in, but he had his suspicions. He'd been heading in that direction when he got the call from the payphone: Could they meet in the woods by the lake instead? Gavin had a drop-off nearby later, so aye, it would do, although Mr Dead had another thing coming if he thought this was him dictating the terms of their every transaction now.

By some mad fluke, Gavin arrived first. He reset his dad's old bunnet on his head, and stared at the lake, which had a rumpled supernova of algae blotting the surface. He sent a moody text. Fucking Dead. The fella looked scunnered at the best of times, hence the only name anyone ever had for him. About five six, not tall, Mr Dead had always been a labourer. He would always *be* a labourer. Pure sunburn on the neck and forearms and all kinds of daft tattoos with hazy lines, the spiciest of which was etched onto Dead's neck: a severed head with a hammer above it, driving in a nail. Mr Dead's saggy cheeks were skinned by a cross-hatch of purple, and, who knew? He might have been blond once. Now his scalp was veiled with ragged grey and he had a tannin of plaque on his front teeth. The guy hardly spoke and when he did he called you *pal*. When he was pished they said he took against whatever you'd said and came out with stuff like, What you looking at, you? What the fucking hell are you fucking well doing that for?

Gavin re-checked his phone. Ruth was up his arse again about those light bulbs. She and him had gotten mates first, and yeah, he reckoned she loved him now. Things had been better since they took over the parlour. Gavin had won the business in a game of Texas Hold 'Em from Ricky Cheung, who also lost his internet cafe that night. Gavin hadn't told Ruth about putting her savings and their engagement rings up to stay in the game, because it had turned out fine, better than fine, at least for Ruth. Before the parlour she'd been work-shy, she had. Work-shy. The parlour had given her some much-needed purpose – it had been just the ticket. The shifty punters, the tenants, all of them seeing themselves as undefeated, inconspicuous, on the verge of something new, Ruth had them all forgetting they were stuck in an endless consort between where they wanted to be and where they were actually going. She seemed to derive a squalid satisfaction from that.

Which was a shame, because, truth be told, the parlour bored Gavin. It bored him to fucking tears. It was better than being on the broo, but milling around listening to that racket all day? And the inane bloody chatter? *Please.* He was drowning in handbags, and as for being the one who had to clean the bogs every time ... He spat on the floor. It was a matter of time. He knew. Fucking *knew* it was a matter of time before there was a tight cunt who might decide not to put his hand in his pocket one day, and it would be muggins here who would have to deal with it. It hadn't happened yet, *but it would*, and Gavin was no strong-arm. He hated confrontation. Fucking despised it, in fact. He was counting the days, waiting for when Ruth would have to mop him from the tiles. But maybe that would make her sympathise with him. For once she might pity him, like, in a good way, like, a *you were so brave* sort of way. She'd realise what she had on her hands then. The value of his love. The gravity of his esteem. Because at this moment she saw fuck all, or what she chose to see, which were basically the same things. Ruth was always on at him. Re-stock the oils. Get the candles in. Whatever useless thing she could think of just now. It was all a facade. Fakery. Course the cops knew what the parlour really was – they certainly charged enough to pretend that they didn't.

Which was why Gavin was out earning extra cash by flogging gear in this dingy wood. He didn't want the polis shutting the place down. Ruth getting ideas about kicking him to the kerb.

A stir in the trees. Maybe it was Dead. But it wasn't Dead. It was six lads with local accents, a metal baseball bat and a plank of two-by-four between them. Gavin hated youngsters. They were unformed, which made them vulnerable, but they were also unregulated, so they posed a threat. He about-turned up the clough. Scoop Lake might look natural but it was a man-made former gravel pit, the banks made of this weird clay shite, chalky composites laddering the mound and eventually reaching the outer reaches of the Circuit. They offered hand-holds up the hill, which Gavin scaled with ease, hiding behind a tree and spying out from behind it.

The lads stank of fire. One of them, the chubby one, took a tester swing with the plank, then with a vicious swipe smashed a wedge of fungus free from a fallen tree. The lopped fungus skimmed into the middle of the lake and was sucked below. As the boys cheered, Gavin found himself smiling, because you had to smile.

These lads didn't seem aimless like most valley teenagers. No, they were waiting for someone. Gavin watched as a hollering noise sent them scattering in the bushes after barely a minute, all but two going into hiding, the remaining pair sticking where they were: a few yards away from the lake.

The voice belonged to a final boy in a red denim jacket and green trainers. He entered the clearing and said *They're here*, then, when he stopped by the water, his chubby mate clapped him manfully on the shoulder, despite the fact that this new kid was wearing diamanté fucking earrings.

Another group arrived. Four of them, counted Gavin. Rough lads. Ones for going off on their own. They had a BMX with them. One of them rode it while the youngest, a kid of maybe ten, stood behind him on the stunt pegs. This youngest kid was wearing a striped black-and-white T-shirt – he looked familiar. Gavin tried to place him. That was it. He'd been in the park before, mucking about with one of those ratty mutts that kept going for people, boy and beastie alike darting in and out of the caravans near the parlour in that bounding wee way weans have for only a finite period of fucking time.

Words. Gavin couldn't hear anything. As the new arrivals approached the lake, the other boys hidden in the bushes suddenly pushed into view and surrounded them. The dull sound of the plank. The metal bat shimmered like a car flashing past a window. *Fuckin' hell*, whispered Gavin, fondling the crack baggies in his pockets. Soon the boy on the BMX was pedalling away, the youngest one in the striped T-shirt fleeing on foot into the trees with a whooping gang thundering after him. Gavin watched the two oldest travellers as they lay in the dirt awhile, before, to his relief, they picked themselves up and staggered into the shaggy pines as a dappled rash of shadow spread over Scoop Lake.

*

The show was tonight and his stylus was missing. Reggie didn't have a spare – quality needles were expensive. Course he had the rest of his gear: the compressor, chaos pad and synth. Then there was the Macbook Pro that had made a hermit of him, which had the latest version of Logic installed. The thing was, without the stylus there was no deck and without the deck there was no set, and he hadn't time to put something new together at this hour. Why the fuck had he agreed to perform live?

Reggie had been recording as Polonium 210 for ages now but had only just started to attract label interest. He was convinced this was down to his latest podcast: a tight-as-anything set of bright, tunnelling crisis music that someone from the forums had said invoked crystal dimensions, ice planets, and that had all been pre-recorded – a very different thing to a live performance. Polonium 210 had gathered a real mystique about himself recently. No interviews. No social media. Oblique messaging delivered only by third party. It all abetted a sound that, in all honesty, Reggie felt could be improved. His dad would have agreed on that front. Bobby Bonucci, bawling at him from upstairs. Since the restaurant had folded Reggie's dad had turned into such a crabbit.

Reggie toyed with the idea of emailing the guy who ran the online station. Jesse was one of the only people who knew his true identity and could probably sort a replacement act if he was given enough notice. But let's face it, if you took what you did seriously, you never cancelled. If you cancelled, all was for naught. Reggie considered all art to be an abstract expression of its creator, and if he was right about that then what did it say about him that he was so tempted to drop that expression of himself? It was like he was trying to drop who he was. Quit the one thing he could never not be.

He climbed the basement stairs, entered the kitchen and opened the fridge door. After joylessly evaluating the spartan shelves he went to the window and the view of the mini-roundabout, the draped outline of low hills and the fluted exterior of a nearby warehouse. Post college course in music production, Reggie had spent six months at the fish market, packing the staring fish into the crushed ice and sprigging them with clips of parsley. After that had commenced his aisle-pacing stint at Pound World, trading shelf-stacking, terse customer service and stock checks for that vital creative headspace, hoping for the opportunity to make a mark on life and maybe even get to the bottom of a few truths. He was certain of it now. Backing out of the show would be game over.

Leaving the kitchen he remembered his dad kept another stylus in the box of disco paraphernalia stashed in the utility room above the washing machine. It would be a shite needle but it might do. Reggie lugged the container towards himself but in his rush the box slipped off the shelf and emptied its contents behind the machine.

Oh, come on.

He reached behind the washer but his freckly arms were too fat and the machine resisted any attempt to haul it out. How had it even slotted there in the first place?

He was losing his rag, he could feel it. He shifted the fucking machine to and fro, roaring as he heaved until at last the washer lurched towards him, loosening out *way* too easily.

Reggie fell back onto his arse, wetness swarming around him and soaking his grey joggers. He'd snapped the supply hose clean off and a jet of water was battering from the exposed pipe in the wall.

Frantically he moved the nearest perishables to safety, then he shut the door and tried calling his dad.

No answer.

Where the hell did Bobby keep disappearing to?

Reggie googled what to do: find the stopcock, crank it clockwise. It took him ages to find the tap, but eventually he got the water off. Bemused, soaked, he returned to his basement refuge where he discovered that the deluge had soaked through the ceiling, drenching all of his records, all of his equipment.

A primal shriek erupted from somewhere deep inside. Reggie hurried his precious gear off the desk, the steady leak driving the dust left behind into a paste. *Boff. Boff. Boff*, he punched the wall three times. He realised he was running. Upstairs, pushing outside. He had no idea where he was going. His feet kept moving but in no way could he describe himself as being in control.

Reggie hit the woods near Scoop Lake. It had rained relentlessly that month, the ground sliding under his weight. From the Circuit came the tinker of a jackhammer, the smouldering scent of bitumen. Reggie had a stitch. He sank to his haunches, his hand killing him, and that was when he saw it: a twitching shape lying among the ferns.

It was a young boy in a striped black-and-white T-shirt. He couldn't have been more than ten years old. His legs were in crazy spasm, arms doing the same thing. Whitened eyes. Head bopping. Foam. Was it foam? Did you get foam when you were having some kind of fit?

A man was coming.

A man.

Reggie hailed him, sticking both hands in the air, but the man continued his loping trajectory up the path.

Hey! Reggie trampled his way through the bracken. Hey, mate, wait!

Reluctantly the man halted. There was something cloudy about him. It was hard to tell how old he was, he could have been anything between thirty-five and fifty-five. His eyes were heavily canopied by lids that looked like clam shells, and he wore a builder's mac, neon. He exuded magic and danger. His tattoos suggested stories. The faded one on his neck depicted a boggle-eyed freak having a nail hammered into its weirdly thrilled head.

Mate, have you a phone I could use? asked Reggie urgently. I don't have mine on me.

The man gazed at him like some farm animal. Now that he thought of it, Reggie realised he'd seen him before. This was one of those semi-legendary characters that roamed the valley and places like it, talking to themselves, acting bizarre, recognised by all yet known by few. An air of mental illness surrounded these people. They lived lives you didn't want to hear the truth about, in case it undermined the essential joke of their existence.

A phone, repeated Reggie. There's a kid there. He pointed at the bushes and the fitting boy. There's summat up with him.

The stranger squinted into the trees as drizzle began to polka-dot Reggie's T-shirt. I've no battery, pal, he eventually said, then carried on walking up the hill.

Reggie had to block his way again.

Please, he begged. *Will you please just help me?*

Together they waded through the undergrowth, the stranger kneeling by the fitting boy. The man selected a stick from the ground, dusted it as clean as he could get it and pressed it in the boy's mouth, on top of his tongue. I'll wait here, he said, dumping a load of change in Reggie's hand. Then, holding the stick in place, he pointed. Payphone's that way, pal. In't Circuit.

Reggie took off. As he arrived at the phone booth a short-haired, burly man in a polo shirt with the collar flicked up came around the corner. He barged into Reggie on his way past, but Reggie knew better than to protest. He let his dark shaggy bowl of hair fall over his eyes, and deferentially stepped to one side.

Watch it, the man growled.

Reggie did watch it. He watched the man head for the pineys and Scoop Lake. When he was gone, Reggie slid into the phone booth and dialled the ambulance. After the call, he returned to the wood where he was stunned to see that the fitting boy had vanished, as had the stranger. Reggie bent over the ferns, his hands parting their tactile fronds, some still furled like tentacles, until he saw a dirty work boot in the undergrowth. *Shit*, he said. *Oh, shit*. The stranger's neon builder's jacket sounded like a tent in the pattering rain. The man's face had been reduced to a bloody pulp. It looked like an overripe plum that had been chucked against a brick wall.

*

Already Nurse had got mud on the motor's upholstery. Manx watched him in the rear-view mirror: lying on his side, taking up the whole back seat and grazing muck on everything he touched.

He should have made the fat cunt get changed. How did an amateur like that end up with cauliflower ears? Training Wednesdays and matches Sunday, that's a couple of hours a week Nurse would be playing at most, less since Manx had been in charge. Manx supposed Nurse had been a prop forward since he was a teenager, the squad's vanguard ... *still*. The sheer size of him. Imagine sharing a scrum with *that*, having to stick your head behind an arse so huge, your hand having to grope between such broad, chafing legs, trying to grasp the waist-band of Nurse's shorts, unable to find any purchase amongst the flab. Manx had never in his life been out of shape. He'd played for England under-seventeens, trained with the seniors at Sale. That lot could justify a cauliflower ear. They were more than lads, them boys. They were men.

Speaking of which, Manx was grabbing the kid. Doing the dad thing. Stu had said he'd been involved in some sort of argument up at Scoop Lake, and now he was shitting it. Practically begging for a lift, he was. *A lift?* Manx had walked everywhere at Stu's age. Course where he'd been raised on the Isle of Man, it was easier terrain, he'd give Stu that, but five miles was five miles. You had to wear the soles of your shoes down if you wanted to get anywhere in this life.

A couple of months ago Stu and his cronies had been involved in an incident with some traveller kids in Bacup. His BMX had been nicked and he'd been shit right up. Initially Manx had been worried, but he'd become glad of the mugging because it seemed to have given Stu some much-needed balls. For one thing, since the mugging Stu had finally got shot of that awful long bleached barnet, and now Manx had high hopes for the rest of his sorry get-up: the bright colours, the moisturisers and poofy smells. You had to wonder whose blood was running through the kid's veins sometimes. Manx would never forget the day he caught Stu wearing concealer. Make-up! A son of his. Youths got spots, it was a fact of life. Leave him alone, Shelley had said. So it was her idea. Fucking tidelines, Stu had: tan frills stopping short of his pierced ears. First the hair straighteners, then the earrings and make-up. Manx had sat the lad down in the study over coffee. *Stu*, he'd said. The boy wouldn't hear it – I don't even like coffee, he said, sliding his mug back to Manx over the desk then sauntering off in those diamanté fucking earrings to listen to R&B in his bedroom, crooning in front of the mirror. Auto-tuning, they called it. *Oh, Baby*. Pass the earplugs. Manx had seen Stu, Scott Deakin and the others heading out with the metal bat between them earlier this morning. He'd approved of that, and had said so to Shelley, even if the kid's sport of choice had to be a wet sport like baseball.

Nurse's eyes were closed. He must be asleep. A guy like that probably spent most of his life dozing in one form or another. Nurse had said he didn't mind collecting Stu before he was taken to hospital. Typical, thought Manx, typical bloody Nurse not standing up for himself. All the guy had to say was that he was hurt, *genuinely hurt*, and could they please leave spoilt bloody Stu to make his own way home for once? And Manx would have done it. But no, Nurse couldn't rise to the challenge. He wouldn't do it. He never said zip about zap.

The guy was a passenger in every aspect of life, really he was. A waste of space, and as for his game, Nurse's tackling was weak, he couldn't run and he was easily turned over in the maul, no matter how hard Manx had tried to coach him. Nor did the lad bring anything to the dressing room. When the banter was flowing, where was Nurse? Every week Manx took part in training and sometimes when he was drying himself off after the showers he'd catch Nurse watching him. They'd make eye contact and Nurse would look hurriedly away. Manx would too. He'd no longer be smiling.

Ossie said Nurse worked in an office. Facilitating paper clips, no doubt. Being the guy who knew how to fix the photo-copier or volunteered to take the minutes rather than chair the fucking meeting itself. Manx would never take orders from anyone else. He had his own haulage business. Well, technically it was Geoff Tatt's name on the deeds, but it was Manx who'd built the company up. He'd pulled himself up by his own bootstraps, he'd ... There was a whimper in the back seat.

You all right back there? Manx said.

Yeah, okay, boss.

You fucking sure?

Yeah. Thanks. It just hurts.

Manx cackled. Ah, you'll be reight, Nursey-boy. Probably only a sprain. It'll put hairs on that chest. Well, a few more anyway. Match the ones on your back, eh, you fucking beast.

The state of the mud on the leather back there. Manx cursed himself again for not forcing Nurse to get showered. He'd only just had the motor valeted as well. He could sense those docile eyes on the back of his head. *Nurse.* The polite core of the guy padded by that endless crust of dumbness. Differentness. Not-botheredness. He looked like a walrus, a brown fucking ... Manx pinched his nose ... a *lazy* fucking walrus who could be found chowing down on the Gutbuster breakfast every Saturday at the greasy spoon. People like Nurse had brought this country to its knees and told it to start sucking. You couldn't trust them. Parasites. Meddlers. And, let's face it, potentially dangerous. One of them could have a bomb strapped to their chest any minute, the bloody maniac. No, you never knew with a guy like Nurse. A watcher. An internalised sort of person. Manx particularly didn't trust the fact that Nurse never sank more than one beer after training, whereas he, after bossing every session, necked at least four pints then did an easy sixty home down the dual carriageway, headlights fixed to fog, twin beams slanting like javelins into the other drivers' eyes.

Manx directed the Range Rover into that godforsaken estate, picturing Nurse returning home to his flat, empty save a bed, chairs and hundreds of crinkly foil trays and greasy Tupperwares containing stagnant puddles of takeaway curry sprinkled with MSG. He imagined Nurse savouring the metallic taste of blood from chewing the insides of his chubby cheeks, heading, not to his usual spot in front of the telly, but to the kitchen instead, opening the fridge, his attention caught by the bulb bleaching the top shelf with its pure wintery light, staring at that electric glow like Manx had started doing recently. Would Nurse feel the same thing? That magnificent displacement?

The distance had come for Manx more and more of late. At 4 a.m. in bed, matrix of thought, Shelley asleep a million miles away by his side. Or on Saturdays at Harvey Nick's: that mausoleum of chrome, spotlights and glass, an escalator to carry them in silence through it. Where did your consciousness go at times like that? And where was Shelley, for that matter, when they cuddled on the couch, oblivious to the fact that Manx was at her shoulder, transfixed by the hollow glare of her phone? He didn't know ... Oh, how could he put it?

Even at work he had that feeling. Avoiding Geoff's endless flirtations with the warehouse manager, Sharon, by heading to the Portakabin step to listen to the rain splattering the lorries, wandering into the yard and gazing past the needles glued to the warehouse roof to stay the pigeons and seeing the louring sky in all its coldness and feeling, *say it* ... So bloody lonely. This was not a position Manx could budge from, no matter how many people he surrounded himself with. And there was a truth in that, he felt, something pure you had to face. Like grasping hold of a blade and learning to squeeze.

Stu waited beneath the awning of the corner shop. Hop in, Manx said, twisting the air-con dial towards the red spot.

Cheers, Dad.

You all right?

Think so.

This is Nurse. Say all right, Nurse.

Hiya, Stu.

What happened? said Manx.

Them lads tried jumping us again. In't woods.

Oh not them bloody animals. Same ones?

Yeah, them from Stubbylee, Dad ...

Flaming gypsies!

Manx clocked Nurse glancing up. What happened? said Manx. Did you say summat to 'em?

Stu was already on his phone. Dunno, he said.

Stu?

Huh?

You wanna watch yourself.

They arrived at the hospital, which reeked of disinfectant and uncertainty. Piled in a tower by the A and E reception were cardboard bowls for puking in. A cleaner bleached the vacant chairs next to Nurse, who sat in a wheelchair with his leg up. He'd need an X-ray. They were going to have to wait hours for a doctor, thought Manx. NHS was in a right state. He glared at the dumpy pisshead dozing in the corner. The guy had a compass tattooed to one arm and a huge congealed wound on his slumbering head.

Manx loosened his tie. He was late for the annual do but Geoff would have it covered. They'd only organised the flaming thing for tax reasons, paying more now so they could pay less down the line. Geoff had even shelled out for an earnest soap star to come and hand a giant cheque to a grateful representative from a kiddy hospice. Manx pictured Geoff's casual applause, off his tits on the codeine he took to muzzle the jaws of the gout that would consume him one day. Geoff had already texted, and Shelley was on the warpath. Manx switched his phone off and frowned at the ceiling.

You don't have to stay, you know, said Nurse, evidently nosey-parkering. I'll be all right, boss.

Manx patted Nurse's healthy knee. A good coach never shirks a duty.

Stu sniggered.

Go fetch the bloody brews, Manx commanded, slinging a handful of quids in Stu's lap. What had put the lad in such a good mood?

On the way to the machine, Stu was nearly hit by some paramedics bumping a bed in through the main doors. An awkward, flat-faced young man followed the bed into the A and E. He looked like a Mormon or a Scientologist, thought Manx, a shapeless basket of black hair halting above huge letter G-shaped ears. The young man's joggers appeared to be patched with wet, while the patient wore a reflective neon-yellow builder's coat. As the patient was steered in, the younger man stood awkwardly near the main doors. He was still for a moment before performing an instinctive movement with his hands, laying them against his cheeks just like the figure in that famous painting Manx often thought about. What was it called again? *The Shout. The Shriek.* Whatever the fuck its name was, the kid looked easily as horrified, and Manx had to turn away, craning to see the patient as he was wheeled past.

Bloody hell, Manx said to himself.

The poor bugger was in a bad way, a deep wash of blood coating a severely pummelled face. Manx had no idea who it was but judging by the annihilated workboots and dirty, burnt-sausage fingers, he was a *not-right*, as Manx's mother used to say.

The nurses manoeuvred the patient into a curtained area, while the dark, worried Mormon lad spoke to the receptionist, passing a scrap of paper over the desk. A moment later he sat opposite Stu and began checking his watch.

Emre Ergoli, called the doctor. Mr Emre Ergoli.

Manx was shocked to see Nurse's hand shoot up. He'd completely forgotten the guy's real name.

In the examination room the X-ray resembled a bird's-eye view of a bay at night. An archipelago of bone. Manx shuddered. He and Stu waited in the corridor while Nurse spoke to the doctor. The hospital porter wheeled the bloodied patient in the builder's coat past, and positioned him over the way. The young Mormon stood awkwardly by the gurney.

After a few minutes a squishy fellow in a flat cap arrived, followed by an attractive blonde-haired woman with bejewelled fingernails and red-rimmed sunglasses. Manx swore under his breath, and covered his face.

The man in the cap spoke with a Scottish accent. Guessing you're my pal? he said to the young man, who nodded.

All he had on him was your number.

The Scot removed his cap and combed his thinning hair with signet-ringed fingers. You're lucky the boss picked up, he said. I'd have telt you where tae go.

The woman glowered at the Scot. It's okay, she said, we'll stay with him ... Is it serious?

Dunno, replied the young man. He's had a right pasting. He began collecting his things. I found him like that. Up in the woods.

Manx recognised the emotional distance between the couple, and pitied them. The madam from the brass house hadn't noticed him yet, but the Scot was eyeing Stu suspiciously. Manx contemplated saying something but was pleased when the stern gaze he issued the Scot with was enough to have the guy interested in the floor. That's right, he thought. You've still got it.

At last Nurse finished with the doctor. As the big man wheeled himself out of the room, the bloodied patient in the builder's coat shook awake with the most terrific, lurching groan. Everyone jumped. Manx even stood up, accidentally making eye contact with the madam. That fucking brass.

Shit. She definitely remembered him. The injured man groaned in his gurney, louder, moaning awfully until he succumbed to consciousness and broke down in tears. At the same time the corridor lights began to flicker. Each panel stuttered and blinked, wonderfully, thought Manx, *hypnotically,* and they kept on doing it. He dared not climb on his chair to get a closer look but there was a spider's web in front of one of the lights that was just *glowing.* It was fascinating, the webbing's structure, its strands calibrated, configured by instinct, nature, defined by a single unity of purpose and design. Perfect, really, when you thought about it, and mad as well, that every web turned out the same every time: the constant repeating gossamers crucially linked yet only ever touching to the most *minimal* degree.

Just as Manx had set one foot on the chair, wanting, no, *needing* to be close to that truth, every light in the hospital winked out. The darkness made it seem as if the injured man's racking sobs were the last remaining sound on earth. Manx could hardly breathe – he was terrified. He only managed to unfreeze when the back-up power kicked in and the lights ticked on again. He removed his foot from the chair, leaving a muddy imprint behind. Here was Nurse: the big man had wheeled himself across the corridor in the gloom, and had halted beside the bloodied patient's bed, his head lowered, holding the man's hand, comforting him. Manx desperately sought Stu but his son had disappeared. Manx was alone, he realised, surrounded by people he didn't know and a woman he'd only met that one time, *for Christ's sakes*. The smug *tart* was watching him, judging him over his one solitary slip-up, never mind how she took advantage of poor bastards like him, never mind how she led them on, people who needed something, a moment to connect, be held and understood, that parlour of hers dragging the whole bloody borough through the muck. She was a disgrace. That's what she was. The smile that had begun to tweak her lips melted away as Manx shook his head at her in disgust. Serves her right, he thought, striding away towards the reception. The *way* she carries on.

Far From Then

———

MARTIN BAINES HAD A HABIT of going out at night and coming home a couple of days later with a cold and no explanation as to where he'd been. He'd joined the army straight from school, went on to become a fireman after he was discharged from the forces and spent most weekends cracking skulls on the stands of Elland Road, a member of the Leeds United Service Crew. Anything to avoid the wife and three caterwauling kids.

Martin admitted all this to me when we were travelling together in Asia. He also said that his whole life had changed after a wall collapsed on him when he was fighting a blaze at a shoe factory back home. Although he was originally from Armley, Yorkshire, home to Martin was an area over the county line that he simply referred to as 'the valley'. His then-wife Ada was from the valley, and she'd wanted to raise their children there because she thought they wouldn't take as much watching somewhere quiet as they would in a city. Martin was easy to persuade. I always agreed with everything, he told me. That's just what I did. I always said yes.

When Martin came out of the coma much was changed. He quit the fire service, attempted a beard and booked a one-way flight to Asia, minus Ada and the kids. I first met him in Thailand on one of those shrouded evenings where the sun only seems to set when you're not looking at it. After a few beers Martin asked me what had brought me overseas, and my response was that I had the vaguest memory of stumbling upon what had seemed like a cheap return flight to the other side of the world, a story that Martin found hilarious. He roared with laughter as I confessed that it felt like I'd woken up and found myself backpacking on a month-long sabbatical from work. Were you drunk or something? he said to me.

I wouldn't be surprised if I was.

That's one weird hangover.

Oh, you know. They usually are.

What you tell an interesting man is one thing. In truth there was no sabbatical, there were no accrued holidays to be cashed in, this was no romantic getaway and there was no pursuit of culture or experience. If I'm honest, I wasn't even curious about Asia. The continent had never once seemed like a viable holiday destination to me. It came across as dangerous, underdeveloped and too hot. It was a place for people who liked dance music, spicy food and had threesomes. The fact was I was immersed in what I regarded then as a *slump*, but what I now recognise as the most severe case of depression I would ever have. That is, until the recent episode that I will describe to you in a little while. When you're in that frame of mind you'll either sit around not caring enough to get out of your chair, or you'll fall hungrily upon the first thing that might feasibly jolt you into a better frame of mind. For some people this might mean meeting a friend for coffee, getting a haircut or taking a shower. In my case it meant shelling out nearly five hundred pounds for a midweek flight from Heathrow to Bangkok with a four-hour stopover in Bahrain.

I got my GP to sign me off work with stress. I knew I wouldn't be missed. I was an underused executive support-ing three bombastic account managers employed by CPA, short for Collins, Peacock & Astley, a business process innova-tions company based outside London, not far from Wembley

Stadium. It was CPA's job to organise a crack team of freelance troubleshooters who were paid vast sums of money to parachute into corporate businesses, helping them to streamline processes and reduce costs. Coincidentally my three managers were all Irish. Eamon, Kieran and Gerard were their names, and they would scout for clients and manage relationships while I booked hotels and trains and raised payment orders so that our agents could go around the country telling already spectacularly wealthy conglomerates what they had to do if they wanted to make yet more profit, and recommending low-grade workers for the sack.

But I was talking about Martin, Martin Baines. For an older man Martin really threw himself into travelling. He wore tie-dyed baggy linen trousers, flip-flops, straw hats and whatever shirt he had on would never be fastened above the third button. When I first met him he was travelling with a short, overly tanned girl named Kerry Coakley who, as it turned out, came from the same valley where Martin had lived with his family. Kerry, Martin informed me, was the youngest of the Coakley family, who to this day are famous in the valley for producing boiled sweets in a factory outside Blackburn. I would lose count of the number of times I heard Kerry tell people that her family's factory was home to the world's largest pear drop. Apparently they kept it in an alarmed vitrine in the lobby by the reception.

It was Kerry who introduced me to Martin. She was outside the Iguana Bar down Roi Sambuttri in Bangkok when I first met her. She was reading a novel while sitting on a plastic chair that she had balanced on two legs, and I was immediately struck by the demonstrative way she had of reading. For instance, if a character in her novel gnashed their teeth, Kerry would do the same thing. If a character happened to flick a stray French fry from their table, Kerry would replicate that action on the quiet.

Up until then I'd been travelling alone, mostly getting lost and when I wasn't getting lost, spending an obscene amount of time failing to cultivate interactions with my fellow travellers. Jesus, the effort I spent trying to engage with people. At the beach, making a big deal out of needing someone to rub suncream on my back. In town, approaching couples at dinner and prattling on about needing directions to whatever-place-it-was-this-time, when really I was hankering for an invite to sit down and *talk*. In hostel lobbies filled with bamboo canes and Formica, on dance floors wreathed in dry ice and on packed buses where I should have been watching out for my stop, I abased myself in search of confidants. Once down the Kao San Road, I even cosied up to a couple of gym bunnies from Sydney who were mocking a street vendor for selling badly carved wooden frogs. The ornamental creatures produced a vague *ribbit* whenever the vendor dragged her tiny wooden mallet down their tiny corrugated backs. I practically herniated myself laughing at that poor woman, but the drunken Aussies were appreciative enough to buy me a few drinks, which was something, I suppose. I think that experience was what gave me the confidence to approach Kerry that day.

Seeing her gurning at her page, I adjusted the rubber bra straps digging into the burl of my shoulders and headed over, reeking of the tiger balm I'd used to salve the constellation of mosquito bites covering my lower legs. Twin bottles of Chang Lager clinked and frothed as I sat down next to Kerry, took one look at the cover of her book and said, *Hemingway*.

We spent the afternoon drinking, and that evening I was introduced to Martin. He and Kerry had met in an ashram in Rishikesh, bonded over their shared northern pedigree then skipped India for Thailand. It was obvious they were sleeping together. Sex to Kerry, I soon learned, was a sort of forbidden loft space that she couldn't keep from entering.

Do you know how some words don't look right when you see them written down? That's how I felt when I first met Martin. *Friend, gauge, definitely, Tokyo*. Here was a thirty-eight-year-old with a Stanley-knife scar on his cheek and a tattoo of the Om symbol on his back, and he was courting a twenty-year-old, who, the moment she had a drink in her, was anyone's. My view was that Martin hadn't done well for himself, he'd picked low-hanging fruit.

I know it wasn't fair to wonder about him in this way, but you meet so many new faces when you're travelling – it really teaches you the value of a snap perception. A week into my trip I was able to categorise the tourists. The first group created a rod for their backs in search of 'legitimate' experiences that no longer existed. The second were essentially there to pillage the place, treating a foreign land like an unrulier extension of their own, the locals regarded with contempt or not at all. Within these two categories were extremities, yes, but that is the nature of a Venn diagram and generally I think the model holds true. At the very least it helped me to manage my nerves during those first lonely days abroad, because I can't stress how little I had understood that no matter where you go in this world, life really isn't that different. It was ironic, going away to transform yourself then stumbling into a distortion of the same futility you felt back home. Don't get me wrong, there was language, architecture and history, all that, and I was finding out how a place develops according to climate and money. What I was realising , however, is that all of that's just fluff, and it's the people that are interesting. This is why I was so curious about Martin. He was a man who seemed to defy all categorisation.

A good deal older than Kerry, I vowed to protect her from Martin, but as my presence was accepted and the three of us travelled through Thailand's beachy south, drinking through our trip assumed priority. We did the common Westerners' circuit. Tubing in Laos where I caught pink eye from a mud bath in a bar and had to wear a cotton patch for three days. Vietnam, where Martin had a suit tailored for him in Hoi An that he later lost in a drinking game to a local who had a puckered sinkhole where once had been an ear – you should have *seen* the fuss when I joked about this – then on to Cambodia, one of the only places I've ever been where I believe that, truly, you can do anything you want.

I fell in love with that motorcycle country. Cambodia, where nearly every white girl you saw had an exhaust-pipe burn on her leg from carelessly riding on the backs of bikes with no passenger pegs. Cambodia, where we tied our hair into buns to keep our necks cool, where we hitch-hiked on the backs of trucks with live hogs strapped to the roofs, making their final squealing journeys to the abattoir. In Cambodia we became pogrom voyeurs. We hit the Killing Fields, S-21, we visited firing ranges where you could shoot animals with machine guns, then later we traipsed a delirious slick of rock leading to a waterfall, leaping into a plunge pool edged by mustard-coloured spume and an abundance of thirsty leeches.

By night we'd return to a township where I would feel invisible as strangers sought Kerry's attentions, and although I was used to this sort of thing, it never gets any easier to see someone prettier than you, thinner than you, someone whose hair isn't as dry and curly as a wheel of tangled string, effort-lessly soaking up the possibilities in a room. Kerry had never suffered, or so it seemed. She had never lost anyone, she had never envied others or had to discover that her parents were poor. Nor had she ever, I assumed, thought about herself in relation to someone she knew and had to say, I'm sorry, I can't compete with that. I just do not measure up. Not everybody thinks like I do. I have to believe that. I was trying to teach myself that there is a way of living that involves letting go, that in the face of everything I knew, I could still walk into a bar and say, I'd like a drink, please. I could still sit down and enjoy that drink: a multi-layered fruit cocktail in a funky glass, and I could marvel at the decor: the chrome bumper of a 1950s Cadillac mounted on the wall, the glowing dollops of wax morphing in a giant lava lamp positioned behind a beautiful topless barman while a soldier's blood-spattered uniform has been cut up and used as wallpaper. In a place like that I like to think that a girl like me could rest her arm on the tablecloth. She could smooth her leopard-print skirt against her thighs and say to herself, Well, this is a place. This *is* a place.

The DJ's played riff-heavy Cambodian psychedelia from the sixties and seventies before the Khmer Rouge wiped all the musicians out. I was never confident enough to give the dancing side of me any sunlight, but I did enjoy sitting on a bar stool sucking on a gin and tonic whilst Kerry had her fun. She tended to dance with one hand in the air and, like it was some kind of antenna, the drunken advances kept coming her way. This happened over the course of several evenings. Men, local and tourist alike, treated her like some sort of blonde-haired sexually charged spirit, perhaps as attracted to her vitality as they were to the prospect of another lay. I passed right through jealousy into amusement. It was like watching a mating ritual on a nature documentary. A macho sortie that went on, and on, *and on*. The male imbibes his intoxicant. He dons his regalia then performs his bizarre courtship dance. Like a lot of men, Martin had problems letting himself go. Rather than strut his stuff with Kerry he sat with me pretending not to mind what was going on. Maybe on the third or fourth night, I can't remember which, when Kerry went off with a humour-less eighteen-year-old from Maryland, Virginia, Martin left his beer on the table and didn't come back.

I found him at another club. We sat at the bar like veter-ans discussing war stories that had changed us, and drank beer after beer until the place closed. Martin was pretty out of it by then. In the car park I followed him, and in a blurry collision of cigarette fug, Martin's cheap aftershave and my own hesitant excitement we were suddenly having sex on the gravel scrub. I will never forget the tubby slap of our liquid-filled bellies, nor the column of exhaust smoke illuminated by Martin's scooter lights. The fumes created a smog template around the back tyre, and afterwards, as I picked the twigs and debris from myself, I asked Martin if we should tell Kerry what we'd done. He set the scooter to face the road and directed me to ride pillion. There was a monkey in the trees as we hurtled back to the hostel. It bared its teeth at me before scampering into the jungle.

*

I awoke the next morning to a fierce pain where Martin's exhaust pipe had scorched my leg. A swampy light poured through the square window as I fumbled with the kind of tensions I hadn't dealt with since God-knows-when: wanting to be alone and loved, wanting to be held yet pushed away. I could not orientate myself. I had dreamt of a bird of paradise, its beak parted so wide that I could see the red plectrum of tongue glistening at the back of its throat. Although there was no sound I could sense the creature's overwhelming desire to be fed.

We were off to Phnom Penh, and as we boarded the bus I knew Kerry had noticed the bandage I'd dressed my burns with. She and Martin positioned themselves a few seats away then disappeared as soon as we checked into the hostel, returning at midnight, seemingly more bound by the codes of courtship than ever. This was the beginning of them leaving me behind. It was like they had eloped without actually going anywhere. Outside 7-Elevens, beach bars and food stalls, beneath all kinds of neon-bolstered signage, in-jokes were made and not explained. Stories I wasn't in on were recalled. Martin and Kerry also started planning the next stages of their *journey*, poring over the travel guide, knowing that in a matter of days I was returning to the UK and a thunderhead that constantly threatened to overwhelm me.

I spent those final nights in Phnom Penh in a sweltering room with a bathroom that basically amounted to a hole in the floor below a scratched vanity mirror. I wanted to understand what had happened. I wanted to graze Martin's knee with my own under a table and have him remember how my body felt. I remember playing with the zip of my money belt while Martin and Kerry fucked in the next room, perspiration pooling in my belly button, a fan whirling above the mosquito net I lay in. There was a straw mat at the base of a wall that might as well have been made of rice paper, and a lizard skeleton was splayed under my bedside drawers. I kept padding to the window to stare through the iron bars at the rickshaw drivers congregating on the corner of the road, street dogs battling in dusty passages while a party I hadn't been invited to throbbed just metres away. It was a heavy meridian, and it exacted its force upon me as I tracked Martin and Kerry's repetitions and adjustments in the next room. I placed my fingers against the ticking in my throat. I counted the number of beats in ten seconds. I multiplied the results by six.

I didn't hear from Martin and Kerry again until about a year later, when Facebook told me they were home. They were living in the valley by then, engaged. I waited for an invite to the ceremony that didn't come. Not that I would have gone. I was back at CPA by then, really, just tremendously busy, because by that time I had met a man of my own and married him. I had a devouring affection of my own to be getting on with.

My new husband was an account director for a print company. Born in Northampton, raised in Southampton, Judd Taylor-Walsh was attractive in the way that a wildebeest or buffalo is handsome: staunch-boned and serene-looking, but he was so aware of it that it made him ugly. Of course I didn't realise this at the time. Mainly I was flattered by Judd's attentions. I always say that people who hate the way they look are prone to victimisation, and so it has proved in my case. I suppose it's because some of us have a dark need to put others down, and some of us have a deep well where we draw upon the need to think we deserve it. At university I would often catch male friends nudging one another if I happened to mention someone I liked, and I became cannon fodder for the reckless matchmakers in life. I was never sure if these do-gooders were pushing me into a relationship because they wanted me to be happy, or because they hated to be reminded of how things might have gone for them if they were less fortunate. It makes me think of my childhood. Me, a girl playing on the carpet while my bog-eyed father stared at me listlessly from the couch – or at least it *looked* like he was staring – and releasing the occasional *tut*. As I got older the *tut* became such-and-such-a-body is doing this, such-and-such-a-body did that: why can't you be like them? I never said a thing. Matters don't come to a head in my life. Generally, they taper away to nothing.

Still, my name means *friend* in Gaelic, which might be why I get on so well with people. I met Judd via a dating app that I signed up to as soon as I got back from Asia, using this charming fact about my name as a tagline, allied to a suite of strategically lit headshots that were filtered to make it look as if I had rabbit ears, a rabbit nose and huge babyish eyes. Me, in the kitchen. Me, in the shower, a pink tongue edging between pinker lips.

This misrepresentative profile generated the kind of localised interest that, while it wasn't quite passion, delivered more than the usual yield of dick-pics, humiliating silences and one-night stands that my honest ones had gotten me. I was matched with Judd – that was enough. Never mind that I should have realised how things would turn out when I read his opening gambit:

Did you know Cara also means expensive in Spanish?

And what does Judd mean?

Praised. Judd means praised, in Hebrew.

We met at the kind of noisy bar where sags in conversation could be papered over easily. I knocked back a Michelada, a drink Martin introduced me to, while Judd sipped a glass of Pinot Noir. We talked about childhood, work, TV, and after we'd eaten we caught the tube back to Judd's place where I tried to steer things towards the sofa, or the floor, anything to avoid the telling intimacy of the bed. Unfortunately Judd was a traditional sort of guy, and we started seeing one another regularly after that. Don't get me wrong, I knew our relationship was based upon reduced expectation and low self-esteem, on both our parts, and I also knew that this dynamic rarely ends well, but Judd seemed keen and at forty-two years of age I wasn't getting any younger. His doggedness and my compliance carried us to the registry office.

All of Judd's family, all of his colleagues and all of his friends attended the ceremony. The reception was at the King's Arms around the corner from Judd's office, and from its rafters the reprographic guys under Judd's employ had arranged for a banner to be strung upon which our blissful faces, I *thought*, seemed blurred. The pool table was covered in pebbled tissue paper on which the most egregious buffet was spread. Sausage rolls the length of my thumb. Potato salad. Cubed things on sticks. And the cake. Oh, the tiered cake. When I cleaved that first wedge free, people cheered. I ate an extra portion alone in the bathroom.

As soon as our married life began, Judd took to cardigans, he cultivated herbs in sill pots and every Saturday he listened to the afternoon play on the radio. During this time he also volunteered at the local library, and he encouraged me to join the National Trust, so I did, the two of us spending bank holidays remarking on the free parking at country estates over expensive bricks of flapjack, making cutesy goo-goo noises at pensioners' terriers and sustaining eye contact with various overindulged brats.

I stopped taking my citalopram altogether, and I began to eat lunch in the park near my office in order to drink undetected. This was followed by wine with dinner and wine when Judd was washing before bed, and if I finished the bottle and opened a second? You get the picture.

Drink made the internet chat rooms so much more *involving*. Because by then I had brought the PC into my own loft space, while downstairs Judd read the paper before he slept. I'd joined a chat hub, a digital enclave populated with sports rooms, music rooms, *whatever*, places where you could talk and indulge in the physical absence of present strangers. In the hub I toured initial worlds and subordinate worlds, each filled with so much partial disclosure that I felt giddy. I particularly enjoyed the X-rated rooms where I could sit until the early hours bathed in the glaze of a dawn that would gradually leak through the skylight of my suburban garret the way moisture fills a cloth. The staccato *hards* and *yeahs* and *sucks* puttered in the message windows before me.

I should also say that Kerry lost a lot of weight around this time – the bridal diary she posted online confessed as much. Anything Kerry could do, I could do, I told myself, so for breakfast and lunch I downed sudsy protein shakes and for dinner I ate eggs, a lot of eggs, plus fish and salad with no dressing and sometimes a bowl of boiled broccoli or spinach, all the time pumping iron whilst making new friends online. Judd had no idea what was going on, despite the fact that every now and again I would emit sounds he must have heard: a clinched roar or a tempered groan as I bench-pressed a broomstick with paint cans hooked onto either end of it, just like Bruce Willis does in that film where he discovers nothing can hurt him.

I lost four pounds, and decided I'd had enough of Judd. He was someone who picked his fingernails then left the remnants for me to find: minuscule slivers of cream-coloured kindling piled on the armrest of the sofa, or the side of the bath, or scattered at the bottom of an empty teacup. Pork made Judd belch, he broke every wine glass and whenever he went for his post-work drink on Fridays, he failed to come home when I asked him to. Also, if there's a bigger hogger of the duvet on planet earth, I'd like to meet them. Judd never hit me – he didn't have to. It was enraging to discover how answerable the great question of his adequacy as a husband was. By night came affection, amendments to the facts. We agreed that I was needy and sensitive. Forbearance was a huge thing to ask, Judd said. He would never ask it of me.

I stayed with him (it wasn't like I had any other option) and as Martin and Kerry's nuptials drew closer the days began to balloon around me. I kept abreast of Kerry's bridal diary, wondering why on earth I hadn't thought to write one myself in the run-up to my own big day. When I mentioned the diary to Judd, how happy Kerry seemed, he asked me why I didn't write to my travel friends if I missed them so much. The cracks in our facade were deepening. At a garden dinner with his work colleagues, surrounded by the stench of incense from a citronella coil positioned in the middle of the table, Judd told a story about how my hair had caught fire at a local restaurant, embellishing the moment when I strayed too close to the candle in search of my phone. To hoots of laughter from two subordinates and their spouses, Judd re-enacted the waiter smothering the flames with the wine towel. That night I took to the chat rooms with a new fervour, meeting a user named STAR in one of the X-rooms. Most users tend to commence a dialogue with a request for age, sex, location ... STAR was different. On a scale of one to ten, he wrote, how happy did I rate myself? (Ten) How close to my family was I? (Ten) How confident was I? (Ten) Was I popular in school? (Yes) Had I ever lost anyone close to me? (No) Had anything bad ever happened to me? (No) If I could be any famous person in the world, who would it be? (The Queen)

STAR said he was living up north with his ailing grandfather, who was dying peacefully at home. He went on to tell me sage things. Beautiful things. STAR's grandfather wasn't really in a coma, he said, but existing on the deepest level imaginable, hyper-aware of the universe. Unconsciousness is a kind of meditation, STAR typed, a heightening of the mind's interior dimensions where a person's true self has reverted to its natural state, which is to dream. STAR said that when we fall asleep or get knocked out, we are actually entering into a state of preparation for the next stage of an overarching scheme: the plan for each of us: to be reborn and die again. Apparently STAR's grandfather was at the apex of one of these rebirths, which I have to say made me feel grateful because it meant that I could at last anticipate the night rather than fear it, for STAR had taught me that sleep was not a time for awful thoughts, nor was it a time for sadness or allowing the brain to rest. It was a dress rehearsal for death. It was a preparation for when I could finally no longer be me.

While STAR and I grew close, Kerry's hen-do came and went. I commented on every picture she posted, wished her well, and asked how Martin was. She didn't reply. I had to chivvy her along in the end, telling her I'd love to come and visit. Kerry just said she didn't think that was a good idea. Martin's grandfather was ill. He'd come to live with them and things weren't looking good. Not good at all.

I shut down the computer, in a tizz. It could have been a coincidence, but the more I thought about it, the more sense it made. STAR's tone, his phrasing. It was similar to Martin's.

It was the same.

I told Judd I wanted to go for a drive. Anywhere, okay, just take me anywhere. We got caught in traffic. The windscreen wipers moaned rhythmically up the car's windscreen, a game on in Wembley Stadium to our left. There'd been an accident, silhouettes milling in front of the emergency lights by the crash barrier, where a corpse was being fed into an ambulance. The crowd in the stadium roared, and I was thinking of STAR, of Martin Baines breaking noses and extinguishing fires. I don't know what made Judd grow so contemplative – maybe he sensed my shift in thought, maybe it was the corpse – but he touched my thigh and said he couldn't think of anyone who'd make a better mother than I would. I smiled at him. I smiled all the way home, where Judd and I attempted to make a baby in the back seat whilst parked on our drive. After Judd left for work the next day I swallowed the morning-after pill then uploaded some photographs I'd downloaded of a woman from the Marks & Spencer's catalogue, and sent them to STAR.

Here I am baby.

When will u visit me Cara? When will u come?

This is how I came to take wing, heading north by saturated Pendolino, on my way to meet Martin, my STAR. There is nothing worse than a wet train. A scudding of light brown film coated the standing area by the doors, down every aisle, and each window was obscured with condensation and rain trails shaped like cracks of lightning. I sank a lot of beer, stuffing the empty cans into the seat crevice as I was transported through Milton Keynes, then Stafford, eventually arriving at what I can only describe as crow country. Here I saw collared and carrion crows. I saw magpies, jackdaws and rooks. They circled terraces and farms, suburbs and chimneys and, later, after I'd boarded a bus in Manchester, I saw them gliding above the winding belt of motorway, perching on roughshod drystone walls, squabbling in the fields that bordered this stretch of humble towns, this windy valley.

When I stepped out of the ancient bus station there was a sheep licking salt from the middle of the road. A few prosaic stone buildings rose on the other side of traffic that calmly drove around the sheep: an office and a taxi rank, a funeral director's. Behind the station was a supermarket, and on my person were two maps: an A–Z and an ordnance survey on which the settlements of Rawtenstall, Waterfoot and Bacup looked like a trachea riven through a set of lungs. Flat-topped hills blossomed on either side of these parochial towns, each with their respective contours, their triangulations.

I couldn't decide what kind of place this was, and neither could the place by the looks of it. I tightened my scarf against the moody wind. It was cold. Colder than down south. Martin and Kerry were living in a converted barn somewhere on the Yorkshire border, towards Todmorden. My guess was that the Coakley family had something to do with this arrangement since Martin was earning a scant living as a painter and decorator. I had a vision of the couple living in a giant sweet. A rhubarb and custard, perhaps. An Everton mint.

When I phoned the house from the heaving supermarket café, Kerry answered. I was in the north, I told her, to see a friend.

There was a long pause. *Okay.*

What did she think about me coming for a visit!

The views were unavoidable. Plains of peat, sweeps of heather and uninteresting, broken-coloured summits. The taxi made good time along a route interposed by telegraph poles that flickered by so quickly that I could have been in the middle of a zoetrope, a coated horse capering in a nearby field, its mane flowing from its neck like greasy streamers. At the smell of rotting flesh I opened a window. Over the hill was a maggot farm, my driver explained, raising himself in his seat and winking at me in the rear-view mirror.

Outside Martin and Kerry's I stuffed my wedding and engagement rings in the pocket of my trousers and undid the upper buttons of my blouse to show off a little chest. Something was happening. It took hold of me as I knocked on the door and it threatened to overwhelm me as Kerry appeared. I nearly bawled *Hello* into her stupid little face.

She wore a tight woollen jumper, striped, and black leggings and slippers shaped like monkey heads, where you slid your feet into the unfortunate monkey's mouth. Her now-dyed dark hair was bound on the back of her head in the shape of a croissant, and lacerations of mascara were painted around each eye, her nails shellacked purple. I had a flinty feeling inside as I apologised for the short notice of my visit. Kerry replied that it was indeed a surprise. She had no choice but to invite me indoors.

I got the grand tour, escorted up the kind of stairs I could see myself falling down, viewing one bedroom with netted windows – the other presumably occupied by Martin's grandfather – then moving on to the bathroom where slugs had mounted the base of the sink and crawled in the direction of a bar of soap that was attached to a magnetised holder.

The house was a work in progress, Kerry said. She wasn't wrong. The bathroom tiles were wonky and rimmed with bacterial orange gunk that clung to the grouting. Here I was, in Martin's home. Oblivious to my excitement, Kerry directed me towards the kitchen with its whorl-knotted pine table where an array of toby jugs leered like china gargoyles from hooks screwed into the roof's spinal beam. I asked for wine, and, glass in hand, gazed out at the garden, which was unremarkable save the pediment on which a birdbath stood. To the buzz-thrash of a chainsaw in the pine woods nearby, a crow settled in the water and began to wash itself. Hearing its merry *caw*, I began to giggle.

Martin arrived. His hair was completely grey now and cropped short. He wore a decorator's raiment: the overalls, the malformed trainers. I imagined him dipping brushes into pots of garish paint. Every day rotating colour up the wall with a roller. Yesterday's dinner stowed in a Tupperware with a dodgy lid.

Surprise, said Kerry.

Hi, Martin, I whispered.

Kerry, you never said we had visitors, said Martin, brushing paint flakes from himself.

If you checked your phone you'd have seen the messages, answered Kerry.

Martin took his phone out, scrutinised it.

Aren't you going to say hello? I said in a voice that didn't sound like my own.

Sorry, Cara, Martin replied. How you doing, love? The corner of his mouth grazed my cheek. You good?

Oh, you know. Same, same, but different. I winked. How's the old man?

I'm sorry?

Your grandad.

Martin stared at Kerry, who'd flushed scarlet.

Yeah, she explained. I told Cara we weren't having visitors. You know ... because of your grandad ...

Oh ... right, Martin said ... Oh, right, yeah.

I gave his arm a squeeze.

After they'd entered the kitchen and the kettle had steamed into action, I hurried across the room and spied on them through the space between the door and its jamb. Kerry slid her arms around Martin. Martin shrugged her off.

I dived back onto the couch as a branch clacked a window and tickled the glass. On the horizon was the spindly outline of wind turbines. I thought of that ceiling fan back in Phnom Penh.

Your house is huge, I said to Kerry when she returned. It must have taken you ages to save up. I wafted my hand at the lounge's rafters.

My parents helped us.

You're so *bloody* lucky.

I'm paying them back, Martin offered, sitting down and squinting at his lap.

I had a slug on my shoe. Wine dribbled down the bowl of my glass, marking the carpet with little spots. Neither Martin nor Kerry noticed, and this made me wonder what else they did or did not see. Did they think about the fire at the shoe factory that had changed all our lives and no doubt many others? Did Martin think about things like that? Did he remember that night, the smell of molten rubber, the wall's compromised structure as it teetered above him?

Because I did.

Kerry sat cross-legged on the couch, the space around her littered with tiny feathers tugged from a cushion. I tried to catch her eye but she was swiping at her iPad. Martin's hand was close to mine, so slack and open that I reached out and took it as dusk invaded the tawny outdoors, as soot began to sprinkle down the chimney onto the coals. It was a crow up there. It had to be. A bone-dry scrawl of wing, beak and claw perched atop the chimneypot in all its strutting equanimity. I couldn't help it. I began to laugh as I listened to the creature shift and depart, as I pictured it swooping in a thermal, soaring powerfully, beating its shabby wings in majestic flight.

Effigy

———

FRANCIE MORGAN WATCHES THE DEEP ARC of the golf club. Its sweet sound is like the thrum of a bamboo cane, or a whip.

Swoosh!

The club strikes the fluorescent ball, sending it kiltering at a wild slant in the direction of St Cuthbert's, where it disappears. Never mind. A packet of replacements sits in the dirt between Francie and his cousin, Callum Tinker, who's just taken his first shot at the school.

They've nothing else to do. Callum readies for his second go. St Cuthbert's seems vacant, like a brooding beast with its back turned.

Go on then, says Francie, his hands wrestling in the central pouch of his hoodie as Callum's second ball blasts over the tarmac playground, piercing a pane of glass in the science block.

Shit, says Callum.

The lads drop to their bellies.

Lucky shot, says Francie, peering through yellowing quills of grass.

A lone figure comes to the broken window. Is that Loveland? asks Callum in a tight voice.

Hairy-nostrilled bastard, probably is him. Loveland used to

go jogging during lunch-break, taking a selection of favoured students along, lads like Callum. Francie, who once trapped Loveland in a store-cupboard, pictures the visible vest under the teacher's shirt, the sweat refusing to dry under each armpit. He gets up and pulls a moony.

Francie.

Fuck off me!

Francie tugs his flower-pattern surf shorts up and unleashes a beige slug of spit into the undergrowth. Fuck they gonna do anyway? he says.

Callum sits heavily on his new skateboard, the wheels sinking in the grass up to the trucks. It's all right for you, he says.

Too right it is. Back in December, Francie cemented his place in the annals of St Cuthbert's by holding a burning stick of dowel in front of an open gas tap in the chemistry lab. When the flame ignited the gas, a frayed spear of fire was thrown onto a cardboard box of magnesium strips that Francie had set on an adjacent stool. Although the iridescent glare ball was almost worth his expulsion, Francie won't admit to missing St Cuthbert's. He's recently sat his GCSE's at Slatten Fold High. *Sat* being the operative word, and he's just glad school's finally all over with.

He holds his hand out for the club. Honest, Tinks, you wanna sack this place off, he says.

And do what? Callum sends the club up.

Fuck should I know?

I could come work for your Uncle Pat.

Francie clicks his tongue, making a thing of it. Callum has no idea that his unsupported confidence has only developed because he's always got what he wanted, and he's always got what he wanted because of his looks. The fact that Callum thinks this won't count against him in Pat's world speaks volumes.

Why not? says Callum indignantly.

No need for an answer. A lurid yellow ball winks at Francie. Better yet, a rock of suitable size is only partially wedged into the clay next to it. Francie shakes his head as his cousin makes an offended posh little clucking noise, then he nudges the craggy lump into the open with his trainer. The club has the most satisfying weight. Francie takes a huge, shoulder-aching swing then smashes the rock in the direction of the school. It makes a *tack* sound. A tally mark is apparent now, blighting the brick.

Callum smirks. Missed.

Did it heck, says Francie, though certainly there's a feeling of failure. He tears a knee-high clump of grass out of the ground and cobs it, roots and all, onto a patch of scrub where it rests like a discarded knot of scalped hair. What a scraggy patch of land this is. Hobbit Hill, where common mallow and cowslip grow; pink Himalayan balsam and probing tiers of bindweed. Not far are the remains of campfires, copses littered with cans, bottles, homemade bongs and all sorts of plastic wrappers. Once, Francie found a syringe here next to a scraped-out pot of KY jelly.

He aligns his next shot, this time with a ball.

Swoosh!

Another window breaks. Francie raises the club in celebration, but Callum is already legging it into the woods with the skateboard floundering in his hand.

Tinks!

The school doors burst open. It's McGinley, the caretaker. Oh, he of the blow-job lips. Francie goes to ground like a dropped marionette, his nose about a centimetre from some cuckoo spit. He can see McGinley's shadow lengthening across the playground, but there's no need to hide from it, not any more. He gets up, takes aim with the club and *thwocks* another ball in the direction of the school, the speck of colour gliding, fleet and true, before bouncing off the tarmac into McGinley's face. As the caretaker ducks, Francie flees into the woods, hollering. He can sense McGinley watching. Each hand will be placed against the small of the caretaker's back.

Use of the skateboard is the penalty for Callum's cowardice. The expensive new toy was his reward for doing well in his mock exams. His mother Harriet, *the General*, as Francie refers to her, is always buying stuff for Callum and his little brother Jim. She'd go spare if she knew Francie was using the skateboard, which makes him ride it all the harder. He propels himself along the pavement with one foot. He pushes himself *again*, before leaping onto the deck and coasting downhill through the snick towards Edgeside Park, passing beneath a wrecked pair of trainers that have been tied by the laces and slung over a phone line, to indicate to passing skag-heads where they can get their fix.

Skating is easy. Francie pops an ollie from the kerb. Hidden among the interweave of houses is Uncle Pat's place. Paddy Morgan has a live-in girlfriend with a son of her own and nails that *skree* whenever she files them. Today Elspeth's doing burpees in the lounge in front of a laptop set on a footstool. The computer's plugged into some portable speakers, amplifying the aerobic instructor's chipper American voice. The sound drifts into the kitchen, drowning out the boys' entry via the back door, while Floyd, a Boxer-Staffie cross, yawns from a massive cage by the bin.

Callum opens the cage door and begins to knead Floyd's deformed jowls, his ragged ear. The dog chewed one of Francie's firecrackers a few months ago, the detonation mangling its face. Francie can't go near Floyd any more. His culpability for the animal's hideousness is overwhelming.

Leaving Callum to coo and fuss, Francie leans the golf club against the lower cupboards and roots in the fridge for the ingredients for cheese-and-brown-sauce sandwiches. He's just salvaged the margarine when the door closes against his arm, trapping it.

It's Eddie Grinstead, Pat's business partner. Grinstead's a Merseyside pilgrim with an appalling gum-to-tooth ratio and a severe case of monkey breath. Now you've a choice to make, he says, forehead creasing like the draining board by the sink.

Francie tugs his arm free of the cold, the fridge door leaving a harsh mark on his forearm. The Buckfast bottle, where the milk is supposed to be, clinks gaily.

Grinstead's far too old for the Adidas tracksuit and Rockport shoes combo he always wears. His greying ginger hair is slicked into a duck's arse and most of the time he has a hand down his pants, fondling his cock. Eddie runs a door-dipping business along with a few more lucrative ventures operating from some lockups on the moors over Cribden. He and Uncle Pat keep five bitches in one of the sheds, chained to a pipe on some straw matting. The dogs are sealed into a continuous cycle of pregnancy and whelping until they can take no more. Pat's also a doorman in town – *going to war*, he calls it – he knows people who'll take the pups. Francie feeds the unfortunate dogs their chow. He takes them on frail ambles around the boggy field.

So how's the wayward roadster? says Grinstead, playing with the drawstrings of his tracksuit bottoms.

Francie sneers. Typical of a petty chump like Grinstead to pick up on the fact that his full name – Francis Austin Morgan – makes him sound like a model of vintage car. Same as last time you were here, he says. You gummy prick.

The golden stud lodged in Grinstead's ear has a vapid shine. You always speak to your betters that way? he says.

Not seeing many betters round here.

Francie raises his middle finger.

Grinstead's obviously fuming but all he can do is turn to Callum, who is no blood relation to Uncle Pat. He says, How are we today, sweetheart?

Fine, thanks.

This one got you in bed yet, has he, or what?

Callum realises Grinstead isn't joking and doesn't know where to look. Thankfully Elspeth enters the kitchen, vines of fringe hair plastered to her forehead. Oh, leave off, Grinny, she says, shouldering Grinstead in the back. Her tongue protrudes impishly from her mouth. Elspeth is a good few years younger than Uncle Pat yet way beyond her late twenties. A T-shirt is knotted above her abdomen, hammocking her breasts.

Take no notice of him, she says, flashing her top teeth at Callum. How you doing, handsome?

Good, ta, says Francie.

Elspeth fixes him with a stare.

I'm all right, yeah, Callum says, glancing at Francie apologetically.

Tinkered any keys recently?

Callum chases a blush across his neck with both hands, fingers interlocking behind his head. He is a talented pianist but since his father's affair with that nurse came to light, has recently given the instrument the elbow. Poor misled Tinker, floundering in the midst of the only kind of certainty Francie has ever known. Francie doesn't blame Callum's dad for giving that nurse one – if he was married to the General he'd have done the same thing. The Tinkers have been trying to keep their marriage alive but if Francie knows the General, they're wasting their time. He's related to the old bat through his mother Claire, who is as highly strung as her elder sister, her brittle nature manifesting in a more unruly, though no less suffocating way.

A part of Francie's mum has been overfed somehow, he senses that. He dearly wishes one of them knew what part that was. As it is, she's always on the pull. Thursdays to Saturdays, she goes out – it's just something that she does. Over the years it's got so that Francie can't smell hairspray and red wine without thinking of his mum. He can't hear the clop of impractical shoes or glimpse an item of sparkling, billowing clothing heading out of a door. He has never felt like he belonged to his mother, and he reckons she feels the same. They look nothing alike and Francie has always had the idea that whatever he's doing around her, he's doing it wrong. At least he's not the only one. Scores of men have been driven from their lives, including Francie's father, Ryan. Francie hasn't asked why his dad left and Claire doesn't really discuss him, or indeed any of the men she's taken up with over the years now that they're gone. Francie's aware that being ignorant about your heritage isn't normal but the assumptions, the not-knowing, seem preferable to a deeper, long-term letdown. Fuck the truth, he tells himself. Fuck what happened.

Anyway, there's plenty of photographs of Ryan Morgan to be getting on with – Pat's made sure of that – but surprise, surprise, Francie looks nothing like his lost father either. Whenever Francie is out with his uncle, Pat is at great pains to point out the places where he and Ryan used to go. The swing in the park that Ryan jumped off, resulting in a fractured collarbone, the corner shop they crashed their first joyridden car into, the gravel pit in the pine woods where they swam once, ending up with the shits. When he regales Francie with these sorts of stories, Pat seems to be saying that the valley only belongs to people like him who think for themselves, gleeful chancers who might know their roots are tangled but will never be caught up in them. Pat seems to be saying that if your only claim is to freedom, if you've the guts to not leave anything in the tank for the journey back, then you have the right to immortality. A kind of greatness. This stands as truth even if you come from a corner of the world as indistinct as this one.

Callum would never understand an idea like that – he'd only pretend to. Still, he's Francie's best friend and Francie doesn't know what he'd do without him. He extends one leg and trips Callum as his cousin passes to drink directly from the tap.

Francie.

Francie shrugs at Elspeth. Is Pat in?

Elspeth blanks him.

Gumbo, me uncle in?

Eddie Grinstead blows his nose into a coagulated bit of tissue he's had secreted somewhere, and studies the Sudoku puzzle lying unfinished on the table.

Grinny—

Well me and her are hanging about, snaps Grinstead. So what the frigging hell do you think?

The boys sack off sandwiches in favour of crisps and take the golf club to the spare room that's made up so Francie can come and stay whenever he likes. They kneel by the bed, and from the shoebox in the wardrobe Francie removes a drawstring bag containing his Stanley knife, the tins of spray paint and the last of the firecrackers. He's also managed to acquire a deck of porn cards from the newsagent by the bus turning circle. Zaf, the proprietor, is all right. Pay him enough and he'll sell you anything.

This is the first time Callum has seen the cards. *Whoa*, he says, removing the pack and easing the contents free. Check her out ...

The eight of clubs suckles a finger and wears nothing but a pair of glossy, turquoise stilettos. Never mind that she's presenting what looks to Francie like a thatch of gorilla hair, she's another Elspeth: burdening him with the powerful yoke of her sexuality.

Gorgeous, says Callum.

Tenner to you, replies Francie, as footsteps get louder on the other side of the door. Francie stuffs the golf club and drawstring bag under the bed seconds before his uncle sticks his head into the room.

Were you planning on saying hello or just coming round then doing one?

All right, Pat.

Where you been?

Out, says Francie. Raving it up.

Paddy Morgan rushes into the room, delivering a series of mock rabbit-punches to Francie's kidneys. The big man has a too-often-busted beak and scars on both eyebrows from where a boxing opponent who didn't know any better once cut the padding from their gloves to get an edge. In homage to Pat's scars, Francie has shaven tramlines into his own eyebrows, although this has never been as acknowledged as he would have liked.

How were Job Centre? asks Pat.

Good, yeah.

Owt doing?

Nah, not much.

A frown zigs across Pat's forehead. The big man has always been one for the salvation narratives in life, never mind how heavy and on the hoof he earns his own crust. Pat has it in mind to set Francie on some noble path, though of what sort, Francie isn't sure. *Do as I say, not as I do,* is a favoured utterance of his uncle's, a hypocrisy that must help Pat justify the ways he makes his living, especially since the cash-in-hand labouring jobs he once spoke freely about have, over the years, been replaced by the clandestine work with Eddie Grinstead and acting as a freelance strong-arm in town. Along with their puppy factory, Francie knows that Pat and Grinstead have been making money by installing jerry-rigged diversion systems onto the gas and electric in local houses. This is so people can bypass their meters and get their energy for nothing. Making the community more efficient, Pat says. Putting something back.

You need to get a job, France, says Pat, especially wi' your birthday coming up. He winks. Francie is seventeen tomorrow. Because believe you me, you're not coming here for handouts once you've your present.

Francie has long since discovered the quad bike hidden under the dust sheet in one of the Cribden lockups. It is a thing of great power and beauty and now that the summer holidays are stretching way past September into an open future with no school, his entire landscape has been challenged by its presence, by its possibilities, by all it represents.

He starts picking dog hair from his hoodie. I know, Pat.

Well pull them socks up.

I am doing.

You'd better had be. Pat finally acknowledges Callum. The doctor's boy.

Francie reaches out and flicks Tinker's ear.

I'd watch out for this one if I were you, Pat says, nodding at Francie, who's having trouble hearing over his mouthful of crisps. He'll do you down if you're not careful.

That's what my mum reckons, Callum says, smiling up at Pat.

Now it's Callum's turn to get one of Pat's looks.

What, your mum says that?

Callum's expression falters. Well, sometimes she does, yeah.

How come?

Ah, she's just not his biggest fan, is she.

What, your mum's not Francie's biggest fan?

Well, not really, she's—

Your mum chats shit about our Francie?

It's nothing serious, Pat, she—

Your bitch mum fancy a knock on her door one night?

Pat crouches in front of Callum and slaps him in the chest with the back of his hand.

You think I'm messing, Tinker?

Pat...

I said, do you think I'm messing, boy?

Callum looks like he's about to spew, but Pat is smiling, dimples like parentheses.

Well, I am, he booms, slapping Callum again. I'm pulling your pisser, mate.

Francie exhales.

Seen his face, Francie!

Shit, Pat.

Seen him blushing!

No way you thought he were serious, Tinks.

I couldn't resist, could I, Pat says, slapping Callum a final time then cocking his head at Francie, who joins him out on the landing.

The top of Pat's uncarpeted stairs is lit by a dusty bulb that illuminates a poster of Eric Cantona performing his infamous kung-fu kick. The smoke alarm on the ceiling was ripped out a couple of weeks ago because it kept making bleeping noises. Pat found out later that this was because the batteries needed replacing.

Pat just comes out with it. Were you playing through on the back nine at St Cuthbert's earlier? And don't answer with your fucking mouth full.

Francie swallows the last of his crisps. What you on about?

Pat nods at the spare-room door.

Were we heck!

So if I check my clubs, they'll all be there?

Course, says Francie. The stairs are so steep.

I can't be having the bizzies round 'cause you're acting the goat.

I haven't touched your clubs, Pat.

Pat grabs Francie's collar, twists it. Well swear it then.

Pat!

Swear it. Pat sticks out a hand and spits on his palm, glaring at Francie until he copies him. Swear Jeff McGinley's a liar.

I swear, Pat.

The two of them shake hands.

Pat gives it a few more seconds before ruffling Francie's hair. You're a good lad.

Cheers.

I mean that.

Francie smooths his hair back into place. I know, Pat.

Don't you mean, *Thanks*? Pat says, messing Francie's hair up again, then he disappears, cackling, into the bathroom, where he will wash away the traces of the gym.

Francie waits until he can hear Pat's naked echo and the loofah's sop, then fetches the golf club and returns it to the bag in Pat's wardrobe. His uncle's domain smells of antiperspirant. There's a wall-mounted TV, some CD decks on either side of a mixer on the drawers and a framed photo of Floyd when he was a puppy. Next to the digital clock radio that Pat bellows groggy curses at whenever Elspeth gets up for work, is a shelf Elspeth uses as a dresser. On the shelf among the potted ablutions and creams is a boxing trophy topped by a kinetic-looking figurine with both its fists raised. Francie lifts the trophy, roaring softly for his jubilant fans. His uncle's jeans are on the bed so all he has to do is lift out the wallet and remove three twenties. He stands in front of the mirror holding Pat's shirt against himself. He looks at his own reflection, which displeases him. He shuts his eyes then opens them again. He lifts his T-shirt, tenses his stomach.

No definition.

He and Callum bus it up Bacup Road. Francie has never lived anywhere else. His mum's flat in Whitworth feels too small for them now he's grown up, and right next to the building's main doors you can always smell the bins. Claire works in an office. Francie thinks she's got something to do with the council. Certainly she's always griping about how work have no money to do anything these days. It must be something like that.

Cars, cars, cars. His belly rumbles and he feels sleepy. He can't stop thinking about his mum. She's got a flexi-time contract at work meaning that although she's supposed to do forty hours a week, how she chooses to complete that time is up to her. Claire's always valued the extra hours in bed over getting home to spend time with Francie. As a kid, Francie went to his gran's every day after school. His gran would fix him tea: mainly something from the freezer but every now and again a treat like toad in the hole with baked beans, chilli con carne on a jacket potato, or on the very best days, nachos. Once his gran had resumed her position in front of the telly, the remote control duct-taped to the arm of the chair, this week's TV guide doubling up as a coaster, Francie would sit with her until the soaps had finished, then make his way home.

Since his gran was reduced to a wisp of smoke petering from the chimney of that tumbledown crematorium, Francie has made dinner for himself. Conversation with his mother when she gets in usually amounts to how the traffic has been or the weather, yes, the weather is very changeable. Up until Francie was expelled, Claire even occasionally asked about school when the truth was she didn't even know what subjects Francie did. He'd told her as much when she tried to confront him about the expulsion. *Like you give a shit.* He had made her cry – finally something genuine – and now they don't discuss the future. Things aren't too bad at the minute. With Claire single, there are no pissed-up voices in the front room at four in the morning, she's not forever pouting at herself using the camera in her phone and Francie doesn't have to wake up and discover the empty baggies and white powder trails left on a plate on the kitchen worktop. Still, most nights, once their conversation has evaporated and Francie's heart is racing and he feels like he might explode if he doesn't say, I can't reach you, I don't understand you, I'm so *angry*, he sits in his room or goes out until it gets dark, or he stops over at his Uncle Pat's house.

Usually he walks it to Pat's to conserve the pocket money his uncle gives him. He can never be bothered with the trek but the valley is no longer than ten miles end to end: a cup of life in a big green mess of slopes and towns and farms, a bypass tearing out of it, leading the fuck out of here. At Pat's house there's a stack of old *National Geographic*s. Pat loves them almost as much as Francie does. Francie's recently read an article about Scandinavia. Depending on the time of year over there it stays light or a night comes that won't leave. The valley feels similar in its way. There's that same certainty, that same black and white. All the days jumbled into one. It's been an okay place for serving out a boyhood but for teenagers like Francie who hate sport there are no youth clubs, no cinemas, nothing. There are scrubby parks to fill the time when it's dry. There are other people's houses when it isn't. There's buying eggs by the dozen, spending your evenings throwing them at passing cars and hoping for a chase.

Francie says he's hungry and Callum is too. They take a shortcut into town through the Circuit. The estate is another of the valley's limbo places, a sprawl situated above the main road, yet bordering a wood. Some of the houses are still owned by the council, most have been bought on right-to-buy schemes. From the bottom street Francie and Callum can smell coal smoke and see the stitching of tracks leading to the final outpost of the East Lancashire Railway. Today the Flying Scotsman's due, so Francie supposes what you could call crowds are gathered on the platform. It doesn't take long for him and Callum to sneak down to the station, fill some bottles they find on the floor with piss and hurl them over the fence at the daft geeks huddled over their flimsy notebooks like they're in some laboratory.

They hit the Circuit, jostling and taking turns on the skateboard, passing windows filled with England flags, past chunky kiddies' toys strewn around angled squares of lawn, driveways with weeds sticking between the paving and the odd wheelless car set on breeze blocks. Along the way Francie spies a hanging basket full of stealthily dying plants. He takes a run-up, leaps and catches hold of the basket's metal rim, tearing it from the wall in one swing.

To get to town they have to go past Crustyman's place. Crustyman was a hairy oddball who walked his Rottweiler about and foraged for scrap metal, slaughtering twitchy animals with his shotgun and tagging up the area. CRUSTYMAN, says the underneath of the flyover. CRUSTYMAN, inscribed in four-foot-high letters above a painted figure riding a scrambler motorbike. Further out there's the word CRUSTYMAN and a drawing of his dog on a drystone wall. Elsewhere, CRUSTY-MAN is scrawled on a bench, tiny portraits scratched here and there: a mystic face on a post box, a fertile thatch of man on a bus stop. White slashes for eyes. Lines and blobs form a beard. CRUSTYMAN.

On the way to Crustyman's house the lads stuff every dog-shit and lamp-post bin with firecrackers, the detonations puncturing hot sticky melt holes in the plastic. They spread the dog shit on the handles of decent cars, duck from passers-by, dive into hedges and stomp random beds of shrubbery until they're outside the puddle-green house where a full-blown police operation once took place.

This is where he did it, says Francie, imagining the sensual gun barrels protruding from the window.

What happened? Callum almost whispers.

Mad-head lived with his mum. When she died, the council said Crustyman had to leave the place. He went sick an' set his shed on fire. A neighbour complained, Crustyman said he'd do same to her. Burn her to fuck. She phoned the police – Crustyman shot one. There were a siege, petrol bombs, the lot. Francie takes an imaginary shotgun, sticks it in his mouth and mimes blowing his brains out.

One thing this shithole has going for it is the supermarkets. A Lidl's behind the bus station, a two-storey Asda's up the road where the furniture warehouse used to be and a small Tesco rises near the river to accompany the huge Tesco on the round-about near Haslingden. Not far from here is a retail park they had to stop building thanks to the recession. Francie wonders if they're ever going to do anything with the place or if it will always be this stark, empty shell. He kind of likes it in this unfinished state. There's power in the vacancy, something haunting, and he trespasses here all the time, navigating the elevated steel girders, leaping over the hole in the ground where the escalator was supposed to go and chucking detritus into the abandoned slab of car park. He's sprayed CRUSTYMAN up the building's interior next to the outlined shape of a man, and he's particularly proud of the enormous gaping mouth filled with flat herbivorous teeth that he's drawn. The yawning spray-paint mouth is framed by a straggly green beard that gropes and strives towards a mural of a sun descending westerly above a vast, tenanted moorland.

Through the Tesco by the river the lads charge. A crate of beer from one aisle, all kinds of munch from another. The till girl barely registers their presence until Francie tries to pay with one of Pat's twenties. No good, she says, taking a special pen from a drawer and marking a line down the eternally sug-gestive expression sported by the Queen.

Why not? says Francie.

S'fake.

Ah, come off it. Francie hands over a second twenty.

I'm telling you. The till girl draws another line with the special pen. *See?*

Give it here.

Francie inspects the notes. Ashen lines mark both the Queen's faces. The till girl is so smug. She has yolk-coloured hair, and one of her teeth is edged ominously, rotten.

Fuck it. Francie hands over Pat's final twenty, which turns out to be another fake. He daren't face Callum. The cavernous air of fiasco hangs over everything. This feeling, in many ways, is all he has ever known.

Francie? says Callum.

What?

Here. Callum eases a credit card from his wallet. My mum gave me this ... for emergencies.

Francie eyes the life-changing slice of plastic. I never knew you had one of them.

Callum blanches. I did tell you.

Bollocks you did.

I did!

Well go on, give it her then.

Callum does as he's told but the till girl is squinting at Francie. You got any ID?

Francie can feel himself blushing. No. Come on.

I'm sorry, I'm gonna need to see some ID, mate.

You were serving me a minute ago!

That were before.

I'm eighteen!

Yeah, right. You want the rest of your stuff? Your food 'n' that?

Oh, thanks, says Callum, but Francie knocks his cousin's arm away, picks a sandwich up and chucks it at the till girl's chest.

I wouldn't eat this shit if you *fucking* paid me!

Outside, Francie spray-paints CRUSTYMAN up the car park wall in massive red letters, then he gets Callum to paint around him using his body as a stencil. His outline is exaggerated, agreeably monstrous.

It's a short climb over the fence into the back lot where the dismal men unload the pallets from the lorries. The first few bins are padlocked but the open one is all Francie needs. There's all sorts of goods inside, and most of it's only just out of date. Loaves of bread, all sorts of seeded rolls, pizzas, quiches, ready-made curries, yoghurts, chocolate bars, crisps and cakes, sandwiches and pâté. Francie chucks a load of stuff over the fence for Callum to collect before hopping over himself, landing directly in the trolley along with their treasure, vandal paint smearing his hands as he stands like a Viking at the prow of a longboat, while Callum, shitting it, scoots them across the car park towards the main road.

It doesn't take long for a security guard to give chase but the fat bastard's got no chance of catching them. The lads make it to the scrub down the side of the building where they finally eat their lunch behind the brambles. Francie, cigarette in mouth, has just sent the trolley into the river when a policeman arrives. He escorts them to his bullet of spinning light, that blue reminder.

Of course no one was in at home and because he can't be dropped off just anywhere, Francie's at Eddie Grinstead's yard, slumped in the back of the panda car waiting to see if Uncle Pat's about. The young Asian police officer is at the shutters calling through the open hatch, but no one answers. Francie sits quietly, praying to be let go.

Callum was dropped off first, shepherded indoors by the General, who, whilst the policeman was talking on his radio, marched down her drive with that cauliflower of hair wobbling madly and the stick up her arse growing by another metre at least. She rapped on the car's window. Hot breath steamed the glass. Dribs of saliva. Francie isn't to see his cousin any more. He's a tearaway, a horror, *just like his mother*, and why do kids like him have no respect? Why can't they just get out there and *do something* with themselves for once?

Like what? Francie bellowed, slapping the window with both hands.

Uncle Pat arrives as they're about to leave. He's on his phone but hangs up at the sight of the panda car. Floyd, practically perched on Pat's desert boots, begins to bark at Francie who has stepped from the car and fallen in behind the police officer.

Francie makes eye contact with his uncle and wishes he hadn't. His mouth is a gyre of chalk and quicksand and on the horizon are the castellations of derelict houses and old cotton mills with their brick lumbs. The past is everywhere. There is no future. Above it all, surrounded by a blue thread of wispy light, are the electric lather of storm clouds.

What's up? Pat says cheerily, the cords and ligaments in his neck standing out like appliance wires.

I'm here to talk about Francis, says the officer.

Why, everything all right, mate?

Pat wraps Floyd's chain around his hand, drawing the dog to heel. Floyd's lumpen feet scrabble in an effort to get at Francie. The dog is whining, wheezing.

I didn't do it, Francie says, almost to himself, but no one hears. I didn't do it, he repeats. Then, much louder, *Uncle Pat.*

Pat finally looks at him. His mouth is a thin white line. You what?

The guy's chatting shit. I didn't do it.

Pat tips his head to face the sky. *Fuck's sake ...*

I didn't do nothing!

You're a liar.

I'm not. *Uncle Pat*, I'm serious.

Floyd's lead clicks as he's drawn closer still to Pat's boots. The hoarseness of the dog's wheezing is becoming a real distraction and the police officer can't take his eyes from the drool and spit dribbling from Floyd's scarred jaws. He only snaps out of it when Pat addresses him directly.

Maybe the two of us should go talk in private, Pat says, then, glowering at Francie, he hands him Floyd's lead.

The wait is sickening. Francie watches the men stroll across the yard. Floyd is mercilessly pulling on the lead, actually tugging Francie along a couple of steps until Francie yanks him back. Francie tries to spit but hardly anything comes out.

He needs the toilet and nearby, a rat is skittering around a Rentokil box, escaping into a hole in the wall. Jealous of a rat. Francie boots the box as hard as he can, sending it against the metal shutter doors. The doors resonate, ringing.

Well, I think we should at least hear the boy's side of things, Pat is saying as he and the police officer return. He raises one arm.

Francie!

Francie staggers over, tugged by Floyd. I'm telling you, Pat, honest to God it weren't me.

You'd better not be kidding.

I'm not.

You'd better not be.

Blood thumps in Francie's temples. He almost believes himself. It wasn't me, he repeats, miserably. *Uncle Pat ...*

Pat accepts Floyd's chain and turns to the policeman. Well ... you heard the lad. You've got the wrong man.

The policeman has his notebook out. He looks at Francie. You're denying it was you?

Francie manages to nod.

I saw you haul that trolley into the river myself.

Floyd whines.

Then there's the matter of the CCTV.

Pat steps forward. Listen, mate. If our kid says he didn't do it, I believe him.

Mr Morgan—

But I'll pay your fines, Pat snaps. As a goodwill gesture.

Francie doesn't listen to the rest. All there is, is Pat's solidity: an awesome, commanding and impenetrable force that governs everything. He imagines himself cast as the figure on Pat's boxing trophy: Francie Morgan, electro-plated, *golden*. As he bends to pet Floyd, the dog barks at him.

When the police car has finally gone, Pat ties Floyd up and beckons Francie into the workshop. It's a corrugated-steel vault, its floor dusted with paint flakes and sawdust, varnish polluting the air; machine lubricant. Solvents. A song Elspeth's always crooning to her kid when cooking him tea blares from the radio. Eddie Grinstead is in the upstairs manager's office, watching.

Well, Pat says, hand descending to Francie's shoulder and squeezing hard. In light of today's events I think you'd better start getting used to your new place of work.

Ah, Pat, nah—

Why you laughing?

I'm not doing this shit. No way.

Oh, come off it, France, Pat says, even a fucking dumb-arse like you could manage a job as easy as this. Here, he says, hoisting a cupboard door from a rack and slipping it into an open tank of liquid as if he's placing a slide under a microscope. First they go in the caustic soda, then you leave 'em: forty-five minutes.

Eddie Grinstead emerges from the office at the top of the metal stairs, one hand stuffed down the front of his pants. I'm just showing Francie the ropes, Pat calls up, whilst at the same time removing the sopping door from the tank of soda. The door has a highly distorted look to it now, not that Pat has noticed. He opens a colossal box oven in the corner of the workshop and sets the door inside. Eddie Grinstead stomps along the landing, muttering.

Please, Pat, Francie whispers. *Not with him.*

But Pat isn't listening. No one ever listens. Next you cook the fuckers, he says. So they can be stripped.

Grinstead whistles. Hang on, Paddy.

Oh, come on, Grin, the lad's good as gold, Pat calls back. Every word that comes from his mouth's gospel!

No, it's just that door's MDF. It doesn't dip ... *Paddy!*

Pat hits the button.

Fuck. Grinstead clangs down the steps, shouldering past Francie on his way to switch the oven off. The hinges of the hatch scream as an immense fetid stench billows out into the workshop. The cupboard door has been reduced to a glooping, bubbled mess.

Jesus, Paddy—

Pat backhands Grinstead across the mouth. Your birthday's cancelled, he yells, rounding on Francie. Forget your present, you haven't earned it, you haven't earned a bloody thing!

He kicks the wall on his way out, leaving Francie alone with Grinstead in the chiming, stinking workshop. Grinstead, clutching his face, fans the molten fug of door while blots of MDF drip fatly on the metal.

If you think I'm working here wi' *you* … begins Francie, but Grinstead strides over, cups him by the balls and squeezes.

Did someone say summat? says Eddie. His chin is smeared richly with blood.

Up Cribden Hill, dusky light casts jagged shadows against the rickety lockups. Francie has copies of the keys so he's able to open the final hut caging the quad bike, which glints menacingly. He takes bolt cutters to the collars of the pregnant dogs and frees them, then he uses the tools under the workbench and an internet video off his phone to get the quad going. In the field, the watching dogs, those perpetual mothers, wag their tails as Francie teaches himself the quad's basics. He gets it down easy. It's a matter of throttle, a coordination between wrist and clutch, and it's something. It really is something. He pulls doughnuts in the bog and beeps the horn. I AM CRUSTYMAN, he smears in peat-mud up every lockup.

He bombs into town, the quad's front wheels lifting off the ground. He cuts into the cemetery built in the middle of the housing estate. There are no burials here. The council can't sell graves any more so the place has fallen into disrepair. These days the people that frequent the cemetery are kids, lovers, Polish men who come to get smashed in tranquillity after work. Respect for the dead, Francie's gran might have said, had she known why people now came here. You've got to respect your dead. Never mind that there are the living. There are the lost.

Francie bends a metal pipe free of the wall of the lodge house near the gates, a listed building, now a ruin, and hurtles down the gangway of the cemetery, those overgrown lanes. He takes weltering chunks from every grave he passes.

Whoosh!

A tombstone is decimated.

Whoosh!

Another memorial, totalled.

The quad mounts shattered rock. Francie speeds down the holloway, whacking graves. Here is the cemetery's exit. It's blocked by a massive barrier that's been painted black, but Francie veers towards it anyway, gunning the throttle. As he approaches the formidable metal bar, Francie prepares to duck, a fearsome battle cry escaping him. He'll be up the road soon, burning, magnesium-bright, going faster, *faster*, burning until he's completely out of sight.

Sick of Sunsets

———

1

Jodie's jumper looks like it's made of TV static. It's a knit crew-neck, way too big for her, so it must have come from Adam, probably grabbed on the way out to the removal van or something. She reaches past me and dumps the knives and forks in the sink, some oily dishwater splashing into my face. I roll a shoulder across the wet cheek as Jodie's bare feet make a gluey sound on the tiles. I can sense her wanting to make a comment to me, and of course she cracks. About time we did something about this, she says, leaning against the oven and flicking my ponytail. What are the other kids gonna think, seeing you looking like the back end of a rat?

The sunset's tangerine, so bright I can't see myself in the window above the taps. I squeeze the last knife clean with the coloured sponge and drop it in the cutlery basket.

Oh, right, I say.

Truth be told, I haven't given my hair much thought up to now. I have been thinking about my new classmates though. I unstopper the plug and drag it from the water by its chain. The drain makes a boggy sound and a tide of orange scum's left on the inside of the sink, some soap-bleached spaghetti trailing from the plughole.

I didn't mean to, Gem, it's just … She puts her hand on my arm. I'll make you an appointment for tomorrow, shall I?

Okay. I move my arm away. Nice one.

My treat. Jodie tucks a dark frizzy bang behind one ear. We can walk it, it's not far. Probably do us good, getting to know the area a bit.

Suppose it will, yeah.

I know it feels odd us being here.

I don't mind it, actually.

Well, that's good then, says Jodie, doing that *moving swiftly on* thing with her thin, tattooed-on eyebrows. After a minute she shakes her head. Mad time of life, this.

I don't know if she's talking to herself, or me. Resisting the urge to shrug, I dry my hands on some kitchen towel, the moisture pulling the tissue apart. Jodie's put on quite a bit of weight recently. Whether this is a sign of improved spirits or the exact opposite, I'm not sure, because she hardly confides in me any more. She's trying to put a smile on things and this makes me melt a bit because she's one of those people who, when they smile, everything about them flowers. Almost Mediterranean in complexion, Jodie is the colour of biscuits when it isn't sunny. A rich tan when it is. The problem is that as long as I've known her, she's been tired-looking. That's what it's like, Jodie says. The medical life is like that.

Not that she really goes on about it – a natural busybody like her wouldn't know what to do without the rigours of a nursing life to spur her on. I came into that life around the turn of the millennium when Jodie was a sister on the maternity unit where I was born. My real mum, she shouldn't have been a mum. She was my age when she had me, so I'm beginning to understand what that must have been like for her. She and Jodie kept in touch because my real mum didn't have a real family. When I was three and becoming a proper handful, I came to live with Jodie and her husband Rory, and she adopted me the year after that. Rory was all right, I loved Rory. I know he found me difficult but as I got older he had me on his shoulders whenever I asked him to carry me, and he was the one who taught me how to ride a bike. I once heard Jodie telling him that with the internet waking all the youngsters up these days, you don't get as many teenage pregnancies. I guess that makes Gemma one of the last of her kind, Rory said.

Jodie dumped Rory when I was about ten. He did used to moan a lot. Like, when we were having tea or sitting down the pub, he'd start talking about how messy Jodie was, how she never paid for anything, and he'd do it in a jokey way when it was obvious he was being serious. I think he was stressed with work. I'd often find him in the back yard smoking tabs and talking on his phone. He had his own business, something to do with fixing computers, and it wasn't going well. I used to keep him company out there. We'd kick an air-flight ball to each other whilst Rory spoke to clients and creditors, booting it against the wall so it rebounded between us. From me to the wall to Rory, from Rory to the wall back to me. We used to cheer at each other silently whenever we got a decent rally going.

Now it's just me and Jodie. She started at Walshaw General a couple of weeks ago, and I'm off to St Cuthbert's on Monday, going straight into year eleven halfway through the first term. We came here for a new start. To try living properly, according to Jodie, whatever that means. Her big sister Susan lives nearby, so that was a big draw, and Jodie's home town of Burnley isn't far either. Apparently that's where I'm from too, which I guess makes a pair of us who don't know what to make of a return to dud weekends, cleaner air and a whole lot of space to think.

Get you a little makeover, says Jodie. Sorted for school. She nudges me in the shoulder. For all them fit lads.

Jode.

I turn on the tap and wash away the last of the bubbles. Jodie obviously wants to say something else but the sun's fading and I know we're both thinking about Adam. I wonder if she keeps his memory in a box, like I do. I wonder if she challenges herself to go near the box sometimes, like I do. I watch her play with her nose ring and spark a roll-up. She won't admit to missing how things were but only yesterday I saw the message drafted on her phone. *Ads*, she's typed. *You just popped into my head and*

Finally I can see myself in the window. Everything about me's hidden behind the shape of another teenage girl. My outline watching me from the glass like a stalker.

Branches bat the bus roof. Once we're through the trees we loop a roundabout above the motorway then head downhill past a playground full of charging sprogs. An estate's under construction as you arrive in Stubbins. Identical orange brick houses spread up the new streets like a rash working its way up an arm.

You okay, love? asks Jodie. I know we went for a different look in the end, but that's what this is all about, isn't it?

She flits a hand at the evolving view: a cluster of thin houses below a rutted gradient clad with trees resembling florets of broccoli.

That's why we came here, she says. Remember?

Classic Jodie: only remembering to act protective after the event. I summon a nod because I can see what she means, then I touch my newly exposed neck. I'm unrecognisable. Blonde. I'm a snobby, middle-aged-mum blonde.

Seriously, you look great, Gem. I wouldn't worry about it.

I'm not worried.

Well, that's good then?

Course it is.

The moment I saw the crude neon of the salon's logo, I should have known. *A Cut Above the Rest*, it was called. Beige walls with ribbon borders stencilled in blue. Overpowering citrus candles, a plant with leaves like swords and a woman who looked like she was exhaling all the time pushing a broom around the wonky chairs.

The Irwell's low and I can smell the chippy. The bus tilts under a railway bridge and a hulking paper mill spreads ahead of us, the cloying stink of farts filling the air. Susan lives in

Ramsbottom, which is a town of a few thousand people that supposedly gets its dumb name because of all the wild garlic, ramsons, that grow in the surrounding woodlands. From pretty much anywhere here you can see Peel Tower, a stone folly that stands on Holcombe Hill: a cross between the last turret of a ruined castle and an industrial-age chimney. The tower was built to honour local hero Robert Peel, who, Jodie tells me, was the founder of the police force. It does look like a sort of guard up there, a lonely sentinel that's been condemned to watch over everyone, waiting as patiently as the truth.

Susan's terraced house is over the road from the local swimming pool. It has pink gutters and a bay tree in a ribbed pot by the front door. When she lets us in she relaxes her head in a practised imitation of delight and tells me I look like the lucky Gwyneth Paltrow. You know, she says, from *Sliding Doors*.

I don't need to have seen that movie to know Susan's a shit liar. She makes a knowing face she thinks I won't get, then glances over her purple glasses at me. She works the reception at an optician's and always seems to have a new pair on.

I know you don't like cuddles, she says, offering me her hand.

It's fine, I reply, submitting to a very stiff hug.

The TV's more of a home cinema, and Susan's splashed out on a brightly coloured sofa and an armchair that she refers to as 'the yellows'. *Careful of the yellows. Watch your shoes on them yellows. No eating on the yellows.*

Is Ben in? asks Jodie.

In his lair. Go say hi if you want, Gem.

I make a polite noise but stay where I am. Ben's a couple of years older than me and the first time I met him he was making Action Man and Barbie do it while Ken watched. I think his big sister Becky must have been mean to him growing up or something because he's, I don't know … There's just this way he is around me. He's a good example of how knowing someone and understanding them can be very different things.

Susan has the uniform draped over the yellows. I've some of Rebecca's shirts dug out. A couple of skirts and her old blazer, she says. I think they're the same size. Well, roughly they are, anyway.

One look at that uniform and I just know it's not going to fit. The blazer smells like the pages of an old book and the red tie has blue-trimmed white stripes. Even I can see that when she was my age, Becky was bigger than me, plus all her shirts are grey-white and in need of a good iron.

Why don't you try it on? says Jodie, offering me the blazer.

Okay.

I slip into it, my arm hairs collecting a static charge from the nylon sleeves. Loose threads straggle out of all three buttons and the inside pocket's been torn, creating a passage into the lining.

Thanks, I say, as Jodie rolls my cuffs up roughly.

We'll take these in, she says. Sorted.

You all right, love? asks Susan.

I'm fine, I say, looking out of the window at the tower. I've known for a long time that we're all separate people. Now I think that teenagers are the most separate of all.

What do you say, Gem?

Nice one, Susan.

You can call me Auntie Sue, dear.

Auntie Sue.

Susan clasps her hands. Don't you look *smart*.

The steaming mugs of slightly burnt instant coffee come out. Susan and Jodie sit at the dining table behind me, breaking squares off a massive chocolate bar, agreeing that because they've 'been good' all week, a treat won't hurt. Caffeine sets my headaches off. I slump on the yellows with a glass of apple juice, pretending to watch telly and eavesdropping on the conversation.

So how's work been? asks Susan.

Oh, mental busy, replies Jodie. Thought it might be more chilled this way, but no.

Susan titters. I bet. What about your colleagues? Are they all right?

Yeah, everyone's been dead nice, thanks. There's this doctor. Oh, he really makes me laugh, Sue.

Sounds dreamy.

Oi, it's not like that.

Susan doesn't say anything.

Honestly, adds Jodie, he's happily married.

So?

Suzie.

Go on, what's his name? Susan asks. Your good doctor.

You'll only laugh.

I won't.

You bloody will.

There's another gap in the conversation and Jodie sighs like she used to do when she talked about Adam. I feel wizened. Two hundred years old.

Tinker, she says.

Susan stifles a laugh.

I know, says Jodie.

Tinker?

Yeah.

Dr Tinker.

His first name's Mervyn as well.

There's a blip of quiet before the sisters burst out laughing. I'm laughing too, into my fist with my back turned.

Once they've calmed down, Susan clanks her mug on the table. And how is ...?

Jodie lowers her voice ... Good, yeah. Well ... She laughs nervously. You know how it is.

I can feel their eyes on me. Susan's going to ask about Adam. She was going to ask about him the minute she opened that door.

I hurry upstairs, my insides knotting. One way of describing what happens at times like this is it feels like a layer of cling film has come down, and it stops me from getting my words out. According to Jodie I was thrown against a wall by my mum's boyfriend when I was six months old, which might explain why I get like this. It really weirds me out thinking about that. Something that's had such an impact on my life and I can't even remember it.

When there's no reply from the other side of Ben's door, I enter the room where I'm met by the rhythmic chug of heavy-metal guitars. My adopted cousin sits in front of a desktop computer. His cap of greasy ginger hair flicks out behind dorky ears with very large lobes, and he's topless and spooning a pile of chocolate cereal into his mouth. Unsurprisingly for someone who lives opposite a pool, Ben has a swimmer's body, although I find something inhuman about him. The outsized bumps of his spine. His supple frame. He makes me think of the smell of chlorine.

Shut the door, he says.

I'm not your slave, Ben ...

Shut the fucking door!

What's up with you?

Ben lurches forward and kicks the door shut. Returning to his spinning chair, he points at the bookcase next to my head. Gizmo.

Oh.

I turn around and come face to face with an inquisitive piebald ferret leaning towards me from the shelves, its cloth-like nose twitching about a centimetre from my own. *Shit.* I duck backwards. Oh, Ben!

Ben spits chocolate milk everywhere. It dribbles down his chest as he rocks in his chair, laughing. I'd forgotten about Gizmo. A slippery furry tube that scampers all over the place. Under the bed and that. On the windowsill.

I wondered where that stink was coming from, I say, moving to the window.

Yeah, yeah.

Why don't you keep it in its hutch like a normal person?

How would you like living your whole life in a cage?

Ben turns back to his PC. He's ignoring me but, after a minute, still staring at his computer, he says, What've you done to your hair?

I don't reply.

He sets his bowl down. You look like a boy.

Fuck off.

Or an ugly Princess Di. What have you done to yourself?

You're one to talk, you ginger bastard.

I know who I am, Ben says. I've come to terms with that. You, though … He smirks, setting his hands behind his head. Look at the state of you.

He reaches for his phone. Man, for once I'm glad you came round, Gemma.

The camera flashes, snapping a picture of me with both hands held in front of my face like stars.

I suppose I should ask how it's going.

You're too kind.

Looking forward to the joys of St Cuthbert's?

Can't wait.

They're gonna love you, Ben says while typing something on his keyboard. Honestly you'd have been best off sticking where you were, Gem. You're gonna get muntered round here.

Gizmo's fur is patched with a yawning white. I go to the door and listen for Jodie. Surely she's finished her brew by now.

Hey, Gem.

What do you want?

Any more pervs touch you up yet? Bet you'd like to do this to Big Ads, wouldn't you? Teach him for giving you one, once and for all.

Ben rotates his monitor to show me a video of a poor Arab surrounded by a crazed mob. The guy's arms are tied, his trousers at his ankles, his withered dick exposed on a chopping block. As the machete thuds down, I cry out and swipe Gizmo from the shelf. The ferret hits Ben full in the face, and I'm rushing downstairs, bleeding from where the creature's desperate claws raked my wrist. Now I'm in the middle of the road and beeping traffic. No way am I going back indoors.

I end up catching a couple of random buses into Burnley, which is fine because I've never been to my home town before.

I wonder if it's always been this dead. Maybe it's the weather. Hard, noisy rain falls on a bandstand with no band, there are loads of vacant shop units and even the big high-street brands seem to have pulled out, so things must be bad. I follow a pensioner towards the market, eventually stopping at a stall with knackered table edges. It's a snide place with crocodile clamps holding everything in place – the tarp, the tablecloth, the lights – and it's flogging a mishmash of remote controls and batteries, novelty air fresheners, cleaning products, smoking paraphernalia and accessories for mobile phones. I make a fist and hope my wrist will stop hurting.

The stallholder's sat in a foldable camping chair with his feet on the table, swigging from a can of cider. He double-takes when he sees me and stands up. No way you've got one of them, he says, nodding at my phone. How long you had that brick for?

He's got a broad Lancashire accent: round accentuated R's and harsh drawn-out vowels, and I can tell straight away he fancies me. This sort of thing has only happened once before and… what I'm saying is, you know it when you see it. He's actually not bad-looking, although he does have quite a thin nose and traces of stubble mark the apples of his cheeks. Acid-green waterproof. Burberry scarf (probably fake), smart black jeans and spotless white Reebok Classics. He could be Greek, maybe Italian. His cropped hair's shaved in a fade up the sides, waxed neat and forwards on top, unlike the lads in school who all look like they've got sponges glued to their heads. I can't tell how old he is. He's original though. Mature. It's like he knew a crisp urban look would suit his slender frame, so that's what he went for.

Even though I'm shielded from the worst of the dribbling tarp, no way am I pulling my hood back. Dunno, mate, I say. It's cheap to run though. Gets loads of battery.

It's a museum piece, is that.

Suppose you'd know.

His bum chin sinks into his collar. Business isn't mine, he says. I'm only manning it for a mate.

With it being late in the year, it's hard seeing anything in a positive light, but I have to say that the plastic ice-cream tubs of rolling papers, USB wires, phone chargers and sat-nav holders look especially pathetic today. I must be making a face because the guy says, *Seriously*, and the breath rushes out of his nose in jets. It's only for a bit, he says. Cash in hand. You can't argue with cash in hand.

I shrug in half-arsed concession, spotting a weed grinder with a cartoon of a stoned Rasta on it. I pick the grinder up. I always wonder how you guys get away with selling this stuff.

'Cause everyone does drugs and no one gives a shit?

The guy spreads his arms, and we both laugh. I'm surprised by how relaxed I'm feeling. Maybe it's because for once I've met someone on *my* terms. Everyone else there's always been baggage. To Adam I was Jodie's moody kid, at least at first, and to Jodie I should have been someone else's problem. Right now, what I am to this smiling guy is just between him and me.

What you up to then? he says. You chose a mint day for it.

The rain's getting heavier. Together we watch it fall, the water smashing into the crazy paving, bouncing back up.

Nothing much to be honest.

Me too. He smiles. You off work? He pats his hair with one hand.

Nah, just mooching about.

The fruit-and-veg man looks like he's singing a hymn. *Pears, five for a pound. Pears, five for a pound.*

How come? the stall guy says. You on the tick or summat?

I pause. What's the point in lying? I'm still in school, I say.

Get out.

I shake my head.

You're still in school?

Apples! Get your apples!

Here comes the cling film, and with it, that first blast of shyness. I examine a bottle of floor cleaner as the Belisha beacons over the road flash.

You look well older, the guy continues. Like my age. Seriously, I'd never have known if you hadn't said.

I feel well squirmy. As I put the floor cleaner down, the guy says I look mature and tells me again that I could be his age. Like proper *easily*, he says.

All I can do is make a dumb face. If I could speak, I might tell him I'm not surprised I look his age. Actually, mate, I might say, after what happened with Adam, I can't believe I don't look way older than I do. Thoughts of Adam keep beetling all over me. He came on the scene about a year or two after Jodie and Rory split up. Jodie had found him on a dating website *because that's how love happens these days*. It turned out he'd come from a strict Christian family, and although he'd rejected the faith and in fact went on a massive rant about organised religion if you gave him half a chance, his background had made him really particular about stuff. I mean, Adam actually came into my room once with a tangle of wet hair pinched between his fingers, and he was like, *I'm trying to have a shower, Gem. Do you think I like having to pick this shit from the plughole?*

Him and Jodie used to shush each other and giggle whenever they were shagging, and the next morning they'd be overly affectionate to the extent that I felt like I was being taken advantage of, my awkwardness being used to make things more exciting between them as a couple. That gross forbidden naughtiness, know what I mean? Adam won me round over the next couple of years. When Jodie worked weekends he'd take me to a museum or a gallery or a football match, and we'd talk like adults over lunch. He said he'd never had true faith in anything, and I recognised that. I even understood it. He also confessed that he'd run away from home at seventeen. He said, I had to fend for myself, Gem. Grow up fast. A lot like you have.

What was it about that mutual feeling I had about him? There was an awareness there, a hopeless knowledge, dark as cinder, that I recognised and flocked to.

You're being daft now, I say to the stall guy, Adam's memory shaking me from my funk. Stop taking the piss.

Sorry, the guy says, even though he doesn't seem sorry, nor does he seem fazed by anything, actually. He hunches to my height. Squints. Hang on, he says, clicking his fingers. It's not that we're that close in age. It's more you're an old soul. That's what you are.

How do you ...

I clear my throat.

How do you mean an old soul?

The guy takes a breath then says a lovely thing. You can always tell with eyes like yours, he says. I dunno. They're just full, aren't they. You see things in 'em. It's rarer than you might think as well. You've got a deepness. It's ... it's wisdom is what it is.

He jangles his money belt. Bloody hell, he says. Listen to me on a Tuesday afternoon. You must think I'm mental.

A lot of words are seething inside me ... mental isn't one of them. Oh, man, I whisper.

My mum was into all that, the guy says, apparently not hearing me. We lived out in the sticks. He points in the general direction of Pendle. Plenty of time for stories up there.

I want to say, *You don't have to justify anything,* but I'm so flustered that I push my fist into the table, and its metal legs creak.

I take a mood ring from their cardboard box. This stall all you do?

No chance, I want to run parties, the guy says, looking relieved to have changed the subject. Well, one day, I do. I wanna run my own club night. I wanna start my own label.

I've never met anyone who wanted to do something as cool as that. The guy says he's done house parties, a night here in B-town. But what I really wanna do, he says, is put on a rave. Like they used to have back in the eighties. Stand Lees Farm. Deeply Vale Festival.

What, sort of like they have in Embassy, do you mean?

Embassy ain't about music, he says fiercely. It's about boozing. Having a fight, getting a shag. Raves are outdoors. Or you have 'em in warehouses. Spaces no one knows what to do with. We do 'em by ourselves, for other people. Act of kindness. Proper civil disobedience. Protest, man. You stick two fingers up to the void.

That's well sick, I reply, then, holding my hand up with the mood ring balanced on a fingertip, I ask him what the colour green means.

The guy checks the code paper from the ring's packet. Deciphering your feelings from this, he says, I reckon you've got mixed emotions. What's your name, anyway?

Gemma. Gemma Glove.

The guy just grins at me, and after a stupid silence, we keep talking. I was born here, I end up saying, but I don't remember it. Mainly I'm from Manchester, but I don't feel like I'm from there either. I'm not from anywhere really.

The guy listens when I tell him about school. He says education did his nut in as well. It's just another arm of the state, he says. School. Uni. Job. The same old conveyor belt designed to teach you to tune in and shut your trap whilst the toffs keep their boots on the throats of ordinary working people. Anyone with a brain hates being told what to do. I sacked it off. Best thing I ever did in a lot of ways.

Bet that was amazing.

Aye, it were well good, yeah. Always is, pushing everything away. It's not for everyone though, I can't lie. For me it were the money or the freedom. He raises his can. Guess which one I went for.

I don't think there's ever been a time when I haven't had things decided for me. The idea of making my own choices is that new I almost don't believe in it.

That's so crazy, I say.

Honestly, I think we'd all be a lot happier if we took control of ourselves from an early age. I mean think about it. What do we need? Like, *really* need. A roof over our heads. Food. Something to give us a bit of purpose. Beyond that it's all just bollocks. Why waste your time doing some bullshit job, doing what you're told. Bringing some wanker his coffee.

I gesture at the wall of phone cases in their plastic sleeves. So?

Bare minimum, the guy says proudly. I can work any time I want. I can tell the customers to shove the business up their arse an' all, if I like. It's up to me. I don't work any more than three days a week. Twelve till six. That's me done.

Do you not get bored?

Only boring people get bored.

Other than the stall he loads lorries. Casual, like. Warehouse shit. Zero-hours contract.

That the haulage place, Tatt's?

How d'you know that?

It's near my house, I explain, the unspoken invitation to come visit me sometime feeling as if it's been yelled full volume. I revisit the phone cases. Ocean vistas. Studded sparkles. Cute pets and Man City winning the league title the other year. Adam was a big City fan. I think about the day he walked in on me when I was in the bathroom in my bra and knickers. That was the turning point. Our mistrust morphing into something else.

Another customer arrives. The stall guy ignores her and comes to my end of the table. I'll have to keep an eye out for you.

We scan each other.

You gonna give me a discount, or what? I reply, even though it feels like the boldest thing I've ever come out with.

He laughs. Dunno if we've got owt to fit that relic. Pass it here a sec.

I hand him the phone. I haven't bothered setting a password because it's never off my person, and who's going to rob a piece of shit like that? The guy walks to the other end of the stall, ignoring the cases and typing something on my phone's keypad. He's got a great arse and I want to explode when he winks at me. He puts the phone down, serves the other customer and when he doesn't come back, not wanting to lose face, I grab my phone and say, *Laters*, then I wander off with a mixture of excitement and loneliness splashing in my stomach. The Christmas decorations are up. Coloured bulbs. Holly. Santa. The text comes later that night. His name's Kayden and what am I up to tomorrow?

2

The washing machine's not been emptied, so the turtleneck I wanted to wear stinks of fish. With Jodie putting the tea on, every cupboard door is open in the kitchen and the extractor fan is noisily sucking up smoke from our burnt chicken nuggets.

I go into the bathroom where wet towels are balled in the corner like giant scrunches of bog roll. It's that misty after Jodie's shower that I can't see myself in the mirror and I have to clear a space in the condensation. It's still a surprise to see the one side of my hair grown back to reach my chin. Last week, I shaved the other half off: clipped it away in a scalp-hugging fade, a bit like Kayden's. Why not try something *really* different, he said. It'll be sexy tied back in a knot. That sold me on the idea. Now I'm bleach blonde, as short-haired as long, plus with the kohl eyeshadow and red lippie I've started wearing, it's a new me: watching myself in the mirror, still half a stranger.

Jodie's contact-lens packets litter the sill, the solution crusting the wood like a salty coastline. Her underwear's strewn all over the landing, empty teacups have become ornaments and by the sink a clouded pint glass she stole from the pub last week has dregs of beer drying in it. It's no wonder Rory used to get pissed off. *Jodie*, he was always calling up the stairs. *It's like living with a kid.*

If she was a kid then, she's a teenager now. I often see her lying on her bed texting Merv the Perv. Merv with his hairy knuckles – that's how Jodie described them. *Oh, and what he does with them, Sue ...*

For God's sakes, I shouted the other day. *Will you shut that door?*

Don't get me wrong, Jodie has as much right as anyone to be happy. I just wish her happiness didn't involve this masquerade.

The doctor comes to our flat to get his end away whenever I'm not in, which means I'm out a lot. Thank God for Kayden. He's the only reason I'm not *really* kicking off about the situation. He's why I've got sympathy for Jodie, because now I know what it means to want someone's whole attention all the time, and to get it too.

Thankfully the Fred Perry polo-neck's clean. I put it on, a lithe black, and step into my denim skirt and Nike Air Max 90's, completing the look with an orange-lined green bomber jacket.

Where you off to? asks Jodie, dumping a hot baking tray of oven chips straight onto the tabletop.

Cinema, I say, opening a tinny.

Oh, with Dec again?

Hmmm? Dec, yeah.

Jodie empties a shitload of vinegar onto the chips, and the fumes make her sneeze. She says, You and him getting on well.

Suppose we are, yeah.

The TV's showing a movie: *The Curious Case of Benjamin Button*. I turn the volume up to detract from the fact that Declan Kirklees is actually one of the main knobheads from school, and excuses are the only thing he's good for. Him and his mate Nathan Wray get through life by turning cruelty into laughter. First they took the piss out of me for my mimsy haircut, then it was because for some reason Nathan decided I was frigid. After Ben avenged Gizmo by telling everyone I'd slept with my stepdad, even though people laid into *him* about it too, I got dragged over hot coals for being a slag. Paedo-shagger, they call me. Dec even set a blog up so people could write stuff and post pictures of me: my head spliced onto the bodies of porn stars, sucking old guys off and shit. I went to the teachers and the whole year group got a letter home. We had to sit through a special assembly about cyber-bullying and now I get dogged for being a grass.

Without Kayden I wouldn't have handled it nearly as well as I have. I haven't told Jodie about him yet. She'll only make out like what I'm feeling is nothing more than a sugar high. I can almost hear her. *He's more than double your age. You're giving your love to the wrong person*, anything to put me off, all because she's never had what I've got. She didn't have it with Rory and as for Adam, well, how could she? It's tough shit, Kayden said when we chatted about it. She's a good example of how people always want more than there is. People like your step-mum hate thinking about what they wanted. They hate not having it as much as remembering what they've lost.

This is why Jodie's affair with Merv the Perv could be a good thing. Along with making her feel good about herself again, it might stop her resenting me and that way I might be able to stop resenting myself. She's gone to get herself ready. Whipping off that silk kimono. Blast of hairdryer. Make-up applied in smudges. Back downstairs she ups the sexy by forcing her feet into a pair of high-heeled black leather Chelsea boots.

How do I look? she says.

Chef's kiss.

Thanks, love.

The hairdryer clicks off and I realise Jodie's gazing at me gloomily.

Gem?

What?

I know it's a welcome novelty, you having a mate and everything, but can you not wait till I'm out the house before you start drinking? It might give me the vague idea I don't have to worry about you all the time.

This is how things are between us. It's Friday night, I reply, snapping the straighteners at her. And it's only one beer.

Sighing, Jodie takes the straighteners and applies the heated plates to the hysteria of her curls. You're only sixteen, she says. You seem to forget.

Least I'm not a smackhead, I say, draining my can.

Small mercies.

Or preggo.

Don't even joke about that.

Come on, you know I'd never.

I hope that's true. Jodie gives me a soft smile. Yeah, I know you wouldn't, love.

I crush the can and leave it on the table. Anyway, I say. You're the one who smokes. What does the dirty doc think to that?

His name's Mervyn, and he smokes more than I do.

Shut *up*.

I'm telling you, he does.

I don't reply. That wasn't how I saw Merv at all.

A horn sounds.

Kayden.

I rush out to the Mini Cooper. The number plate ends in BRN so Kayden's named his car Bernard. He's funny like that. Bernard's British racing green. He has a fat spoiler, alloy wheels and an awesome set of neons.

We kiss the way Kayden likes it: shitloads of tongue. I love how fast he drives. Especially in a classic Mini where you're that close to the ground that sixty miles an hour can feel like a hundred. We speed into Rawtenstall, past Marl Pits Sports Centre, then take the swooping road into Burnley past the windmills up Crown Point. There's not a jot of traffic here. We're going way above the speed limit between an expanse of bog, turf and open country, an emptiness that's kind of scary when you think about it.

All over here, says Kayden. You get shrooms. Every autumn, liberty caps. World-beating trips, they are, Gem, as long as you get 'em before first frost. My mum used to take us here after it rained. We used to go foraging wherever there was sheep shit.

So everywhere, basically.

Pretty much, yeah.

Kayden's got tons of stories about his childhood. His dad was a joiner and his mum made jewellery that she sold at markets across the north. They liked Kayden and his brother to call them by their first names. They were into shamanism, they did mushrooms every day and meditated when they weren't fire-juggling, doing poi and hula-hooping. Kayden's parents taught him and his brother how to make a wicked dhal and they also taught him how to tightrope, knit and sew. Considering how much air time he gives them, I find it strange that he never sees them. He says that if they'd worried about giving him and his brother a more conventional upbringing like they'd worried about being so right-on all the time, the family might have been a lot happier. I've never said this to Kayden but his youth sounds all right to me. Learning sitar and didgeridoo, living in an ivy-laced cottage in the woods. He belonged to someone. He wasn't abused. He had as much freedom as he liked and no one pressured him down a set path that didn't suit him. One thing: Kayden never had a TV or normal music growing up, which I wouldn't have liked. Plus he told me he fainted once after dislocating his knee falling off a tightrope. Apparently it was his dad's fault. Off his head, Kayden's dad pushed the joint sharply into place like you'd reset a broken pipe.

You did shrooms with your parents?

Sometimes, says Kayden. In my teens I did. That's my mum and dad for you. They met in Morocco. Dad had done time in the seventies on drugs charges. He never talked about it. It were him who gave me my first pill. To be fair I were going out that night anyway, I'd probably have found 'em one way or another. It's just weird though, innit. I'd never get high around my kid. Dad said he'd prefer I got my drugs off him safely rather than off some random scumhead.

Suppose that makes sense.

It's fucking depressing.

Your parents still together?

Are they heck.

The car skids around a corner, careering into the grass. Splashed mud fills Bernard's windscreen and is gone a second later, slicked clean. The two of us whoop as Kayden thrusts us into first gear, regains the road then stamps on Bernard's accelerator.

But it weren't weird all the time, says Kayden. We did loads of healthy shit. Like, we used to bake our own bread. That's wholesome, innit?

Oh, definitely, I say, as the evening shoots by. How were that? I wouldn't know where to start.

To be honest it were a pain in the arse. I don't do none of that shit no more.

Still though.

Aye, probably why I dress the way I do. I might be a scally on the outside but I'll always be a crusty on the in.

I love how Kayden dresses – he looks well smart. Down into B-town we go. Kayden's got me rolling the spliffs. I'm a natural, he says. A fucking joint factory. I pulled a whitey and spewed the first few times but Kayden taught me how to pace myself and now we get so high, it makes the sex crazy-good. The other day I saw Dec and Nathan and a few girls hanging around outside the Tesco supercentre in B-town. I pointed them out to Kayden and he stamped on the brakes. He's not even that tall. It's just the Mini, when he climbed out he must have looked well mad. *Oi!* he shouted. *You little pricks.* Dec's dropped face. Me laughing my head off as I got out and chucked a can of Fanta at them. It burst, sprayed right up Nathan's legs. Slags! I shouted, climbing into the passenger seat and perching on the lip of the window. Slags! Then I flicked the V's and beat Bernard's roof with my elbows as me and Kayden tore off, excitement's dream. I'd fallen for Kayden then. I knew I had. We reached fifty miles an hour going uphill in a car that's so small that we can squeeze it through the gates of Towneley Park, and we razzed it down those slim paths, *High as Hari Krishnas*, as Kayden says, listening to fuzzy drum and bass on cassette because Bernard's only got a tape deck.

Slags!

On our way home from the cinema Kayden stops at the picnic benches on Crown Point. It's a renowned dogging spot. We've to be careful, he says. Watch out for flashing lights, Gem.

I can't see no one.

Well, they might still be here. Hurry up before anyone comes.

We sit on the tabletop, our trainers on the seat slats, the horizon partly framed by the distant silhouette of the Singing Ringing Tree, which is one of the Panopticons, these weird sculptures that were commissioned as part of a lottery-funded art project a few years ago. The tree's a twisted sculpture shaped like a tornado, and it's made of steel pipes that echo in the wind, sending a blend of ethereal notes out across the countryside on evenings like this. I'm listening out for a song as Kayden racks a stonking pair of lines on the screen of his phone, my hands cupped over the top to prevent the expensive powder from blowing away. In the other direction we can see the bowling alley, the shining town and the tiered chocolate box that is the football club. All the towns round here have got left are their footie clubs, is one of the things Kayden likes to say.

There, he says, pointing vaguely at the artificially glowing sprawl. There's my gaff.

Ah, right, I say, making out like I can see it.

The riots were round there. They were well bad down Burnley Wood.

Yeah, I remember you saying.

Well, I am sorry.

How do you mean?

Am I boring you or summat, Gem?

What you on about, you madhead? I never said that.

Well, what are you saying?

Kay. I put my hand on his knee. I like hearing you talk.

He settles low and snorts his line. Happened ages ago now, but it's still well funny, he says after punishing me with one of his extended silences. Pakis and whites versus cops. Probably the only thing that's united us in years.

That's summat, I guess.

Take the fucking piss, man.

Right.

The Pakis.

Oh.

Bombing about, littering the place. Hardly any of them work. Dirty fucking bastards.

Do they not? Surely—

They nail loads of crack an' all, half of 'em. You get 'em parked up near mine. Blue smoke and smashing wank tunes out till four every morning.

I can see chalky coke scuzzing the tip of Kayden's nose. Mad, I say, scratching my head.

Bet it weren't like that in Manchester.

Nah. Well, I mean, I guess people don't mix there like they could. That's true, I say. But there's not nearly as much …

I sniff my line and go quiet.

As much what?

Well … they get on more. People aren't as bothered.

No way. There's well less Pakis in Manny. You're not out-numbered like we are here.

Come on, there's all sorts of communities. You go through Moss Side, Hulme and Rusholme and—

Whatever, Gem. I'm talking about different environments here. Totally different sets of people. Manny's been taken over nowhere near as bad as it has here and in Blackburn. Fucking Bradford, you been up there recently?

Course I have.

Have you heck.

I have!

Princess like you.

Oh, do one, you snob.

Snob.

An inverted snob is still a snob, Kayden. Mr Virtuous, that's you.

No chance! No way am I like that, Gem. Some people, they might be down on their luck or whatever and there's some out there who wouldn't look twice at 'em. Me, I've never judged anybody. If you say hello to me, I say hello back.

I guess, I reply, mainly because I can't be bothered arguing and also because I can finally hear the Panopticon, wind pouring silently into its pipes, coming out as music. I nick the cigarette from Kayden's mouth and take a sweet, husky drag. I know that deep down he only thinks like he does because he's never lived in a city. If he had done he'd have changed his tune because only weak people can't change their minds, and Kayden's the strongest person I've ever met. I don't blame him. Where he comes from, it's not that remote in the grand scheme of things, but it's still further out than where most people live and I've realised that the further out you go, the blunter the differences become. You might think that when you come to the narrow end of the branch things won't be as complicated. Take it from me though, they always are.

My town, Kayden's saying. And loads of others, they've taken what they were and not given them anything to replace it with. What they were built for in the first place has gone. Years and years of taking and never owt decent getting put back. The things we need sold off like we won't notice, like we're too thick to get a say. Everything's been fucking diluted. I were glad them riots happened, Gem. The whole town got bum-rushed that night. I wish you could have been there, Gem. I wish you could 'ave seen it. They deserved it, man. The council. The government. B-town had to burn like it did.

I tell him how brilliant it must have been. I kind of mean it as well because I've got that bursting coke assurance, and also because I'm imagining how mad the twinkling town must have looked with all the trouble and sirens erupting everywhere. Burnley Wood isn't the easiest area at the best of times, let alone in a riot, ask anyone. Loads of houses boarded up, ready for demolition – the place is like a battle zone. There's pure smack about, addicts doing that funny quick walk they always do when heading from one bolthole to the next. It's cheap rent, though. Cheap as it gets. Plus there's no one living on either side of Kayden. He's a loner, which has surprised me. He doesn't like people bothering him, he says. I suppose that's fair enough.

I'm gearing up to ask when I can move in. The first thing I'll do is put pictures up. As it stands, beyond Kayden's Nietzsche and Schopenhauer books that don't even look like they've been read, and the TV and stereo and some basic flat-pack furniture, there's only a poster of what Kayden says is a Fibonacci spiral. He says it's to remind him of what life's like when it's left to its own devices. This, he said when we were stoned one night, keeps my feet on the ground. It's the shape things take when they're allowed to progress, Gem. The golden ratio. Birth rates. Seashells. Black holes. Relationships. All that. Things diminish. They repeat, and once you come round to the idea it sets you free. You know then that you're trapped. You can learn to deal with things.

I agreed with Kayden then like I always do, but as we fall silent on the moor overlooking his entire world, I don't know if it's the weed or the coke or what, but I can see way more patterns than that single helix. I mean, just check Burnley out. Check the valley out. The configuration of our sky.

I wanna stay here all night, I say, snuggling up to Kayden.

He kisses my hair. Sounds good to me.

I'm starting to get a headache. Right across my forehead, I can feel it. I'm yours, I want to say, I've always been yours, Kay, but I can't get my words out. I hope he understands.

See a way off, where them windmills are? Kayden says after a while. That's the kind of place I'm gonna do me rave.

It's gonna be sick. Everyone's gonna come.

Few more shifts down Tatt's. Nail the hours. And I tell you what, Gem, I've been thinking. I'm gonna start flogging some gear.

Oh, Kay ...

Fuck off, don't start wi' that. I've done it before. You sling a bit. You work a bit. We'll get this valley buzzing. One mad night then off to Ibiza.

We share a long kiss, then Kayden shows me the pills. They're dark, shaped like Pharaohs. Tutankhamun.

You want one? he says.

He has such black eyes. I've never had one before and I think he knows it.

Okay, I say. Okay, yeah.

It takes ages for us to come up but the rush is beautiful when we do. Even though I'm cold, it's a sweet cold, a deep and nourishing chill that seems to know exactly who I am. We get the duvet out of Bernard's boot and lie in the grass and it's wicked, so wicked here. It's all it has to be, this place. Above me is a shifting block of nothing, and when I shut my eyes things are full of spirals and flashing honeycombs, and when I open them again I've got a boyfriend with tinges of grey salting his beard, and beyond us is an everlasting network of coloured light.

3

A convoluted string of fairy lights guides the way towards the bass pumping distantly from the PA system. The glowing path was my idea. The route starts down at the main road, wends through the kissing gate and heads into the woods before travelling uphill, cable-tied to barbed-wire fences. Eventually the lights finish in the main field at Shep Summers's farm where the marquee and decks have been set up. They took ages to fix in place but they look ace now, properly magical, and it's time for the fun to start. Already people are enjoying themselves on the way up from their cars, excitably following a guide-rope that looks like a string of captive fireflies.

Kayden's spent the last few months using all the leccy up at our place where we host the rave committee's boozy meetings every Sunday. He's project manager and I'm dogsbody, and other than us two there's a brisk, smoky guy named Smurf who drives a lorry at Tatt's Haulage, Smurf's housemate Samirah, a warehouse colleague of Kayden's who's quite the exception to some of his more forthright views on race, and Hannah, a friend of Smurf and Samirah's. Kayden sorted the generator, the sound system, lighting rig and DJ's. Smurf built the bar and hay-bale seating area and he also booked the marquee.

Samirah's looked after the promotion, namely a Facebook page and an Instagram account (no, we repeat, *no* dickheads allowed) and is manning the burner phone that people are to text if they want to know where the party is.

I get on with them all except Hannah. Hannah's the worst. She's gobby and nowhere near as fit as she thinks she is. In fact, I'd go as far as to say her witchy nose looks stuck on. It's all I can do not to grab it when she's having a drunken roll-up in the kitchen at our place, taking me to one side and being all, Oh, Gemma, I seen Kayden the other night, well out of it, did you not know? And, Oh, Gemma, are you wearing that? I've a gold top you can borrow if that's all you've got. You'll look stunning in it. Oh, actually it won't fit.

Zero cellulite. Zero originality. Hannah doesn't even like music. It's Kayden who she likes, and the worst thing is I think he knows it. She's got a well compact, sheer figure, and she's always acting rebellious, which I know Kayden finds attractive, pretending she's got nothing to lose when it's obvious she gives such a shit it's unbelievable. She's related to Shep Summers somehow and has got him to let us use his land. I've been pushing against this because I've heard things about Summers, and some of it's scary. Sure enough, he's getting the money from the bar tonight, and he's also supplying the gear we're flogging. Kayden stood up for Hannah when I said involving Summers was a bad idea. Leave off, Gem, he said. Without Hanny, no way would Shep let us use his place for free. This way we don't need a public licence.

When Kayden says something's free, it usually means it's going to cost in an unexpected way. Since I left school and moved in with him in B-town, I've found that one out. He must smoke ten spliffs a day when he's in a good mood, and every night he tips vodka into his can of cider, pissed and kipping in a chair while I make him his tea. I actually don't mind. We're love and chaos, us two, and we always will be. Plus the independence side of things is amazing. I've been providing the last five months, getting the food in, making sure the electric's on and everything, all of it paid for with my first-ever job: some sales-type thing where I've had to ring people up about PPI. I lasted there till just under two months ago. My team leader was this nasty, skinny, oily kind of guy, and I ended up not meeting my targets and getting sacked. I've tried getting ESA since then, because of my anxiety and depression which have got a lot worse since leaving Jodie's, and even though I had a doctor's note about what happened when I was a baby, with my headaches and that, I still failed the medical and got bunged on Universal Credit.

The money took *ages* to come through, and when it finally did I was in that much debt to Kayden that it was back to being skint almost straight away. On top of that, only last week I got sanctioned because I'd forgotten to record my job searches in the online diary. Then the other day when I was late for an appointment because of the bus, I got sanctioned again. The worst thing is I've been looking for work. Ages I've spent on those slow computers, sending tons of CV's out, and I haven't had a single response. I've been applying for basic stuff as well, things I can do easily like fast food and supermarket work and even more sales-type stuff. You'd be tempted to pack it in too, which, let's face it, is what they want. They want everyone out on their own no matter what sort of start they've had, people fending for themselves on the other side of a locked door.

I might as well ask Kayden if I can start selling pills. He's got four hundred on him tonight and all kinds of other stuff – him and Smurf have a chemical works each in their glittery bumbags. Kayden's the roving dealer while Smurf's stationed in the marquee on the bar, which is made from some piled-up kitchen units. If you want a pill, you've to ask Smurf for a pint of 'elephant' and he'll drop a tablet in your hand as if it's loose change. Eight quid a pop. Three for twenty. Drug dealing is just about the only way we're going to cover the cost of this venture, seeing as Kayden's insisting the rave's free. Charging goes against everything he believes in, he says. Raves are about the moment. I want to give people the best possible night. Forget the money. It's about having a good time.

Already people are dancing in the makeshift area I built: a cosmic zone created by nailing king-size panels of black cloth to the knitted boughs of some mature trees, dancing platforms made from a few of Tatt's pallets and crates. The cloth I made glow in the dark. Neon stars, day-glo rockets, Cheshire Cat smiles and my old friend Fibonacci's spiral. Right now a lemon-shaped planet is pinging in and out of view above Samirah's head like a light bulb, as if she's having a great idea but keeps forgetting it.

The DJ's really slamming it out on the 12-10s. A load of people in fancy dress are going for it. Wigs and tiger suits. Glitter and stockings. Illuminated hula hoops. I mingle for a while but I'm too sober and I can't find Kayden between the busy lights and a sun that's settling low: gold becoming pink becoming nothing at all. Also, I've eaten half a pill and it's done fuck-all. I neck another full one and do a couple of shots of Sambuca at the bar.

No sign of Kayden. The rave's filling, meaning we've done our job, we did it, and I know I should be thrilled. The thing is, I'm not happy, at least not in the way I should be. I've no one to talk to and the high's climbing and suddenly I'm rushing hard, bloody hell, this half's strong as fuck. How will I be after that full one I just had?

The buzz begins to burrow its way through every part of my body. It's soaring in my being and I'm having to inhale deeply through my nose and it's delicious and the butterflies in my stomach keep folding and opening themselves at a rapid rate. I drink as much water as I can to prepare for what's to come – way too much as it turns out, my belly swilling and shifting until half an hour later, when I have to stagger behind the marquee and projectile vomit in the grass whilst holding desperately onto the guy ropes.

Thankfully no one sees. Less thankfully, being sick sends me into the stratosphere. I'm hurtling madly, blasted completely and utterly into another plane of reality.

I've no choice but to see what happens. I need the toilet.

Well, actually I need somewhere to be fucked and come to life again. Get a grip, Gemma. Focus. Here's the Portaloo. You're always at your most high when you're on your own at a party in the bog. The cubicle stinks and I've to queue for it, blokes pissing in the bushes nearby. I'm proper sluggish. Well hazy and I can't chat to the other girls in the line because I'm that spangled I'm having trouble seeing let alone talking and the heat's bleeding and the techno's pounding out of the speakers erected on a pole next to me, driving, ruthless, the crowd cheering and whistling in front of the decks. My mouth is dry. I'm pouring sweat, trying to relax and enjoy the tunes, but my jaw's rattling, my teeth are chattering and it's good, it's fine, this is fun I'm having. I squint at the flags I made. A spiral. A mayfly. A Galapagos tortoise. A guy with a torch in his mouth walks past, a real sight when I'm wrecked like this – violently lit – the glowing, fleshy hole of his mouth and, ah, the door's open, I'm inside the booth now and my eyes are sledging and everything's tinged green and I'm leaning against the wall, dropping my backside onto the toilet seat, my pants tugged and me trying to piss yet being unable to relax down there, I can't, I'm on the verge of going and it won't, it is, here it comes, hard, the piss, I think it's coming, and I need a drink but there's no water coming from the tap. I have a moment to myself. A couple more. How long have I been in here? I can't make out the screen of my phone to tell the time. There's a banging on the booth. *What you doing in there?* Shit. I stagger outside, so high I've to lie under a tree on my own and feel complete and fully grown yet also like I've been a very silly girl indeed. I feel like crying. I give in to the wave and sob hard and I can't control myself because I'm mad with Kayden for not being here to help, and I'm raging too because after I moved into his place, when I finally told him about Adam, he wasn't bothered, like, he thought I was being daft. It were only a couple of shags, he said, you're well sensitive, you, Gem. Weren't you old enough to know what you were doing?

I know that, Kay, I know that, I replied, hating myself for

agreeing when I didn't agree, and hating having no choice because I had nowhere else to go and no one to turn to, and, *seriously*, who knew what that thing with Adam was all about anyway?

Lying under the tree, more memories come back.

Adam's smooth face bunched in pleasure.

Those measured inhalations.

Jodie's face when she found the slimy condom stuck to the grille of my waste-paper basket won't go away. Adam denied everything and I ran off, returning when it was dark. I found Adam asleep on the couch – he looked irresistible, like an infuriating child. I crept past him, upstairs, hesitating when I saw the lamplight defining the outline of Jodie's bedroom door, a door I would never walk through in the same way again.

Fuck it, I was fifteen. I've never known what I am and that prick took advantage, simple as that.

I'm going completely under here. Where's Kayden? Where is he? I'm on my feet, tottering and I can smell shit. Human shit. It's not mine, thank God. I'm covered in dirt plus leaves from lying under the tree for I've no idea how long, and there's someone juggling fire sticks.

Kayden?

I run over and the face of a stranger stares down at me, licked by flame. A quickening fire. The music is loud and the green lasers are going, bisecting each other against the smoky night sky. I have a dance, or a sway is probably a better description. And it feels okay, like maybe I'm sorting myself out, but then I get another surge of high and I have to crouch down and wait and close my eyes in the staggering fuzz and I'm not in control of my face, and I don't like this, but I've no choice, all I can do is let it pass through me and it feels amazing, actually, oh, it's unbelievable, and I'm on the lookout as I stand up, I have to be, I'm searching until finally, shit, *there*, I can see Kayden behind the decks. He's on the sofa Smurf got hold of, dragged out of the Transit van last Friday.

The strobe lights are flickering a mile a minute. They make

Kayden's movements go all futuristic, glitchy and robotic. On his knee sits Hannah. She's yacking in his ear, Kayden's hand cradling her backside and they're laughing about something. I stumble over the wires and now I'm stood behind the sofa and I can hear them and I know Kayden's face will be grey as a storm. It's deepness, he's saying. Them eyes. You've got an old soul, Hannah. I can see wisdom there. That's what it is.

I stumble off to the marquee, in tears, and there's Samirah smoking a fag. She seems to lean through the music towards my ear. What's up?

It's Hannah. That *bitch*.

Calm down. What about her? What's she done now?

She's after Kayden! She's trying to pull him. She's all over him!

Ah, they're just friends. Look at you, mate. Here, drink some of this.

She passes me a bottle of water, and it's the most incredible thing I've ever tasted.

They are, I say. *They are* ...

You know what, Samirah says. Even if you're right, what you worrying about a guy like that for? He's not worth it, mate. Seriously.

She's trying to get me to sit with her. No way am I doing that, I think. But I stay by her side.

I'm telling you, you don't wanna worry about Kayden, Samirah says. Guy's a destructive prick. Always has been. Only cares about himself. It's reckless, man, the way he goes about.

No, he's not, he's ... you don't understand.

He's blind too. If he can't see what's on his own doorstep, Gem, he's blind and I'm not kidding.

This is too much. It's like Samirah's calling me out for being dumb enough to go with someone like Kayden. I try to get up but she tugs my sleeve.

I'm sorry, okay? Guys are shit sometimes.

My jaw won't stop juddering. I clap my hands over it and

shake my head. Across the way, a girl in a red dress has climbed on top of a tractor, and she's dancing, her face fixed in pleasure. Pure euphoria.

You sure you're all right, Gem? How many pills you had?

I try to push the gurn out of my face. By willing it into my feet, clenching my toes in my trainers, I can just about talk. I'm all right, I manage to say. I'm just mashed. I'm just really, really fucked.

Yeah, I noticed. Samirah pauses. Lights another fag. I've been wanting to ask you, and please don't be offended, but how old are you, Gem? 'Cause you don't look nineteen like Kay's been saying.

She gets me some more water and passes me a stick of chewing gum, which helps a lot.

I'm sixteen.

Shit me.

What do you mean?

I knew it. I knew you was only a kid.

Oh, get lost.

Gemma, I want you to listen to me. Will you do that?

I shrug.

Mate, I'm trying to tell you something here. Are you listening?

Yeah, I am. Sorry.

Promise?

I promise.

You don't have to do nothing you don't want to, right? You can tell a guy to *fuck off* if you want, and they will do. They don't have no power over you. No one has no power over you. Don't listen to the hierarchy, Gem. Seriously.

What you on about?

I'm trying to help you, man. I'm trying to say you've got a choice. You can always choose.

I find myself saying, in Jodie's voice, I thought you were meant to be Kayden's mate.

Oh, come on. We work together—

What you hanging around with him for then?

Samirah pauses. Smiles to herself. I dunno, she says, I guess I like some of his ideas.

Me too.

I mean look at this place. Look what we've done. It's amazing. Do you not feel that?

I'm about to crumble into cheering up. I'm about to say yeah, course I do, but everything I want to say is whipped away as if a gust of wind has taken it.

What else can I tell you? Samirah says. You don't always have to listen to people like us.

I can see the Fibonacci spiral. I can see a wind farm and I can feel the prospect of the valley, the wild black country surrounding everything just a few yards away from this shard of hedonism Kayden has been responsible for this evening. This party is a scream into the night and I'm drunk on profound shit in a world that isn't built to worry about those sorts of questions. Samirah is high, not as high as I am. Her eyes are dilated and her hands clench and unclench, creating, I realise, an idea of how I've always felt.

Look, I gotta go.

Nah, come on, Gem. Let's have a dance.

Honestly, I'm fine.

Where you going? *Gemma!*

I arrive at the bonfire by the circle of standing stones. Tons of people are dancing around them, partying in fields where our ancestors probably worked, connecting with our history, with a real past. I can hear the *whoosh* of nitrous oxide, people falling into each other after they've huffed their balloons. Whoa, they're going.

Whoa.

What am I doing here? I've a sense as I look around me that everywhere there are precious things, singular places and special moments and no one seems to care about them except me. I tread a silver canister of oxide into the ground on my way to the decks. Hannah's lurking around Kayden and in spite of my outsized fluffy-feeling tongue, I march up to her and say You are one vicious bitch, you know that?

What? she yells over the beats.

I said …

Oh, forget it. I try getting to Kayden, but he's playing his set. Kay!

He's concentrating on the mixer, the spinning vinyl. His whole body is bobbing in time to the music. One hand turning the LP. The other on his headphones, tracking time.

Kay.

I tap his arm.

Kayden!

He whirls around, his face a livid simulation of the man I thought I knew. In my smashed state his skin isn't stormy. It's a mushroom colour, elastic in texture. I try to touch his cheek, half-expecting my finger to sink into the flesh.

He catches my wrist. What you doing?

I don't feel well. Seriously, Kay …

Fucking hell, Gem, I'm *playing.* This is my night.

I can feel the tears. I'm crying. Actually crying. I'm sorry, Kay. I'm really, really sorry…

You know what, you're off your head, Gem. Get out of my face. I don't have time for this.

He puts his headphones back on and slips away into the music.

I don't even know what I want from him. What I want from anything. All I know is it's *something*, and I'm striving endlessly towards whatever that is.

I just want to see you, Kayden. I love you … *Kay!*

He doesn't hear me.

Fine, I cry at his back. You know what? Fuck off! You're a prick, man. You always have been, you're—

Gemma! Can you not see he's trying to play his set?

It's Hannah. When she tries to escort me away, I shake her off. Get the fuck off me! I've every right to be here!

Some of the crowd have noticed and I'm getting wolf

whistles. Hannah lets go and practically nuts me. *Do one*, she says, the air from her mouth pelting my ear. Get yourself home, Gem. Go on, get lost. We've had enough of you. Kayden has and so have I. You're just a stupid little kid.

I'm thinking of Adam as I shove her in the chest. I'm thinking of a whole lot of things. I don't mean for Hannah to hit the turntables but that's what happens. The music dies, murdered by me, and people are jeering and Kayden has this awful closed way about him as he helps Hannah up from the ground.

I cock my head at him. *Knobhead.*

You what?

You heard me.

I shove him too then head into the crowd. As the music resumes and the dancing comes to life like an engine that's been jump-started, I disappear into the jaws of the field, past the standing stones and the undergrowth where the nettles are, towards the sterner chasms and the brasher glens, the unforgiving terrain. The grass is soaking. Everything glistens. The air is brisk and clear and I'm high and tearful as I walk until I reach the silent morning. Eventually I come to the foot of a very large oak tree. It's a dear old thing with moss-hung boughs that spread towards me like the arms of a listening, naked mother. There's a cankerous smell of toadstools and as I hug the oak's grooved trunk my centre gives way, and all that remains for me is the sweet oblivion of the moor and the faint design of fallen, forgotten leaves that each tumble to the ground, landing on my face as I lie back and gaze at what's above.

When my mind eventually returns it's the end of the day and I'm lying bathed in the late afternoon sunlight as it seeps through the curtains of the oak. I blink my eyes and rub my lips. My mouth is sore, chewed to death, and my clothes and trainers are wet through. It's over a mile back to the rave site and there's almost no one here save a couple of final casualties giggling to themselves and doing the last of their drugs. A couple are on the sofa where the decks were, and for a moment I think it's Kayden and Hannah. Then I realise it's two guys wrapped around each other, kissing, hands down each other's pants.

I go to the toilet behind the marquee and thank you, thank you, I find a litre bottle of water in the long grass. I drink for a long time. My phone has five per cent battery and I've only two quid on me, barely enough for the bus but it might get me there. All I need to do is decide where 'there' is.

The taxing climb from the rave site to the clean upland plateaus into the most incredibly bright vista. I walk along the tops to the churr of hovering skylarks, keeping the view in sight, the breeze forcing my unzipped coat open, and I don't care. I negotiate cattle grid, stile and field using the brown mass of the valley as my North Star. Eventually I make it to the Circuit. Here the houses have steep raking roofs and a postman is doing his evening round. A car hums past. This is an out-of-body experience and I'm a tripped-out angel with ravaged make-up and bloodied fingernails, gliding about in a bomber jacket and a miniskirt. More than ever I have a sense of the valley as a place that simply does what it does. This place could be anywhere. Babies are born. Lives spool out, stories extend beyond my own and every one of these people, my companions, is close enough to affect me yet somehow too far away for any of us to ever know how close we came to working out the great mystery. This seems to me both a blessing and a curse.

At the main road is a pub where they sell Blond Witch beer. I remember a track not far from here that will take me to the river. It will guide me past the Toby Carvery, past an old mill that's become an office with chromic windows. Yes, that's where I'll go.

I head over the level crossing and squeeze around the end of the steel supplier's chain-link fence, not a soul in sight. When I stamp my feet the sound resonates around the entire complex. I head past a hulking pile of metal planks, reach the sinewy path, then the river itself. This is the valley's basin. A town is in one direction, and in the other direction as well, while in between is a compromised sort of countryside. The fluctuating water puts me at ease, and I head towards its sound. At all times I can hear the road. Red poppies are among the cow parsley. Their petals are like otherworldly eyes while a bank of wild garlic faces me, hundreds of white flower heads reminding me of people in a stadium.

I find myself in a clearing below the bypass, a grey, man-made space where the immense road is carried above the river, slanting towards the ground until it becomes a motorway. Here under the bridge it's huge, artificial and empty. It's a concrete chamber, really, church-like in size. The bypass rushes above me. Sound bleeds through. The rumble of an approach. The rising fade. The bridge is held up by three enormous supports. The middle support is a thick leg while on either side the supports are sharp, broad wedges with slopes flat enough to run up from the shingle floor, each incline reaching into the beams of the bypass itself. I crouch like a sprinter, and, imagining the starter pistol's crack, charge up-slope on my side of the river, haul myself onto a beam and get crawling. The rivets in the beam are as big as cupcakes and the drop gets nasty quick. Still, I'm in a bridge, and a bat wheels in flight as I make my way to the centre of the bypass, above the river.

When I get as far as I can go I push the hump of my back against the dusty ceiling. In this way I can feel the vibrations of the road, its thunder, and I can enjoy the shallow curve of glinting water way below me. I stretch out a hand and touch some graffiti. It's the word CRUSTYMAN scrawled in six-foot-high letters on the central support, almost filling all the space above a tatty old man's face, the face of the seasons, a rough face that has been composed with striking, tearing gestures, a face that follows me, that will always follow me, or maybe it's me that's following it. Traffic. Birdsong. Concrete. It's like the world is breathing up here. It's like it's watching me. I slip my trainers off, tie them together at the laces and hang them about my neck, then I straddle the beam, my toes gripping the chilly ledge. In the shallows is a dumped tyre. Silt is piled high in its middle, weeds growing in that silt, transforming the tyre into a rubber island – an isle of faded hope and fucking glory, as Kayden used to say – while over the way is a football trapped against the river bank, endlessly turning on itself in the current. My phone is ringing. I won't answer it. This place, you can just tell it does well at sunset, and I always say that the day you get sick of sunsets is the day you get sick of life. I read the name on my phone's screen and slide it into my pocket. You know what it feels like sitting up here? It feels like freedom.

Acknowledgements

—

Huge thanks to Eve White Literary Agency: reader Sarah Revivis-Smith for plucking me off the slush pile, Eve for the amazing enthusiasm and drive, and my agent Ludo Cinelli for the unswerving belief and support. I'm also indebted to Hannah Westland, my brilliant editor at Serpent's Tail who did so much to unlock the book, and to Graeme Hall, Mary Chamberlain, Sally Sargeant, Drew Jerrison, Nick Sheerin, and everyone else who worked on the project. A nod to my friend Tom King for providing invaluable feedback during the drafting process, and finally, much love to dearest Lizzy and my family for all the encouragement and understanding.